# -POSTCARDS FROM-
# VALHALLA

*Postcards from Valhalla* is a uclanpublishing book

First Published in Great Britain in 2023 by uclanpublishing
University of Central Lancashire
Preston, PR1 2HE, UK

Text copyright © Danny Weston, 2023
Cover Illustration © Daisy Webster, 2023

978-1-915235-65-7

3 5 7 9 10 8 6 4 2

Set in 10/16pt Kingfisher by Amy Cooper.

A CIP catalogue record for this book is available from the British Library.

Printed and bound in Great Britain by Clays Ltd, Elcograf S.p.A.

# -POSTCARDS FROM-
# VALHALLA

*Danny Weston*

uclanpublishing

# GO DEEPER

There are five different points in *Postcards from Vahalla* where readers are offered the opportunity to 'go deeper.' Simply scan the QR codes with your mobile phone and you will be taken to three locations that feature in the story - you will also be offered the opportunity to watch a scene featuring the book's lead character that is only mentioned in passing - and you will even be given a tutorial on how to make the perfect Greek honey and orange cake!

# PART ONE

# CHAPTER 1
## A DISAPPEARANCE

Viggo was trying to sleep, but it was proving really difficult.

Out on the street, Edinburgh Council's lorries were already at work, emptying the communal rubbish bins. The noise this created seemed completely out of proportion to the task. The sound of it rolled like thunder, reverberating along the entire length of the road.

And the gulls were doing that high-pitched shrieking thing they always did in the morning, a noise to set anyone's teeth on edge. How was anyone expected to sleep through that?

Viggo had been late getting home last night. Jamie's parents had been out for the evening, visiting friends and staying over, so Jamie had invited a bunch of mates over for a D&D evening and had even managed to find a forgotten bottle of alcohol at the back of a drinks cabinet, something with a Spanish-sounding name that tasted really horrible if you drank it neat, but was tolerable if you mixed it with enough Diet Coke. Emma had been there too and Viggo had tried really hard to engage her in conversation, but she clearly wasn't interested in him, answering his questions with a grunt or a nod. She'd been the first to leave.

By the time Viggo walked home alone, it was nearly 1am but, he told himself, school was out now until the middle of August, so where was the harm? He'd let himself in and padded quietly upstairs, noting with a sense of relief that there was no light under the door of Mum's room, so he wouldn't have to suffer her disapproving looks until morning – only now, somehow, it *was* morning and he felt like he'd barely slept at all. When he'd finally managed to snatch a few winks he'd been troubled by complicated dreams that he couldn't quite piece together. Something about a tunnel, perhaps? Yes, he'd been climbing down this long, dark passage and there'd been something waiting for him deep below the surface, something that . . . no, it was gone.

He turned over with a groan, realising as he did so that he was still fully dressed, which was never a good sign. Reluctantly, he opened his eyes and saw that Mum was sitting beside his bed, looking intently down at him.

'Jesus!' he gasped and sat up. 'How long have you been sitting there?'

'Oh, not long,' she said. And then added. 'I like watching you sleep sometimes.'

Viggo shook his head. 'That's one of the creepiest things anyone's ever said to me,' he muttered. He let out a long breath. 'You scared me.'

'Scared?' she echoed, incredulously. 'Of your own mother?'

'Well, no, not scared exactly, but . . .' He lifted a hand to run it through his wild thatch of blonde hair and ran the tip of his tongue over teeth that felt furry. 'What time is it?' he asked. He was all too aware that he was wearing a watch, and only needed to glance at it, but somehow it seemed like too much effort.

'It's late,' she assured him. 'Nearly ten o'clock.' Viggo noticed now that she was dressed in a T-shirt and ironed jeans, and her short light-brown hair was neatly brushed. She paused for effect. 'I didn't hear you come in last night,' she said. It sounded like a reprimand.

'Yeah, well, I *was* kind of late. I didn't want to disturb you. It's not like it's a school night or anything, so . . .' A pause. 'I was at Jamie's house,' he added.

She nodded, but didn't say anything.

'He had a bunch of friends over. We were playing Dungeons and Dragons.'

Now she frowned. Viggo knew she didn't really get fantasy games and that she'd rather he was 'outside in the fresh air' or working at his writing. It irked him that she wouldn't take the time to try and understand the game; it wasn't like he and Jamie spent their time drinking paint stripper and setting fire to things.

'Mum, it's just something we like to do. It's no big deal.'

'And you were boozing, I suppose?'

'Not really,' he said, in as vague a way as possible. 'Not what you'd call *boozing*. Just a couple of . . . er . . . was there some particular reason for this . . . visit?'

Mum sighed. 'Yes,' she said. 'It's Magnus.'

Viggo tried not to let out a weary sigh. Of course it was Magnus. It was always Magnus – something he'd done or something he hadn't done or something he was *thinking* of doing. Magnus was Viggo's brother, three years older than him and, in Viggo's honest opinion, a total weirdo. Viggo had lost count of all the disasters that Magnus had caused but, whenever a new one occurred, Mum always acted surprised.

'What's happened this time?' he asked her.

'Well, he's following in your dad's footsteps, isn't he?'

'Meaning?'

'He's disappeared,' said Mum dramatically, and then, as though realising how it sounded, she went on. 'Well, not disappeared, exactly, but . . . he's still in Shetland.'

Viggo considered this. 'I don't understand,' he said at last. 'I *know* where he is. He's been there for months.'

'Yes. But you remember how anxious I felt about him going in the first place? And the project he signed up to officially finished four days ago.'

'Right, so . . .'

'He was supposed to come straight home afterwards. At least, that's what I thought was happening. But he hasn't turned up. In fact, there hasn't been a word from him in over a week.'

'Have you tried contacting him?'

Now Mum looked irritated. 'Of course I have! I'm not a complete idiot. I've phoned, texted, sent him emails . . . and I've got precisely nowhere.'

Viggo eased himself into a sitting position, keeping the duvet over himself so Mum wouldn't notice he was still dressed. Now he thought about it, he had heard Mum muttering darkly about being unable to contact Magnus over the past few days but he hadn't taken an awful lot of notice. To him it had just seemed like business as usual. He looked straight into her eyes.

'You know Magnus,' he said. 'He's probably discovered something new out there, something amazing – in his opinion – and he's decided to stay on for a while. Or he's met a girl.' He tried not to sound envious about the last bit. 'That's what usually happens. What was he supposed to be doing anyway? In Shetland.'

'I've told you a dozen times. Some reconstructive work at a Viking settlement.'

'Yes, well, there you go. They probably dug up something unexpected. An old sword or a cup or a . . . button . . . something they found exciting.' Viggo tried not to roll his eyes. Unlike his brother, he had never inherited his dad's obsessive passion for all things Norse. Dad had even chosen Norwegian names for his sons, despite his Celtic ancestry. Viggo hated the blank looks he always got whenever he had to give somebody his name.

*'I'm sorry, did you say . . . Vigour?'*

Magnus had got the best of the deal. At least people knew how to spell *his* name.

'You'll see, Mum. He's just decided to stay on a bit longer. It's not like he hasn't done something like this before.'

Even as he was saying it, Viggo knew how hollow his words sounded. After all, Dad had gone 'off grid' in Shetland five years ago and nothing had been seen or heard from him since then. Now he was officially 'missing presumed dead'. Thinking back, it had been a strange process coming to terms with what had happened. Viggo had been twelve years old when his dad had gone away. Now it all seemed like something long and tortuous that had happened to somebody else.

At first, it had been hope that filled his days – the hope that one day the doorbell would ring and Dad would be standing there, giving him that familiar gap-toothed grin. But as the months had slipped by with no word of him, the hope had steadily turned into a kind of simmering hatred, an anger at Dad for running away, for never bothering to get in touch. And in time, the hatred had gradually settled into a kind of empty void somewhere deep inside – the realisation that Dad was never coming back, that he was off somewhere else living a different life, that he probably no longer even thought about the wife and two sons he'd left behind.

So, yes, of course Mum was worried. She'd be crazy not to be. But still . . .

'Mum, I'm not sure I—'

'It was my birthday three days ago,' she interrupted him.

'I know that,' he said, trying not to sound defensive. 'I bought you a card, didn't I? And those nice flowers.'

'Yes. And they were lovely. But Magnus *always* phones me on my birthday, wherever he is. Even that time when he was in America. You remember? Where was it? Montana?'

'Arizona, that time,' Viggo corrected her. 'He was hunting rattlesnakes.'

'Yes. Even then. He never misses, no matter where he is. I don't mind telling you, I'm starting to get a bad feeling about this. And the problem is, he's told us so little about what he's doing over there. Where he's based, who he's working with . . .'

'Well, that's just him, isn't it.'

'And whenever I try to talk to you about him, it's as though you just switch off.'

Viggo shrugged. 'It's not like we've ever been close, is it?'

'That's not true,' Mum told him. "You were really close when you were little. Thick as thieves, the pair of you. And then, after your dad . . .' She left that sentence unfinished. 'After *that*, something seemed to happen to you both. It was like a wall came down between you and somehow, you just stopped relating.' She looked wistful. 'I remember when you were really small, Magnus was almost like your hero or something. You used to follow him everywhere.'

'I did not!'

'You did! You looked up to him. Idolised him. I often wonder . . .'

'Yes?'

'. . . if perhaps the two of you are too much alike.'

Viggo actually snorted at that. 'We're not alike,' he insisted. 'I don't know where you got that idea from. I'm nothing like him. He's . . .' He shook his head, unable to come up with just one word to describe the human whirlwind that was his brother. 'He's so obsessive about everything. And he wants to fill Dad's shoes; be exactly like him. I never felt that way. So I guess I can call him if you want me to, but it won't make the least bit of difference.'

'Oh, I think it's a waste of time calling him. We need to talk to him face-to-face.'

Now Viggo was totally bewildered. 'And how are we supposed to do that?'

'We're going to Shetland,' said Mum. 'I've just been on the computer booking tickets.'

Viggo turned to look towards his bedroom window –

the rain-streaked glass, the grey tenements across the street, other windows staring sightlessly back at him, all those neighbours whose names he didn't even know.

'Go to *Shetland*?' he muttered.

'Yes, why not?'

'Mum, you do realise how far away it is, don't you? It's not like getting on a bus.'

She gave him a weary look. 'Of course I know. I had to go there myself, didn't I? When your dad . . .' Once again, she tailed off, shook her head. 'I appreciate it *is* a bit of a trip, but we haven't had a holiday in ages, have we? And I seem to remember that the place is quite spectacular.'

He nearly laughed out loud at that. As if it mattered what it *looked* like.

'Can we even afford to go?' he asked her. 'I seem to remember you telling me that because the insurance never paid out on Dad, we can't *have* holidays. And you keep getting those letters from the credit card people.'

'I found a deal online,' she told him, as if it explained everything. 'A fraction of the price it normally costs. As long as we're careful, we should be fine.'

'And anyway, I can't just up and go,' he told her, trying to think of a valid reason why he couldn't. 'There's . . . there's the new Marvel film opening on Friday.'

'Marvel film?' She looked puzzled, as if he'd spoken in a foreign language.

'Yes. The next *Thor*. Me and Jamie have been looking forward to it for just about forever. I promised him we'd see it together.'

She smiled. 'You can see it when you get back. We'll only be gone a week.'

'But that won't be the opening night. It'll already be *old*.'

'Thor was a Norse god,' Mum reminded Viggo. 'And Shetland is the land of the Vikings. So why not visit a place where they actually lived?'

'I'd rather visit Cineworld, if it's all the same to you.'

'Oh, really! Since when did you become such a stick-in-the-mud? I thought it might provide inspiration for you.'

'Inspiration?'

'Yes. Perhaps it'll help you to get your writing mojo back. You remember, you always used to say that was what you really wanted to do with your life?'

'I did say that, yes, but . . . wanting to write and actually doing it, that's two different things, don't you think? Anyway, I was a kid when I said that. I'm nearly sixteen now.'

Mum fixed him with a determined look. 'You're not exactly in line for your pension, are you, love?' She seemed to remember something. 'I read an article in *The Guardian* the other day. A woman of seventy-five who's having her first novel published. So you see, it's never too late. Think of that, Viggo. Seventy-five!'

He stared at her. His first thought was that if you could get published at that age then there was clearly no great hurry, but he could see that her mind was made up. There was probably no sense in trying to change it. Nevertheless, he made one last valiant attempt.

'What happens if Magnus is already coming back and we pass him on the way there?' he asked. 'We'll look pretty stupid then, won't we? And you'll have wasted all that money.'

Mum got up from the chair. 'You'd probably better start putting some things into a small suitcase,' she advised him. 'We leave tomorrow afternoon for an evening crossing. Earliest booking I could get. Meanwhile, I'll go and make us some breakfast.' She glanced at her watch. 'Brunch,' she corrected herself. 'I'll make brunch.'

'What about Ruby?' pleaded Viggo. 'Didn't you say her clutch needed looking at?'

'I've got her booked into the garage first thing tomorrow morning. They've promised me they'll make her a priority.'

Ruby was Mum's ancient Kia Picanto, more than ten years old now and thus named because she was a cheeky shade of red.

'Who keeps a car so long?' asked Viggo.

'I do,' said Mum. 'We've been through some hard times together.'

'And how much is it going to cost to fix her? We're skint in case you've forgotten?'

But Mum was already heading for the door. She paused to glance back over her shoulder. 'You'll probably want to change out of those clothes you're wearing,' she said. 'Might have been an idea to take them off last night, *before* you got into bed.'

She went out of the room, closing the door behind her.

Viggo groaned and slumped back on to his pillow, pulling the covers over his head.

But he didn't get any more sleep that morning.

# CHAPTER 2
## HAAR

Mum and Viggo were driving north, sitting side by side in Ruby as they motored steadily along the A90. It was late afternoon and, luckily, there was hardly any other traffic, because the weather, which had been decent when they'd set off, had deteriorated steadily and had now become a 'haar' – a damp, grey mist that cut visibility down to a few metres. Viggo's doubts about Ruby had proved to be ill-founded. The garage had deemed her fit for purpose and she seemed to be behaving herself, eating up the miles without any sign of a problem.

Next stop, Aberdeen.

Viggo was still in a bad mood though, hours after leaving home, and he sat slumped in the passenger seat, arms crossed, scowling through the side window at the grass verges as they slipped by in a blur of greenish grey. Mum, on the other hand, couldn't seem to stop talking. She commented on pretty much everything they passed, no matter how mundane, as though desperate to coax Viggo into some kind of a reply.

'Ooh, look at that hill, Viggo! Doesn't it look like an elephant?'

Or, 'Viggo, can you remember the name of the services we always used to stop at when we were driving north? You used to love their doughnuts!'

And, 'You and Magnus used to play a game when we were driving. I Spy. Remember that? We could try it now if you like?'

But he was having none of it.

This was a waste of time – he was convinced of that – and it wasn't the first time that Magnus had done something weird. While Viggo couldn't actually prevent the trip from happening, he was adamant that he wasn't going to make it easy for Mum. He fully intended to remain silent for the entire journey, or at least until he needed to ask for something – like food or drink or information. Until then, Mum could talk to herself.

As the car motored onwards, Viggo thought about his recent phone conversation with Jamie, who hadn't been pleased when he'd been given the news about Viggo's impending absence for the upcoming *Thor* movie.

His voice had been incredulous at the other end of the line.

'Shetland?' he'd cried, as though he couldn't believe his own ears. 'What's in Shetland?'

'My brother,' said Viggo, mournfully, managing to make the two words sound like some kind of obscure curse.

'Magnus? Oh God, what's he done this time?' Jamie knew all about Magnus and his various disasters. He ought to, he'd heard Viggo complain about them often enough.

'He's not been answering his phone.'

'That's it?'

'Yup.'

'And that means you have to go haring off after him?'

'Yeah. Apparently.'

'But he's, like, what? Eighteen, nineteen? He's a grown-up.'

'I know that. He just doesn't behave like one. And you know, after what happened with my dad and everything, Mum's kind of nervous.' Viggo sighed. 'It's a total pain. But she's got herself all worked up about him.' He paused for a moment, aware that he was about to say something controversial. 'I suppose we could always wait and see the film when I get back?'

A silence while Jamie considered this. 'Yeah, I might be up for a second viewing.'

'No, I meant, maybe *you* could wait too?'

'Me?' Jamie sounded offended and Viggo had to admit it was a pretty stupid suggestion. 'Can't do that, mate. There's a whole bunch of us booked for the opening night. It's going to be great.' Another pause. 'You know Emma's going to be there, right?'

'Don't,' snapped Viggo. 'Anyway, she's not interested. Girls are never interested in me. Why is that, exactly?'

Another long pause while Jamie pondered the question. 'Maybe it's the way you present yourself?'

'What's that supposed to mean?'

'Oh, nothing...'

'No, go on. Say what you were thinking.'

'Well, you know what Emma's like. She'll be looking for somebody... smarter.'

'What, you mean like, cleverer?'

'No! I'm talking about the way you dress. No offence, mate, but you wear the same outfit for weeks at a time.'

Viggo was puzzled by this. 'So do you,' he said.

'Well, yeah, but I'm not after Emma, am I?'

'I'm not *after* her. Not really. I'm just … you know, interested.'

'Right. So if you want something to happen, you've got to make a proper effort, yeah? Dress up a bit. Get some smart clothes. Have a shower every day.'

'Every day?'

'Every other day, then.'

'And if I do all that, she'll be interested in me?'

'Yeah. Well, maybe.'

Viggo had told him he'd think about it and had rung off. It was a bit rich, he thought, Jamie coming out with that stuff. He generally looked like something the cat had dragged in. Viggo favoured jeans and trainers, maybe a D&D T-shirt. And at least he put his clothes in the washing machine occasionally. He tried to picture himself swanning up to Emma dressed in smart threads and some flashy footwear and immediately dismissed the idea. She'd probably laugh her head off. Or she'd think he was on his way to a funeral.

Ruby passed a sign with the image of a leaping deer on it.

'I always wonder about those signs,' said Mum, who still hadn't given up on the idea of coaxing a reaction from Viggo. 'I mean, what would I actually do if a deer leapt in front of the car? It's not as if the sign helps you in any way.' She waited for an answer and didn't get one, so she continued. 'I wonder if it would be covered by insurance?'

This question was baffling enough to make Viggo turn his gaze from the side window to look at her.

'What are you talking about?' he grunted.

'I'm asking, if we ran into a deer, would we be covered?'

'Yeah. In blood, most likely.'

'No, I mean, would insurance take it into account? I mean, I've seen it happen in films. And I've read about it in books, but . . . I can't think of a single person it's ever actually happened to. And I know a lot of drivers.'

'You're asking me . . .?'

'Who would get the blame? The driver or the deer? Whose fault would it be?'

'Well, it's not as if the deer can pay for the damage, is it?' said Viggo. 'Even if it had money tucked away in a wee pocket somewhere. It would most likely be dead.'

'Not necessarily,' Mum assured him. 'I mean, those things look pretty sturdy.'

'Fair enough. It might just be horribly injured or in shock or something. Either way, it isn't going to be much help if somebody asks it what happened. So I suppose the driver would be to blame. That's you,' he added, just in case she had any doubts.

He made a valiant attempt to return his gaze to the passenger window but Mum was just getting warmed up.

'Doesn't seem fair,' she said. 'Does it seem fair to you?'

He could only shrug his shoulders.

'And you know, when you *do* have an accident of any description, the questions you have to answer! Like that time we were in Norway. Do you remember?'

He shook his head. 'Don't think so.'

'Oh, you must! Your dad was intent on visiting some place he'd read about – some lake with an unpronounceable name – and we were driving there in a hire car. Remember?'

Again, Viggo shook his head.

'You must do! This lorry driver came hurtling out of a side road and went right into us. You were terrified. You screamed your head off! Magnus just sat there as though nothing had happened.'

'I really don't remember this,' Viggo told her.

'You *were* quite young. I mean, you were what, five or six years old? But I'd have thought it would stick in your mind. I bet Magnus remembers it.'

'Bully for Magnus! I don't get your point.'

'I'm just saying, the trouble we had trying to get the insurance company to cough up! I mean, the other driver admitted it was all his fault. At least, I *think* that's what he was saying. He was Norwegian and he didn't speak much English. And afterwards, when we got home, I must have had to fill in a gazillion forms, all of them asking the most ridiculous questions . . .'

Her voice seemed to dissolve into a long, unintelligible buzz, like a troublesome insect whizzing around Viggo's head, and he directed his gaze straight ahead at the empty ribbon of road disappearing into the haze.

Except that the road wasn't empty any more.

Because now he could dimly make out something approaching from the other direction, gradually emerging from the mist. Viggo stared straight ahead and was only dimly aware of his jaw opening wider – because now he was able to make out the shape of it, and he was looking at . . .

He shook his head in disbelief.

No, that couldn't be right.

He squeezed his eyes shut for a moment then opened them again, thinking that the vision would dissolve back into the haze, but still he saw the same thing. A man was racing towards them along the open road, not on the other side of it, but directly ahead of the car. He was sitting astride a wild-eyed, white horse and, as they approached at speed, Viggo could see that he was bare-chested and bearded and that he wore his long, blonde hair in a shoulder length tangle.

'No way,' Viggo heard himself mutter.

The rider hadn't changed his position in the road and now he was close enough for Viggo to see that he was holding a huge sword, which he was pointing directly at the windscreen, as though planning to plunge the weapon straight through the glass and into Viggo's chest.

Viggo turned his head in alarm. 'Mum,' he gasped. 'Look out!'

Weirdly, she didn't seem to register his voice. She was gazing straight ahead and seemed totally unperturbed by the approaching rider. She had a calm expression and was still talking in a quiet monotone. As Viggo stared at her, her words came abruptly back into focus.

'. . . and then, of course, we had to find somebody to repair the car and your dad, for all his supposed knowledge of the country, couldn't seem to speak a single word of Norwegian. Not one!'

Viggo snapped his gaze back to the road, panic flaring

within him. Now the mounted figure filled the entire frame of the windscreen. For an instant, the man's fierce gaze locked with Viggo's, as though challenging him, and in that moment he noticed two details: the rider had cold blue eyes and the hilt of the sword he was holding was fashioned in the shape of a bird's head, an eagle or a hawk or something. But there was no time to think, because it seemed that disaster was inevitable. Viggo steeled himself for the impact and then, at the last instant, something within him finally snapped, galvanising him into action.

He let out a frantic yell and reached over to wrench the steering wheel from Mum's hands, turning it hard to the right.

The car swerved violently and the sound of Mum's scream mingled with the long, shrieking squeal of rubber on tarmac as she hit the brakes. Ruby slewed sideways. For a moment, Viggo was sure they were going to skid, go spinning around in a circle, but Mum somehow managed to wrestle back control of the steering wheel, swinging it back to the left. They began to slow down, before coming to a juddering stop.

Viggo fell back in his seat with a gasp of relief and then, remembering what he'd seen, he twisted around to stare back over his shoulder. As far as he could see, the road behind them was completely empty. He made a sound, a low grunt of surprise.

Mum sat hunched over the steering wheel, seemingly trying to remember how to breathe. She turned her head to look at Viggo and, even in the gloom, he could see that her face was shockingly white. Her eyes seemed to blaze with anger.

'What the hell were you trying to do?' she gasped.

'I . . .' He gestured helplessly at the windscreen. 'Didn't you *see* it?'

She glared at him. 'See what?'

'He was right in front of us! I thought you were going to drive straight into him.'

Her eyes narrowed and then widened again as she thought she followed his meaning. 'Was it a deer?' she asked him.

He shook his head. 'You . . . you surely can't have missed it. Didn't you see? It was . . .' But he couldn't say the words he wanted to say because he knew how they would sound.

*'You see, Mum, there was this Viking warrior in the road and he was galloping straight towards us and he was pointing a sword right at me.'*

He even pictured himself saying those words and in his mind's eye saw the look that Mum would give him back – one of sheer disbelief. So instead of telling her the truth he found himself improvising, nodding frantically as he spoke.

'Yes, Mum! A deer! It jumped right over the hedge! It went past us like an express train, but you just kept talking; you didn't even seem to notice.'

Mum stared back at him, shocked, and he felt a twinge of guilt go through him, but he knew he couldn't tell her the truth.

'I'm so sorry,' she whispered. 'I must've let my attention wander.' She took a deep breath and then shook her head, as though trying to clear it. 'I can't believe I didn't even *see* the damned thing! Hadn't I just been saying that I didn't know anyone it had ever happened to?' She gave a strange, shrill laugh, then sat up a little straighter and took a firm hold on the steering wheel. 'It's a good job *you* saw it,' she murmured.

There was a sudden, ear-shattering bellow that made them both jump in their seats and a bright light blazed from behind them. An instant later, an articulated lorry swerved around Ruby and thundered past, its horn blaring indignantly. Viggo stared at the red tail lights moving onwards into the haze and his stomach lurched.

Mum sat there, her mouth wide open.

'I forgot we were in the middle of the road,' she murmured at last.

Viggo nodded. 'Maybe we'd better get moving,' he suggested.

Mum reached obediently for the ignition and got Ruby started up again. She looked long and hard into her wing mirrors before driving carefully away, taking it more slowly than she had before. Neither of them spoke for quite a while after that. Viggo sat there thinking about what he'd just seen – about what he *thought* he'd seen – and he tried to come up with a rational explanation for it.

*A trick of the light*, he told himself, the haar deceiving him, making him believe that he was seeing something that wasn't really there . . . he'd heard about things like that. And yet, thinking back to it now, he could recall it all in such incredible detail.

One more thing. Just as he was about to plough into the front of the car, the man's mouth had been open, his teeth bared, and Viggo had noticed a prominent gap between his two front teeth – a detail that reminded him of somebody he hadn't seen in many years. He thought about it for a moment and felt a chill settle inside him. Because . . . hadn't it reminded him of his dad?

'We're still on schedule,' observed Mum, calmer now, talking with an artificial brightness in her tone, clearly trying to put Viggo at ease. 'If we keep up this speed, we should be there in plenty of time to catch the ferry.'

Viggo nodded but didn't say anything.

'And Viggo, I know you think I'm overreacting about Magnus, but after what happened to your dad . . . I worry, you see. You *do* get that, don't you?'

'I get that,' agreed Viggo, and was aware, as he said it, that for entirely different reasons, he was worried too: about his own state of mind.

# CHAPTER 3

## ALL ABOARD

'You couldn't get a cabin?' muttered Viggo.

'They go really quickly,' explained Mum, leading him along the aisle of seats. 'You have to book well in advance for those, and we were fairly last minute. But these pods are supposed to be very comfortable.'

Viggo didn't feel entirely convinced. What he was looking at were rows of reclining seats – big, padded things with hooded tops that extended out to enclose your head when you leant back. They were arranged in twos in a long line. Mum was studying her tickets, trying to locate the right seat numbers. The ferry was still moored at the quayside but already Viggo was aware of the carpeted floor swaying disconcertingly beneath him. He tried to remember if he had much experience of sailing. He supposed he must have if he'd travelled to Norway as a child – or had they flown? It was odd that he didn't remember any of it, just as he hadn't remembered the car accident that Mum had mentioned. Perhaps a part of him had wanted to blot it out, forget all about it.

Mum finally found their seats and ushered Viggo into the one beside the window before settling down beside him.

She sat there, clutching a chunky paperback novel and looking at the various passengers moving along the aisle to her right, searching for their places. She glanced at her watch. 'We'll be heading off pretty soon,' she announced. Now they were finally ready to leave, she seemed nervous. 'I'm not sure how I feel about going back to Shetland,' she told Viggo. 'Of course, I had to go there to talk to the police when Jonathan went missing. It didn't give me the best impression of the place. You and Magnus stayed with Granny in Dunbar while I was gone. We've never really spoken about it, have we?'

Viggo had other things on his mind. 'Am I all right on the water?' he asked her.

She gave him a disconcerting look. 'You don't remember?' she asked him.

He shook his head and Mum adopted a vague expression.

'You, er . . . did have *some* problems,' she told him. 'The last time you were on a boat.'

'What do you mean?'

'I seem to remember you were . . . a bit seasick.'

'Right. Perfect. Don't tell me, Magnus was fine, I suppose?'

'Er . . . he was, actually. Never seemed to bother him.' Mum reached into her shoulder bag and pulled out a box of pills. 'I got you these,' she said. 'Just in case.'

He took them from her and studied the box doubtfully. He saw it contained something called Kwells. He looked back at Mum. 'When you say "a bit sick" . . .'

Mum tried to look calm. 'OK, very sick. But take a couple of those and I'm sure they'll sort you out. You don't need water, you can just chew them.'

Viggo glared at her. 'You didn't think to mention this before?' he asked.

'No. If I'd done that, I'd never have persuaded you to come with me,' said Mum, matter-of-factly.

'Right.' Viggo shook his head. He opened the box, extracted a couple of tablets and chewed them, trying not to grimace at the odd, soapy flavour. Then he turned and stared out of the long window beside him. There wasn't much to see out there, just a length of dock and a couple of bored looking men in fluorescent jackets, one of whom was smoking a cigarette while his companion watched him intently, as though thinking of marking him on his performance. At least the haar had cleared, Viggo told himself, and there was even a half-hearted wash of sunlight. The swaying motion didn't seem to be too awful but he was pretty sure that it would intensify once they were under way.

'How soon before we leave?' he asked apprehensively.

Mum glanced at her watch. 'Just a few minutes now,' she told him. 'And we'll arrive at Lerwick in twelve hours or so.'

He stared at her. 'Twelve *hours*?' he cried.

'I did tell you before,' Mum assured him. 'You never seem to pay attention to what I say. It's like you're permanently tuned to another channel or something. What's going on in your head?'

Viggo shrugged. 'I dunno,' he said. 'Other stuff.'

'Well, the best thing is just to get your head down and go to sleep.'

'It's ten to seven at night,' he reminded her. 'How am I supposed to do that?'

'You have your earphones, don't you? You could listen to the radio or something.'

'The *radio*?' he echoed mockingly. 'Who listens to that any more?'

Mum stared at him. '*I* do. As you well know. Radio Four, mostly.'

Viggo rolled his eyes. 'People talking,' he muttered. 'No thanks.' He pondered for a moment. 'I suppose I could listen to a podcast,' he allowed.

'Well, what's that but people talking?' she asked him.

'It's not the same,' he assured her.

'How is it different?'

'They . . . talk about more interesting stuff. Cool stuff.' He waved his phone at her. 'There's one on here all about the new *Thor* movie. That's supposed to be brilliant.'

She completely missed the accusatory tone in his voice.

'Yes, that should keep you occupied for a while. And it might help you sleep.'

He was about to say something else but was interrupted by the arrival of a new traveller who came along the aisle carrying a big, solid-bodied guitar case on his back. He was tall, skinny, probably in his late fifties, Viggo thought, his face tanned and grizzled by the sun. He had ragged shoulder-length hair that had once been blonde but was now streaked with silver, a badly-cut beard and he was dressed in a parka and faded blue jeans. Viggo couldn't help but notice that he wore leather sandals from which his huge bare toes protruded – and that the nails were painted red. Now he paused and smiled down at Mum, as though greeting an old acquaintance.

'Hey there,' he said brightly. 'How's it going?'

Mum smiled awkwardly back at him. 'It's . . . er . . . going fine,' she said uncertainly. The man turned his head slightly and nodded to Viggo. 'Are these the sleep pods?' he asked.

'Allegedly,' said Viggo, not really in the mood for pleasantries.

'They are,' confirmed Mum. She pointed at the guitar case. 'I think you're only supposed to bring hand baggage in here.'

The man grinned, displaying rows of dazzlingly white teeth. 'Can't be parted from this old girl,' he said, reaching back to pat the case. Viggo noticed that his fingernails had been left their natural colour. The man had a suave English accent, probably a Londoner, Viggo thought. 'I had a hell of an argument with them back there.'

'Did you?' Mum sounded surprised.

'They wanted me to put her in the hold, but I said, "She's my life support system, I can't be parted from *her*"! In the end, do you know what they did?'

Mum shook her head.

'They made me pay for an extra seat. A seat for a *guitar*. Crooks!' He unhooked the straps and laid the guitar case carefully down on the seat in front of Viggo's.

'You know those are numbered?' Viggo asked him.

'Hmm?' The man looked down at his guitar case as though he hadn't considered such a thing. 'In the end, there was nothing for it but to pay up. Used the last bit of cash I had. But it was blackmail! What would I ever do, if I lost my harp?'

'Harp?' echoed Mum. 'I thought you said it was a guitar.'

The stranger grinned. 'Figure of speech,' he said. 'She *is* a guitar, of course. A Gretsch semi-acoustic.' He said the last bit slowly, as though savouring the taste of his own words. Then he extended a hand. 'Leon Bragg,' he said in a confident way, that suggested he thought they might have heard of him. 'Wandering musician,' he added. 'Actually, I prefer the term "troubadour".'

*Do you really?* thought Viggo, and considered a less flattering term which he thought suited the man better.

After a moment's hesitation, Mum took Leon's hand and shook it politely. He reached across to Viggo and dutifully shook his hand too.

'Always a pleasure to meet fellow travellers,' he said. Viggo experienced a sinking feeling as he realised there was a serious danger they might have to suffer this man for the entire journey.

'Bit of a coincidence, your seat being right in front of us,' muttered Viggo.

'What takes you to Shetland?' enquired Leon.

'This ferry,' said Viggo flatly, and Mum directed a warning glance at him before turning back to smile at the stranger.

'My eldest son is there,' she explained. 'Viggo and I are heading out to meet him.'

'Assuming we can find him,' muttered Viggo. 'If he doesn't hide when he sees us coming.'

'He's joking,' said Mum, but now Leon was looking at her, as though puzzled by something. He pointed at Viggo. 'You're saying that this is your son?' he murmured.

'Er . . . yes, that's right.'

'And you have an older one? Hardly seems possible.'

Viggo felt like snorting out loud at that, but Mum just looked embarrassed. 'Oh, I'm sure that's not the case,' she said. 'You're clearly a bit of a flatterer.'

'Or short-sighted,' said Viggo under his breath, and this time Mum actually glared at him.

'I speak as I find,' said Leon. 'Gets me into all kinds of trouble.' Again, he favoured Mum with that oily smile. 'But what can a fellow do?'

Just at that moment, a middle-aged man wearing a North Face jacket over a grey business suit came to a halt beside the seat where Leon's guitar was. He was holding a ticket and looking down at it uncertainly. 'Excuse me,' he said, 'I think this is . . .'

'. . . taken,' interrupted Leon. He stepped closer to the man and in one smooth movement took the ticket from his hand and gave him another in exchange. 'There's been a mix-up,' he announced. 'Turns out your seat is further along the aisle.'

'Oh, but . . .'

'And I need to be here, you see, because I've just bumped into two very good friends.'

The man stood for a moment, looking as though he might protest, but then his shoulders slumped and with a shrug he moved on again, studying his new ticket. Leon pocketed the other one and turned back to Mum, his confident smile still in place. 'A little white lie,' he said. 'I hope you don't mind.'

Mum seemed momentarily at a loss for words. 'But, er . . . that man?'

'What about him?'

'That was his seat.'

'Yes,' said Leon. 'It *was*.' He grinned. 'It's mine now.'

Mum shook her head and attempted to take the conversation in a different direction. 'So, you're going to Shetland to . . . perform?' she ventured.

'I am,' admitted Leon.

'You'll have to let us know where you're playing.'

*So we can avoid the place*, thought Viggo.

'Oh, I have no professional engagements,' said Leon. 'Not this time. No, I've always meant to visit Shetland and I thought this summer was as good a time as any. I'll busk as I go.'

'Busk?' Mum seemed surprised to hear this. 'You're a street performer?'

'Streets, fields, taverns, hotels, stadiums . . . wherever they'll have me.' He narrowed his eyes a little. 'And what about yourselves?' he asked. He looked intently at Mum. 'I'm sorry, I don't think I caught your name.'

'I don't think she threw it,' said Viggo, and Mum prodded him with her elbow.

'It's Alison, actually.'

'Ah. *Alison*. I *love* the song. Elvis Costello, right? A classic. I may perform it for you later.'

Viggo wasn't sure if this was a promise or a threat. 'That's an old one,' he observed.

'Oh, not so very old. Some of my material is positively vintage.'

'Like cheese?' suggested Viggo.

'The finest Cheddar.' Leon's eyes narrowed. 'So, where are you staying?'

'Us?' Mum hesitated and Viggo found himself repeating the same phrase over and over in his head.

*Don't tell him, don't tell him, don't tell him* . . .

'We've booked a little place just outside of Lerwick. One of those pod things.'

'Ah, I see. You're glamping!'

'I wouldn't say that exactly. It's quite modest.'

*She'll be telling him how much rent she's paying in a minute!* thought Viggo.

'And you're staying there the whole of your visit?'

'Oh, no, we'll be travelling. We're not exactly sure where Magnus is, you see . . .'

'Magnus?'

'My other son. So we'll be basing ourselves there and driving around looking for him.'

'How splendid! You have a car!'

'Er, yes. Just a little Kia.'

'Oh, but to a weary foot soldier like me, any vehicle sounds like a chariot.'

'Well, as I said, we're not entirely sure where Magnus is, so we'll be looking for him.'

'Sounds like you're on a quest,' observed Leon.

'Not really,' Viggo corrected him. 'More of a pain in the backside.'

Leon gazed at him for a moment and then threw back his head and laughed uproariously at a startling volume. 'Oh, he's good,' he told Mum. 'I *like* him. Is your other son as funny?'

Mum shook her head. 'No, he's the serious one,' she said. She made a show of opening her book. 'Well, Mr Bragg, I don't wish to be rude, but . . .'

'Please, call me Leon. And I'm so sorry, Alison, I didn't mean to intrude on your privacy.'

'Oh, not at all. We just—'

She was interrupted by a blast of syrupy music from the ferry's sound system and a suave recorded voice announced that they were about to depart.

'Well, I'm sure we'll talk more in due course,' said Leon, turning aside. But then something seemed to occur to him and he looked back again. 'Will you be dining later?'

'Erm . . . I expect so. There's a cafeteria, *The Feast*, or something. We couldn't get admission to the posher place; you have to have a cabin for that.'

'*Magnus's Lounge*,' said Leon.

'Oh,' she said. 'Is that what it's called? There's a coincidence.'

Leon smiled. 'Forgive me, Alison, but I don't believe in that word.'

'You don't?'

'No. Everything in life – every tiny detail – is preordained, in my view. I was wondering . . .?'

'Yes?'

'Perhaps we could eat together, later, the three of us? We could share our humble traveller's tales as we dine. That is, if I wouldn't be too much of a bother.'

'Umm . . .' There was a long silence. Viggo stared at Mum, willing her to say no, wanting her to tell Leon that he *would* be a bother actually, that they'd rather eat a plateful of their own vomit than dine with him. But, of course, she didn't say anything of the kind. 'Perhaps,' she offered. 'You know, I'm really quite tired. I may just want to sleep.'

'I totally understand.' Leon turned away and settled himself into his own seat. Viggo directed a withering glare at Mum and she could only spread her hands in a 'what could I do?' sort of way.

At that moment, the ferry moved away from the dockside and Viggo felt a corresponding lurch in the pit of his stomach. With inevitable timing, a recorded voice spilled out of unseen speakers.

'Hi there, this is Captain Njord speaking. Just to let you know that we're expecting a little rough weather en route to Shetland and you may experience some buffeting as we go. But rest assured, your welfare is always our primary concern. We will now be running through our safety procedures. Please listen carefully while we go through what to do in case of an emergency.'

Viggo looked glumly at Mum and she made a valiant attempt to put him at ease.

'I'm sure there's nothing to worry about, Viggo. It's just routine.'

'He said something about rough weather!'

Leon's head appeared from around the side of the seat in front of Mum. He had a sympathetic look on his grizzled face. 'Not a good sailor?' he enquired.

'I don't really know,' Viggo told him. 'It's been a while.'

'Let me give you a little tip, my young friend. If you start to feel queasy, get to a place where you can see the horizon.'

'You mean, like, out on deck?'

'Indeed. Sickness happens because your brain can't work out what's happening to your body. As long as you can see the horizon, you'll be fine. Oh, and whatever you do, don't take any of those travel sickness potions. They just make it worse.'

His head moved out of sight again and Viggo leant closer to Mum.

'The pills make it worse!' he hissed into her ear.

'Oh, you shouldn't take that as gospel,' she whispered back. 'He's not a doctor.'

'A chancer is what he is! You realise that wasn't even his seat?'

'Yes, but ...'

'Whatever you do, don't tell him anything else!'

She gave him a wounded look and whispered back. 'I'm sure he's just being friendly.'

'Too friendly, if you ask me!' He thought for a moment. 'And I'll tell you something else. There's no way we're having dinner with him.'

# CHAPTER 4
## ROUGH CROSSING

In the end, they went to dinner with Leon.

Viggo and Mum followed him reluctantly along a swaying corridor. He was striding purposefully ahead of them, talking as he went, and Mum kept flinging apologetic looks at Viggo, but he knew this time it really wasn't her fault.

A short while back, the two of them had got silently up from their pods, thinking that Leon must be asleep by now. They were intent on sneaking away so they could find a table to themselves. But, as they turned to leave, Leon had jumped quickly upright like a meerkat, as if attuned to their every move and had been waiting patiently for this moment.

'Time for dinner, I think,' he said brightly. And, before they had time to raise an objection, he was tagging along with them, seemingly oblivious to their disgruntled expressions. The only other option was to tell him to get lost but, of course, neither of them felt they could do that. Then, when Mum dithered about which direction to take, Leon stepped smoothly into the role of leader, as if he actually worked on the ferry and had done this many times.

'It's just a wee stroll this way,' he announced, pointing.

He glanced over his shoulder at Viggo. 'I know you're not feeling too chipper, old son, but trust me, if you can get some stodge into your belly, it will stand you in good stead. I speak from bitter experience.'

He strode on and Viggo directed a razor-sharp glare between the man's shoulder blades – but had no other option than to follow. *Not feeling too chipper* felt like the understatement of the century. Right now, Viggo's stomach was performing a dance, one that was attuned to every pitch and lurch of the ferry on the increasingly rough sea. He wasn't convinced that eating was a good idea, but neither was staying in a seat that was beginning to feel like a ride at an amusement park.

*The Feast* turned out to be a cafeteria, sleek and spacious, with wooden doors and honey-coloured tiled flooring. On the other side of a long partition, oblong metal tables were arranged on a red carpet. The place was surprisingly busy considering the worsening weather; travellers eating and drinking enthusiastically.

At the top of the room was a long wooden counter where, under a perspex hood, metal containers of hot and cold food were arranged for inspection. Various uniformed staff stood resolutely behind the presentation, faces calm, serving spoons at the ready, as though trying to maintain the illusion that everything here was business as usual. As he drew closer, the smell of fried fish assailed Viggo's nostrils and he had to make a determined effort not to gag. Mum sensed his discomfort and patted him gently on the back.

'You all right, sweetheart?' she murmured.

He could only shake his head in reply. He considered telling her that he felt miserable, but what would be the point of that?

Leon collected some trays from a trolley and handed one to each to his companions. 'Now, let's see what delights they have for us,' he suggested.

'I'm really not sure I want to eat,' protested Viggo. 'Maybe I'll just have a drink.'

'Nonsense,' insisted Leon. 'You need to get some nourishment.' He waved a hand at a veritable landscape of hot food: battered fish and glistening chips, macaroni cheese, curry and rice, great steaming vats of mushy peas and baked beans. 'There must be something here to tempt you.'

Viggo felt a wave of revulsion shudder through him. 'I really don't think...'

But now Leon was taking the tray out of his hands and directing that smug smile of his at a uniformed woman behind the counter. 'My young friend will have the fish and chips,' he told her. 'And I'll have the same. Oh, and some of those wonderful mushy peas. Always had a soft spot for the old Manchester caviar!' He winked at her and turned to look at Mum. 'Alison, what's your fancy?'

'Er... salad of some kind, I think,' she muttered. 'Tuna.'

'Watching your figure? There's hardly any need for that.'

Mum didn't seem to know what to say to this and meekly allowed Leon to place the order for her. Viggo stared at her, mystified, wondering what was wrong with her. She wasn't usually such a pushover. He'd often seen her put other people in their place.

Leon accepted the plates of food as they were handed to him and arranged them on to trays. He gave the first of them to Viggo. 'Why don't you go and find us a table?' he suggested. 'I'll bring condiments. Ketchup, salt, vinegar. Oh, and cutlery of course. We can't eat with our fingers, can we? We're not heathens!'

Viggo shrugged. 'Whatever,' he said. He lifted his tray and turned dutifully aside, gazing around the busy lounge to see if he could locate an empty table. He spotted one and made his way towards it, aware as he did so that the floor was swaying even more alarmingly now, making it hard to balance. He threw a glance in the direction of the nearest window but couldn't make out anything other than water sluicing across it.

He managed to reach the table without falling over and set down his tray, before collapsing gratefully on to a chair. A short distance to his left, a group of young men, all dressed in matching red T-shirts and blue jeans, sat around a long table, clutching pints of lager, from which they kept taking enthusiastic gulps. Every so often, one or other of them would make an oafish comment in an unnecessarily loud voice which would coax fits of laughter from his companions. Some kind of stag party, Viggo decided; he'd seen enough of them in Edinburgh at weekends, though Shetland seemed an odd choice of destination for that kind of thing. Maybe this bunch were into hiking as well as boozing. To Viggo's right, there was a sudden clatter and he turned his head just in time to see a wheeled metal trolley, heaped with trays of discarded crockery, go rattling across the floor, before a uniformed steward intercepted it and pushed it out of harm's way.

'The weather's definitely getting rougher,' observed Leon, sounding almost gleeful as he settled himself into the seat beside Viggo. Leon looked down at his own heaped plate in apparent anticipation. 'This looks great,' he observed. 'Just what the doctor ordered.'

'If you say so,' muttered Viggo, but doubted that any doctor in history had ever prescribed fish and chips to a patient. He watched as Mum eased herself into a seat on the far side of the table and set down a tray containing a plate of salad. The sight of a mound of glistening mayonnaise made Viggo look quickly away as his stomach gurgled in protest. Unfortunately, he now found himself staring at Leon who was in the act of heaping a steaming portion of cod into his mouth. He began to chew enthusiastically, then glanced at Mum. 'So kind of you to step in back there,' he said, through a mouthful of fish. 'Can't *believe* my debit card wasn't working.'

'Oh . . . that's all right,' said Mum tonelessly, though it clearly wasn't. 'It was nice of you to offer to pay for us all in the first place.'

'I expect it's just a technical glitch. If you'd be good enough to furnish me with your bank details, I'll make sure it's repaid the minute I sort things out.'

Mum looked alarmed at this suggestion. She shook her head. 'Really, forget about it,' she insisted, ignoring the exasperated look that Viggo gave her. 'My pleasure.'

'Well, I absolutely thank you from the bottom of my heart.' Leon took another enormous bite of fish. 'Fresh as you like,' he observed. He waved a fork at Viggo's untouched plate. 'Come on, old son, get that into you. You'll feel a lot better if you do.'

'I really don't think that's a good idea,' murmured Viggo. 'My stomach . . .'

'. . . is empty,' finished Leon. 'That's why it feels odd. Fill it with something and it will stabilise.' Viggo looked doubtfully across the table at Mum.

'You don't have to eat if you don't want to,' she told him, but Leon was having none of it.

'Trust me, Alison. I'm a seasoned traveller,' he said. And then, as if to settle the matter, he looked at Viggo and added, 'Your mother just paid a lot of money for this food.'

Viggo sighed and reached out a hand to lift a chip from his plate. He raised it to his mouth and took a cautious bite. It tasted all right and nothing terrible happened, so he repeated the exercise and, finally encouraged, located a knife and fork and began to eat properly.

'That's the way,' said Leon. 'Dig in, old son.' He tore the top off a plastic sachet with his teeth and strafed his own plate with dollops of blood-red ketchup. 'A touch of the old Kensington gore,' he said. 'Excellent!' He looked at Mum again. 'So. You promised we'd exchange traveller's tales.'

'I don't remember agreeing to that,' said Mum, picking delicately at her salad. 'I believe that was your idea.'

'Well, I suppose it was, but . . .'

A bellow of laughter went up from the table to their left and Leon directed a disapproving look at the group of young men. 'We'll see if they're still laughing when the storm hits,' he said, louder than was strictly necessary. One of the men, a big thick-set fellow with hair that had been shaved down to a stubble, directed a hostile glare at Leon, but he ignored it. 'I see a lot of this on my travels,' he told Mum. 'Young men who think that booze is the answer to every problem.

Well, I know where they're coming from. I've been there myself.'

'Really?' Mum stopped eating for a moment and tried to look suitably surprised.

'Oh, yes. In my wild youth, I thought I had all the answers, didn't I? Thought I'd been given the keys to paradise. I had my guitar and my talent and I believed I was untouchable.' He smiled as if remembering happy times. 'I travelled the world, broke the hearts of many lovely ladies and never once stopped to ask the question.'

There was a long pause, before Mum finally felt obliged to ask, 'What question is that?'

'The biggie. What's it all about? Life, love, the universe, everything.'

'And . . . what was the answer?'

Leon shrugged. 'Alas, I never found it. But I did learn one thing. Alcohol is not a solution.' Again, he looked fearlessly at the table of young men. 'For anything,' he added, as if for emphasis. And once more, the heavy-set man glanced at him with a look of annoyance, as though contemplating getting up from the table to take the matter further. But then he turned away with a shrug. He muttered something to the man next to him and they both laughed uproariously. Leon stared challengingly at them for a moment longer, then returned his gaze to Mum.

'Of course, I have connections with Shetland,' he said. 'I spoke before about not believing in coincidence, did I not?'

'Er . . . I believe you did.'

'Well, I have always been destined to go there.'

'Destined, how?' Despite everything, Mum seemed interested.

'You know my name? My surname? Bragg.'

Viggo paused in the act of taking a bite of fish. 'What about it?' he asked.

'Well, many people will tell you that it's of Norman origin. That it means 'cheerful', 'lively' . . . maybe even, 'arrogant'.'

Viggo nodded. He couldn't help feeling the name suited Leon pretty well. 'I thought it meant 'boastful',' he said.

'That's been suggested too. Water off a duck's back!' Leon chuckled. 'Other scholars would argue that the name may be Norse. Did you know that Bragi is a Norse God? A musician, a poet, one of the many sons of Odin.'

'Now you mention it, I think I *do* remember that,' said Mum. She set down her fork. 'And I also recall that you referred to your guitar as a harp. Bragi played the harp, didn't he?'

Leon looked surprised. 'Very good,' he told her. 'I'm impressed.'

Mum waved a hand to dismiss the notion. 'Don't be. It's down to my husband, really. He was the expert on all that stuff.'

'Was?' Leon arranged his face into a look of sympathy. 'Oh, I'm so sorry, are you saying that your husband has . . . passed?'

Mum sighed. 'We don't really know what happened to him,' she said. 'He went missing five years ago.'

'Mum!' hissed Viggo. 'You don't have to tell people *everything*!'

'Oh, don't worry, Viggo,' Leon assured him. 'It won't go any further. You have my word on that.' He looked at Mum. 'How awful,' he murmured. 'And this happened in Shetland, did it?'

'Yes . . . it did actually.'

'How did you know that?' asked Viggo suspiciously.

'I didn't. I just surmised.'

'Well, you're correct,' admitted Mum. 'Jonathan was working on an excavation, you see, for the university where he worked. They were unearthing a Viking burial ground. At any rate, he just . . . vanished.'

'I see. How extraordinary.'

'And this is the main reason why Magnus is in Shetland in the first place.'

'Looking for Jonathan, you mean?'

'Oh no, not that. But he got the Viking bug from his father and studied Norse Mythology at university. He's very knowledgeable on the subject.'

'When you said you didn't know where Magnus was, I didn't realise you meant . . .' Leon set down his fork and reached out a hand to place it on one of Mum's. 'You must be absolutely beside yourself with worry.'

Mum studied her half-eaten meal. 'I *am* worried,' she admitted. 'Of course I am. But it's only been a few days. I may be getting things out of proportion.'

'A mother worries,' said Leon knowingly, as though he had personal experience of it. He removed his hand and went back to his food. 'Well, rest assured, Alison. I will help you to search for your son.'

Mum looked up with an expression of alarm. 'There's no need for that!' she cried.

'No, there isn't,' said Viggo flatly, and Mum and Leon both turned to look at him. 'Besides, there's nothing to worry about. I know Magnus. He'll be holed up somewhere chasing some new thing he's found. It won't have occurred to him to let us know what's happening. He'll show up.'

Leon studied Viggo for a moment. 'It sounds as though you don't like him very much,' he observed with a knowing smile.

'It's not that, it's just . . .' He saw that Mum was about to say something and got there first. 'Please don't say that we're too alike!' he warned her. 'Because we're really not.'

There was a brief silence and then a dull thud as the ferry crashed headlong into a wave, making it pitch sharply upwards. All three of them were obliged to grab their trays as they began to slide across the surface of the table. There were shouts of alarm from their left and a smashing sound as various glasses and bottles went skittering to destruction. The ferry seemed to hang in its elevated position for a moment before crashing heavily back into the water with an impact that shook Viggo to his bones. He felt the half-digested food in his belly rise and fall alarmingly and promptly dismissed the idea of eating any more of it. Leon, on the other hand, seemed undeterred and lifted a mound of ketchup-smeared chips to his mouth. Viggo had to look away.

'It does seem to be getting rougher,' observed Mum, pushing her own plate aside.

'Oh, this is nothing,' said Leon. 'I was on a ferry to Zeebrugge one time and it was blowing an absolute gale. Everybody on the boat was sick except me, and I only managed to avoid it by walking around the deck all night. By the time we docked, my beard was covered in icicles!' He threw back his head and laughed at the memory. 'Happy days!' he cried. 'Oh, hello . . .'

He was looking at the table to their left. Viggo saw that the thick-set man had got unsteadily to his feet and that his face had turned as white as a fall of snow. He stood there, looking helplessly around, as his friends shouted unhelpful comments at him.

'What's the matter, Harry?'

'Feeling a bit off?'

'Here it comes,' muttered Leon.

The man doubled over with a sudden grunt and vomited copiously over the wreckage on the table. His companions leapt frenziedly aside in an attempt to avoid the spray and then two of them went to his assistance, lifting his arms over their shoulders. Laughing, they half-carried, half-dragged him towards the exit. Every few steps, he retched violently and threw up again, leaving a series of reeking puddles in his wake. The other members of the group stood looking down at the table in bewilderment and then began to wander away, leaving the devastation for others to clear up. Viggo could see that several of them were looking queasy and he knew exactly how they felt.

Incredibly, Leon still continued to eat. 'He won't be the last of them, you mark my words,' he said. 'Alcohol is absolutely the worst thing in these cases.' He gestured at Viggo's plate. 'If you're not going to finish that . . .'

'Be my guest,' said Viggo, and watched in disbelief as Leon reached across, took the plate and stacked it on top of his own empty one, before continuing to eat.

'I've been in situations,' he said, between mouthfuls, 'where I didn't know where my next meal was coming from. One summer in Tunisia, me and my girlfriend were reduced to begging on the streets. Begging! I mean, I'd tried playing my songs for them and handing around a hat, but they didn't seem to understand the concept of busking.'

Viggo was about to reply but just then, the ferry hit another huge wave. Mum's plate of salad whizzed out of her reach and went spinning, flinging its colourful contents in all directions. As the boat's hull smacked down on to the water again, Viggo felt his stomach go into freefall and was somehow aware that all the colour was draining from his face. He struggled upright.

'The . . . deck?' he groaned.

Leon pointed decisively. 'Straight to the back and through the door on the left.'

And then Viggo was running, veering from side to side as the red carpet see-sawed alarmingly beneath him. He made it across the intervening space, pushing roughly past other passengers, horribly aware of the meal rising up within him. He silently cursed Leon Bragg and his 'helpful' advice. Just when he thought all hope was lost, he finally saw a metal door ahead of him and managed to wrench it open.

He stepped outside into a tumult, cold air battering him like a series of fists, icy rain bouncing off his face. A low metal barrier was directly ahead of him and he flailed desperately towards it, then found he was clutching the top of it, bracing himself as he stared down into dark, churning waters.

The sickness came out of him like molten fire, burning the

back of his throat, and he gagged violently before discharging what felt like the entire contents of his stomach. In the maelstrom, he couldn't tell in which direction it was going – whether it was falling to the sea or blowing back directly into his face. He coughed, spat and stared grimly out into the darkness . . .

. . . and heard music.

The sound of drums beating a relentless rhythm.

He lifted one arm to wipe at his mouth and was aware that on the horizon, where the sun was setting, there was a weird, purplish glow. He snatched in a breath and stared, because now he could discern something silhouetted against that glow – a long, low shape, the front part of which curved upwards into the air like a serpent. And now, he thought he could see a series of grey circles running along the length of the boat, if that was what it was, metal discs that glinted dully in the dying light . . . and . . . were those oars jutting out from between the discs? Long, wooden oars, stirring the already agitated water into motion as men inside the craft struggled to find purchase on the water?

Viggo gasped in disbelief. This couldn't be real, he told himself, because he was looking at a Viking longship, ploughing through the water as though powering towards the nearest shore, and the sound of the drums was emanating from that longship, as though the rowers were trying to keep pace with its urgent thudding rhythm.

Viggo shook his head. *No*, he told himself. *It can't be.*

Suddenly, there were hands on his shoulders, steadying him, and a voice muttering something that was snatched away by the howling wind, but he ignored that because . . . the boat. The Viking boat! It *was* there . . . wasn't it?

'Mum,' he croaked, and pointed across the water, even though the shape was already losing definition, fading back into the weird purplish light.

'Can you see it, Mum?' he asked. 'Can you see what I see?'

'It's all right, Viggo,' said a voice in his ear. It wasn't Mum's voice, it was Leon, talking persuasively; an unseen hand rubbing his back. 'Just get all of it up, old son, you'll feel much better.'

Viggo shook his head and again he pointed.

'There!' he whispered. 'See?'

But now more sickness was rising within him. His eyes blurred with hot tears and the Viking ship was gone, as though it had never been there in the first place.

# CHAPTER 5
## VELCRO

Viggo and Mum were back in Ruby, in a line of traffic heading slowly away from the ferry terminal. They had abandoned the idea of breakfast that morning and sneaked out of their pods as soon as land was visible on the horizon. Leon, luckily, had remained sleeping soundly on the seat in front of them. They'd headed quietly to the exit that led to the vehicle deck, hoping against hope that he wouldn't come running after them, and, after a tense wait, a voice on the tannoy finally announced that they could descend to their cars. They hurried down the stairs and climbed into Ruby, both feeling weirdly guilty at their actions. Viggo recalled how Leon had virtually carried him to his pod the previous night, but they were determined to end their acquaintance with him here and now.

Viggo felt like a wrung-out cloth this morning and was just grateful to be back on dry land, while Mum couldn't help fretting about what they were doing. She sat at the wheel, staring at the rear of the vehicle ahead of them, her face set into a frown.

'I feel terrible,' she said.

'Me too,' Viggo agreed, rubbing a hand over his stomach.

'I don't mean that,' said Mum. 'We should at least have said goodbye to Leon. It's rude, running off like this.'

Viggo shook his head. 'If we'd woken him up he'd be in the car with us right now,' he told her. 'You know he would.'

'I'm sure he wasn't even headed in the same direction as us.'

Viggo was unconvinced. 'I don't think that man *has* a direction,' he muttered. 'He just sees you as some kind of meal ticket.' He shook his head. 'I can't believe you fell for it!' He went into an approximation of Leon's southern accent. 'Ooh, my debit card doesn't seem to be working!' He snorted. 'You do realise he ripped you off?'

Mum shrugged her shoulders. 'Well, what was the alternative? I certainly wasn't going to give him my bank details!'

'Oh, so you agree he's a crook?'

'I'm not saying that. I think he's one of those people who can talk others into just about anything. And when you think about it, he *was* really helpful.'

'How do you make that out?'

'Well, last night, you were in such a state, I don't know how I'd have managed to get you back to the pods. You were going on about something you thought you'd seen on the sea . . . a boat of some kind? You really weren't very clear.'

'Yeah, sorry, it's hard to be word perfect when you're throwing up. And that's another thing – it was Leon who kept telling me to eat!'

'I expect he meant well.'

'I think he *wanted* me to be ill. He wanted to get me out of the way so he could work on you.' Again, Viggo affected the accent.

'Ooh Alison, you don't need to be watching your figure, I can do that for you!'

'He never said that! You're putting words into his mouth!'

'That's exactly how he was. And all those questions about where we were staying. Honestly, I wouldn't trust him for a minute.'

Mum sighed. 'Well, never mind about Leon Bragg. Now we're here, we can concentrate on finding Magnus. We'll just . . . oh!'

'What's wrong?' Viggo saw that she was gazing straight ahead, her mouth open. He sat up and looked in the same direction. His heart sank. There was Leon, standing at the side of the road, guitar case on his back, a huge red rucksack propped against his legs. He was holding one arm out with a thumb upraised and he had a hopeful expression on his tanned face.

'Go faster!' Viggo urged Mum, and she gave him an incredulous look.

'How am I supposed to do that?' she asked him. 'We're in a queue.'

'Well, overtake!'

'I can't, there's only one lane.'

Viggo groaned. 'We'll just have to pretend we haven't seen him,' he suggested.

'That won't be convincing. And he'll see *us*!'

'That's too bad. We are not stopping. Not for anything!'

'But . . .'

'Not even if he lies down in front of us.'

'That would technically be murder.'

— 50 —

'Never mind that! Just keep looking straight ahead. Pretend you haven't seen him.'

They crawled along at two miles an hour. Viggo took out his phone and pretended to be absorbed in something on the screen. Mum just stared fixedly straight ahead, her face expressionless. Now they were moving alongside Leon. Viggo could almost feel the intensity of the man's gaze burning through the passenger window.

*Keep going, keep going, keep going* . . . The thought blazed through Viggo's mind, a few seconds before Ruby gave an ominous croak and came to a sudden stop.

He glared at Mum in disbelief. 'Why are you stopping?' he growled.

Mum shook her head. 'There's something wrong with Ruby,' she hissed back. She tried turning the ignition key but was rewarded with nothing more than a coughing sound from the engine. 'Oh, no!' she muttered, her face reddening. She tried again. And again. Now Viggo became horribly aware of a tapping sound beside his left ear. He turned his head and attempted a look of surprise as he saw that Leon had stepped off the pavement and was now rapping his knuckles on the window.

'Everything all right?' he asked.

Viggo grinned stupidly and gave him a thumbs-up. Mum tried the ignition again, with no success. Now the passenger door was opening. Leon stuck his head inside. 'You guys having a problem?' he asked.

'Ah, no,' said Viggo. 'No, we just . . . thought we'd . . . pause for a moment.'

'Pause for what?'

'For . . . er . . . to look at this wonderful scenery.' Viggo waved a hand around, though all that was visible was the pavement, a couple of rusting metal signs and the rapidly receding rear end of the car in front of them.

'I think I know what the problem is,' announced Leon. 'I don't believe it's serious. Alison, can you just unlock the bonnet for me?'

'Oh, no, we're fine!' trilled Mum. 'Really!'

'How are you fine?' asked Leon. 'You've broken down.'

'But . . . the garage assured me Ruby was roadworthy,' protested Mum. She registered Leon's puzzled expressions and added, 'That's what she's called. The car. Ruby.'

Leon nodded. 'Of course,' he said. 'She's red. Makes sense.'

'Yes, well, the garage checked everything and said there was absolutely no problem.'

'I'm sure they did say that, but clearly something's gone wrong.' Leon looked thoughtful. 'If you carry on like this,' he said, 'I'll think you're trying to avoid me.'

Mum gave a shrill laugh. 'As if!' she cried.

Leon gave her an odd look. 'Just pop the bonnet,' he said, and this time she complied.

Leon moved around to the front of the car and an instant later, the bonnet lifted, hiding him from view. Viggo buried his face in his hands. 'I don't believe this!' he hissed. 'That guy's like a fart in a wetsuit. You can't get rid of him!'

'Shush!' whispered Mum. 'He'll *hear* you!'

'I don't care, I just . . . he's . . .' The bonnet lowered again with a clunk and now Leon was moving back to Viggo's window.

Behind them, an impatient motorist sounded a horn. Leon glared challengingly at the culprit for a moment then leant in at the open door again. 'Try her now,' he suggested.

Mum reached for the ignition key and turned it. The engine started up instantly, sounding reassuringly normal. She stared down at her own hand as if it had just performed a magic trick.

'How did you . . .?'

'Oh, just a little technique I mastered when I worked for a few months at a garage in Inverness.' Leon grinned. 'I've picked up a whole range of tricks over the years. From time to time one of them comes in useful.'

Another motorist sounded a horn behind them, and a third joined in.

'Well, thank goodness you were here,' said Mum. 'I really don't know what we would have done without you.'

'My pleasure.' Leon rewarded her with a dazzling smile. 'I thought I'd have seen you two at breakfast,' he added.

'Er, well, we weren't hungry,' said Mum. 'As you know, Viggo was sick, so . . .'

'Tell me about it.' Leon transferred his gaze to Viggo. 'You're a lot heavier than you look,' he observed. 'My advice would have been to fill up on a big, greasy breakfast before we docked. But I expect you were feeling a bit too delicate for that.'

'Umm . . . I was, yes.' Again, the clamour of a horn sounded, but Leon seemed to be in no great hurry to step away from the car. Viggo gestured over his shoulder. 'Well, we're holding up the traffic, so I guess we should . . .'

'Where are you guys headed?' asked Leon.

'Oh, our first port of call is the holiday home we've booked,' said Mum. 'Just a few miles outside of Lerwick.' There was an uncomfortable silence. 'What about you?'

'Same area,' said Leon.

'What a coincidence,' said Viggo, through gritted teeth.

'Ah well, you know what I have to say about that subject,' Leon reminded him. 'There's—'

'No such thing,' finished Viggo wearily. 'Right. So where exactly is it that you're going to? In our area?'

Leon gazed at him calmly. 'Not entirely sure yet,' he admitted. 'I'll know it when I see it. Thought I'd just drift.'

Several car horns were honking at once now, but Leon seemed oblivious to them.

'Well, er, why don't we give you a lift?' suggested Mum, ignoring the glare that Viggo directed at her. 'Under the circumstances, it seems the very least we can do. And I can drop you wherever you'd like.'

Leon's face rearranged itself into a delighted grin. 'Alison, you're an absolute godsend! I was beginning to think I was all out of luck. I'll just grab my stuff.' Another car horn sounded an extended blast and Leon sent a fierce stare at the culprit. 'Yes, yes, what else did you get for Christmas?' he shouted. 'Just cool it, OK?' He turned away and went back to the pavement to collect his things. Viggo was still staring at Mum.

'For God's sake!' he whispered.

'What else could I do?' she protested. 'He got Ruby going again, didn't he? I couldn't have done that, could *you*? And we're wasting time. We need to start looking for Magnus!'

'OK, but you realise Leon's going to be with us for the entire stay now?'

'Nonsense. We'll drop him off wherever he chooses and then we'll say goodbye.'

'You make it sound easy, but that guy's like velcro. You can't—'

Viggo broke off as the rear door opened and Leon's giant backpack slammed on to the seat, closely followed by his guitar, which only just seemed to fit in the confined space. Leon came next, squeezing his long limbs in as best he could. 'Well, this is an unexpected pleasure!' he said, settling himself back against his seat. 'I thought I'd lost you back there.'

*And we hoped we'd lost you*, thought Viggo.

Leon slammed the rear door, then reached out a hand and placed it gently on Mum's shoulder. 'I still haven't sung you your song,' he reminded her.

'No,' said Mum tonelessly. 'No, you haven't.' There was an uncomfortable pause. 'Fasten your seatbelt,' she added.

'Yes, boss,' quipped Leon, and did as she'd suggested.

Mum finally put Ruby into gear and drove away.

\*\*\*

They sped onwards across an undulating green landscape. On nearly every horizon, scrub-covered hills reared up under a pale, cloud-flecked sky. They were only a few miles outside of Lerwick and already the land looked ancient and barren and utterly at peace with itself. Viggo thought it was unlike anywhere he'd been before.

'Where are the trees?' he wondered.

'There aren't any,' Mum told him. 'I remember that from

last time I was here. You just don't see them.' She had Ruby's sat nav plugged in and Viggo gazed at a blue line winding like a serpent across the display as they travelled. The delay by the docks had been short-lived. Once out of the little town, they'd encountered hardly any other traffic.

'This island used to be covered in forest,' said Leon. 'But five thousand years ago, the land was systematically cleared for the rearing of sheep – and those woolly rascals ensured that the trees never had a chance of returning.' He shook his head. 'Actually, there *are* a few places where people are attempting to bring the indigenous hazelnut trees back, but you have to know where to look.'

Viggo studied Leon in the rear view mirror. 'You seem to know an awful lot about Shetland,' he observed.

'Oh, just bits and pieces.'

'I thought you said you hadn't been here before?'

Leon considered this. 'No, I don't believe I did say that.'

'But you did! You said that you'd always meant to come here because of your name.'

'I think I said that I'd always meant to come *back* here because of my name. That's not quite the same thing.'

'OK, so . . . when were you last in Shetland?'

'Viggo, that sounds a bit like an inquisition,' Mum told him.

He ignored her. 'Was it recently? Years ago? A few weeks? I'd love to know.'

'I forget,' said Leon, as though it were of no importance. Now Viggo saw that he had picked up his guitar case and, with some difficulty in the cramped rear of the car, was manoeuvring it across his knees. He unhinged the lid and gently, almost reverently, took out the guitar. He pushed the case aside and lifted the instrument on to his lap. Viggo had to grudgingly admit it did look pretty special, the body blonde and a contrasting dark brown marbled fingerboard with the word GRETSCH printed on to it in white letters. 'Perhaps we should have a little music while we drive,' suggested Leon. 'Just to pass the time.'

Viggo couldn't see a polite way to say no, so he just shrugged his shoulders.

Leon brushed his fingers experimentally across the strings, creating a surprisingly mellow tone, which seemed to flood the little car with sound. Then Leon said, 'This is a special request for a special lady – and my way of thanking her for giving me this ride.'

*You could offer to go halves on the petrol instead*, thought Viggo, but somehow stopped himself from actually saying it; besides, he was curious. For some reason, he'd expected that Leon would be completely lacking in talent – a rank amateur with delusions of grandeur – so it was a genuine surprise when he weighed in with the opening lines of Elvis Costello's *Alison* and had a voice that sounded rich, melodic and full of character. Viggo was almost horrified to discover that he actually liked what he was hearing. He thought he had a vague memory of it being a particular favourite of his Dad's, back in the day, though he couldn't have sworn to it.

As they moved on, the mingling of voice and music seemed to fill Viggo's sleep-deprived head like a warm moving wave and the road ahead of him began to dissolve in a shimmering blaze of colour. A warmth rippled through him and suddenly, he was no longer in the seat of a car but gliding across still water – and when he lifted his heavy head to gaze sleepily upwards, he could see the curved roof of a cavern high above him, hung with stalactites and somehow lit by the dull glow of many lanterns.

He stared upwards, entranced, and then was dimly aware of the boatman behind him, standing on a raised platform as his powerful arms manipulated a single oar, pushing the boat effortlessly onwards to its destination, somewhere up ahead.

And then a conviction grew within Viggo, a cold, nagging fear that made him believe that whoever was piloting the boat wasn't entirely human.

And though he tried to fight against it, he felt the muscles of his neck tightening as he turned his head to look back over his shoulder.

The figure towered over him, hidden beneath a long hooded cloak, the face in shadow but the eyes blazing from the darkness like two drops of fire. Now he could see that from out of the hood's shadow, a long, grey beard hung almost to the man's chest. And then Viggo's gaze fixed on the hands that held the oar and he saw, with a jolt of terror, that they were not the hands of a man at all, but of some kind of creature, the fingers clawed talons, the skin a covering of smooth grey-green scales that shimmered in the half light.

A sudden urge to escape filled Viggo's head and he turned back to cast his gaze over the side of the boat, telling himself that the water here was calm, that he could easily swim to shore. But then he saw what lay just beneath the surface. There were cloaked figures drifting on their backs in the shallows, row after row of them, their white bloodless faces staring blindly up at him, mouths open as if to shout a warning. But, as Viggo gazed down at them, he could see movement within those open mouths – bundles of pink, coiling creatures that twisted and squirmed around each other, preventing the faces from uttering so much as a sound.

An overpowering urge to escape engulfed him. He had to get away from here somehow. He steeled himself, ready to fling his body over the side of the boat . . .

'Oh, that was really good!' cried a voice, and Viggo was jolted rudely back to wakefulness, to see Mum beside him, staring delightedly into the rearview mirror. 'I've always loved that song.'

'I actually played it for its composer one time,' said Leon. 'He told me I'd made him see a whole new side to it. I was quite pleased with that. What did you think, Viggo? Did I pass the exam?'

Viggo looked over his shoulder and couldn't find words. He was looking into Leon's eyes and thinking that they were exactly like the eyes of the boatman in his dream, burning with a fierce intensity, one that seemed to see every secret he'd ever harboured.

And then Mum broke the awkward silence by saying, 'According to the sat nav, our destination is just over the next ridge.'

# CHAPTER 6
## MIDGARD

The campsite was nestled in a small clearing in the next valley. It comprised five identical wooden cabins, arranged in a straight line, offering a view towards a range of mist-shrouded hills on the far horizon. A short distance from them, separated by a picket fence, was an open field where a couple of small tents were pitched. Beside that, a children's play area, sporting a set of swings and a wooden roundabout waited patiently, but there was no sign of any children eager to play on them.

A short walk from the cabins stood a low wooden building which sported a handwritten sign reading, RECEPTION.

Mum pulled Ruby to a halt in a small, wooden fenced area clearly marked VISITORS' PARKING. 'Well,' she said. 'This looks charming.' She waited for somebody to agree with her, but when nobody did, she glanced in the mirror at Leon, who was still awkwardly ensconced on the back seat. 'Are you sure there's nowhere else I could have dropped you?' she ventured hopefully. 'We passed a great lay-by on the way in, somewhere you could have picked up another lift.'

Leon was carefully putting his guitar back into its case.

'No,' he said. 'I rather like the look of this place.' He nodded towards the tents. 'There's plenty of room to pitch my little canvas playpen over there.'

'You realise you'll have to pay for that?' said Viggo flatly, aware that Mum was directing a warning look at him.

'Well, of course,' said Leon. 'I don't expect they're running their business on fresh air and promises.' He glanced at Mum. 'I haven't forgotten that I owe you for that meal,' he added. 'Maybe the people here can help me sort out the problems with my card.'

'Wouldn't a bank be more useful?' suggested Viggo. 'Only we did pass a couple coming through Lerwick.'

'Banks!' said Leon, as though it was a curse word. 'Who trusts *them*?'

'Well, it's a bank *card* you're having trouble with, so . . .'

'Don't worry about it, Leon,' interjected Mum. 'And what you said before? About helping us look for Magnus? There's really no need.'

'There's every need,' Leon assured her. 'What kind of a knight abandons a fair maiden in her darkest hour?'

There was a long silence while both Mum and Viggo struggled to come up with a suitable answer to that. In the end, Mum just gave up and opened her door. 'I suppose we'd better check in,' she said and climbed out of the car. Viggo followed her example and, inevitably, when he glanced back, he saw that Leon was strolling behind them like a faithful hound.

Mum pushed open the door of the office and they stepped into a building that smelt strongly of pine. There was a low counter, where a woman waited. She was short and stocky, with bobbed fair hair and ruddy features. She was wrapped in a thick, knee-length cardigan, as though it was the depths of winter. She looked up as they entered and gave them a welcoming smile.

'Ah, right on cue,' she said. 'You'll be straight off the ferry, I expect. Welcome to Midgard!' She had a curious accent, Viggo thought. Scottish but different somehow, with a sing-song tone and a lilt he couldn't quite recognise. He glanced around the small room, noting that there was a glass-fronted fridge stocked with milk, yoghurt and butter; shelves of tinned food and cans of drink; a rack of what looked like maps and booklets. And there were postcards on display, showing vivid images of cliffs and beaches and old stone buildings.

More interestingly, sitting behind another counter at the top of the room, was a teenage girl. She was engrossed in a paperback book, her head lowered, her straight black hair falling forward to obscure her features. Viggo saw with a twinge of recognition that it was a book he knew well and, almost without thinking, he found himself stepping away from his companions, to stand in front of the girl, aware as he did so that it was unlike him to be so confident. She became aware of him and raised her head from her reading. She had intense green eyes, slightly magnified by the black-rimmed glasses she was wearing. She gave him a look.

'Can I help you?' she asked him.

He gestured at the book. '*Dragondarke*,' he said.

She gazed at him for a moment, then turned the book

around to glance at the cover as though to check he was right. 'Well done,' she told him. 'You can read.'

'Freya,' said the woman behind the counter, a warning tone in her voice. 'Play nicely.'

Freya rolled her eyes, but offered Viggo an unconvincing smile. 'Aye,' she agreed. '*Dragondarke*. Book four. You're a fan?'

'Oh, yeah. I've read all sixteen of them,' he told her. 'It's a D&D tie-in.'

'Uh huh.' She sat there looking at him. 'I know that.'

'So do you play?' he asked her hopefully. '*Dragondarke*?'

'Do you?'

'Yeah, with my friends.'

'You have *friends*?'

Again, the woman at the counter lifted her head from the paperwork she was going through with Mum and flashed Freya a warning look.

'Yeah, sure,' said Viggo. 'Don't you?'

'I have some at school,' she admitted. 'But now it's the holidays.'

Viggo struggled to follow her logic. 'Yeah, but . . . don't you see them out of school?'

She smiled patiently. 'I assume most of your friends live within walking distance of where you live,' she said.

'Uh . . . of course.'

Freya nodded. 'My best friend lives on Unst,' she said. She noticed his bewildered expression and added, 'That's two islands away.'

'Oh, right,' he said. 'Tough break.'

'It's not like the other end of the planet, but getting there can be tricky.' She looked pointedly at her mother. 'Especially when nobody ever offers to drive you.'

'But you could play together online, right?'

'Where are you from?' she asked him.

'Me? Edinburgh. Well, not originally, but I've lived there most of my life.'

A new look came into Freya's eyes, one that looked suspiciously like envy. 'Edinburgh.' She said the word slowly, on an exhaled breath, as though it had special significance for her. 'So you'll be close to actual shops,' she said wistfully.

'Sure. But there are shops in Lerwick, so . . .'

'I mean *shops*,' she elaborated. 'Selfridges. Conde Nast. Lulu Lemon.'

'Lulu who?'

'And there'll be theatres, I expect. Cinemas. Cafe bars. And, of course, reliable Wi-Fi . . .'

'Well, yeah, sure, but here you've got so much more. You've got . . .' Viggo broke off as he felt a sudden stab of anxiety. 'Y-you've got Wi-Fi, right? It says so on your website.'

'Oh, it *says* we have,' admitted Freya, 'I'll give you that much. And there's sometimes a signal here. For at least a few minutes every day.'

'A few minutes?'

'If you're lucky. And here's the weird thing. Drive a few miles up the road in either direction and you'll get a signal on your phone. But in Midgard . . .'

Viggo took out his mobile and clicked it on. He stared at the screen, open-jawed in dismay. 'Oh no,' he gasped.

'Told you.'

'Freya!' Now the woman at the counter sounded really annoyed. She looked apologetically at Mum. 'You'll have to forgive my daughter,' she said. 'She's going through a difficult phase. Her teenage years. I'm hoping she'll emerge from them ... *eventually*.'

Mum smiled. 'You don't have to explain a thing,' she said, and the two women shared knowing smiles.

'I'm Agnes, by the way. You'll find me here most of the time, but if I'm not, I'll be in the wee house over there.' She gestured through a small window. 'There's a note of my landline number in the cabin. Ring me if there's a problem. And Freya is right about the Wi-Fi, I'm afraid. There are login details in the cabin but it's patchy. We've tried everything but . . .' She shrugged her shoulders. 'What can you do?'

'It won't be a problem,' said Mum. 'We've not come here to surf the internet.' She ignored the indignant look Viggo directed at her. 'And you have a lovely location here.'

'Oh, thank you. I set the whole thing up a few years back. Bought the cabins from a Swedish firm. My husband, Leif, runs the farm, but this is my own wee business. It's quiet, just yet, but things will soon be picking up. We have regulars who come every year, like clockwork.'

'That's lovely,' said Mum.

Agnes pushed a card payment device closer to Mum. 'If you'll just do the honours?'

'Oh, yes, of course.' Mum fumbled in her purse and took out a credit card. She slid it into the device's slot and keyed in her code. Viggo wondered how much debt she was racking up on this trip, but told himself there was no use in worrying about it now. There was a short silence and then the device beeped. Mum let out what sounded suspiciously like a sigh of relief. 'Well,' she said. 'We'd better get settled in, I suppose.'

'You're all set up,' Agnes assured her. 'Cabin number four.' She handed Mum a key on a little fob. 'I've left milk and newly-laid eggs in there to get you started and we have a few bits and pieces in our shop here. For bigger orders, there's a new Tesco superstore in Lerwick. Everyone's very excited about it.' She ignored the weary sigh that escaped from Freya and looked past Mum to Leon, who was studying some posters on the wall. She was clearly puzzled by his presence. 'The booking is just for two people, so . . .'

'Oh yes,' said Mum hastily. 'For me and my son, Viggo. This is . . .' She waved a hand at Leon. 'We're not together.'

Leon turned away from the posters and directed that beaming smile at Agnes. He stepped closer to the counter. 'I'm considering pitching my little tent in your field,' he said, making it sound like an indecent proposition. 'How does it work, exactly?'

'Work? Well, it's twelve pounds a night for a pitch. How long will you be staying?'

'Not entirely sure at the moment. I'm in a bit of an elastic phase.'

'Elastic?'

'Yes. You know. Could be gone tomorrow, might be here for months. But it looks like you have plenty of room out there.'

'Well, yes. But that's subject to change. I've got quite a few people booked in for next week. So, if you'd like to leave a deposit . . .'

'Ah, now that's where we might have a problem,' purred Leon. 'You see, I've been having a bit of grief with my debit card.'

Sensing potential trouble, Mum stepped back from the counter and gestured to Viggo, who was still staring helplessly at his phone screen. 'We'd better get ourselves unpacked,' she suggested. 'We don't want to waste too much time, but you're probably going to need some shuteye before we set off again.' She looked at Freya. 'I'm afraid Viggo was horribly sick on the ferry coming over here.'

'Was he now?' murmured Freya with a grin.

'Mum!' Viggo shot her a look of betrayal. 'You don't have to tell *everyone*.'

Mum made an exaggerated show of apology. 'I didn't realise it was some kind of secret,' she said. She turned away and started for the door, but Viggo hesitated and pointed at the book in Freya's hand.

'Who's your favourite character?' he asked her.

She looked at the book for a moment, considering. 'I like Brianna of the Woods,' she said. 'She's kind of awesome.' She pointed at Viggo. 'Let me take a wild guess,' she added. 'Your favourite is . . . Gallus, the Berserker.'

Viggo stared at her. 'How did you know that?' he asked her.

'Usual toxic male stereotype,' she said, and went back to her reading.

Viggo couldn't help but laugh at that. He turned away from the counter to follow Mum but then hesitated and looked back. 'We could play a board game one night, if you like,' he suggested. 'I've brought a couple of travel sets with me.'

Freya shrugged. 'Maybe,' she said. 'Let me think about it.'

Cheered by her response, he headed towards the door and, as he passed by, he couldn't help but overhear what Leon was saying to Agnes.

'. . . and perhaps you should think about offering some entertainment to your visitors.'

'What kind of entertainment?'

'Well, I have my trusty guitar with me. I've played for audiences all over the world and I'm sure my fellow travellers would be more than happy to vouch for my abilities.' He turned expectantly towards Viggo, but Viggo was already stepping briskly outside and closing the door behind him. There was no way he was going to be involved in bigging up Leon Bragg. The man needed no help in that regard.

He followed Mum back to Ruby and watched as she unlocked the boot, then started helping her to lift out the suitcases.

'You're a fast worker,' said Mum, not looking at him. She slipped into a seductive parody of his voice. 'I've got a board game with me. We could play, some time!'

'Don't be daft,' he told her. 'I was only being friendly.'

'Hmm. You may not have noticed but she wasn't exactly being very nice back.'

Viggo shrugged. 'I think that was just her sense of humour,' he said. He glanced quickly towards the office. 'Leon is the one who's a quick worker,' he said. 'You probably didn't hear, but he's already trying to sell his services to the woman that runs this place.' He slipped into his approximation of Leon's suave tones. 'I've got my trusty guitar with me. How about I sing for my supper instead of paying to camp here like everybody else!'

Mum tried not to laugh. 'He never said that!'

'Something very like it.' Viggo looked at the guitar and rucksack still lying on the back seat. 'What shall we do about those?' he asked.

As if in answer to the question, the door of the office opened and Leon stepped out, laughing heartily at something that had just been said to him from within. 'You're so understanding, thank you,' he called back. 'I promise, I won't let you down.' He closed the door and strode towards the car, looking extremely pleased with himself. Viggo couldn't help but notice he was carrying a key on a fob, just like the one that Mum had.

'What a charming woman,' he said, as he drew nearer. 'I explained my situation with the card and Agnes said I could use cabin number three until I got things sorted out.'

'But I thought you said you were pitching a tent,' said Mum.

'I had every intention of doing so. And then Agnes mentioned that she can't let cabin three out until she's booked somebody to fix the cooker, so I said, "why don't I do that for you free of charge, while I'm here?" And *she* said I might as well stay in the cabin while I'm doing it.'

'And . . . you know how to fix a cooker?' asked Viggo incredulously.

'Absolutely. I worked as a kitchen fitter for a few months back in the nineties.'

'I expect things may have changed a bit since then.'

'How hard can it be? A thirteen-amp plug is still the same, right?' Leon opened the rear door of the car and slung the heavy rucksack carelessly over his shoulder then, with considerably more reverence, took out the guitar case. He lowered his voice. 'I also pitched Agnes the idea of me performing here when it gets a little busier. She didn't say yes, but she didn't exactly say no either.' He winked at them. 'I'll work on her.' He turned and strode towards the row of cabins. 'If you need any assistance, I'll be right next door.'

Viggo and Mum watched him go in disbelief; saw him unlock the door of cabin three and step confidently inside as though he owned the place.

'There you go,' muttered Viggo. 'That's how you do it. Hey, perhaps you should offer to do Agnes's washing in exchange for a few free nights. It might work.'

'I'm not as persuasive as Mr Bragg,' she assured him.

'Who is?' he asked her.

She locked Ruby and they carried their bags the short distance to the cabins. Mum unlocked number four and they stepped inside. The place was tiny but scrupulously clean, nearly everything constructed from the same blonde varnished wood. There was a compact kitchen with an electric hob and oven, a kettle and a miniscule fridge which, when Mum checked, did indeed contain butter and milk. A carton of eggs stood on the counter top. Through a doorway there was a hall where sliding doors led off to a couple of bedrooms, one on either side and, at the far end, a small wetroom with a shower and a toilet. Mum took her case into the bedroom on the left and ushered Viggo through to the one opposite. He noted that the bed occupied pretty much the entire room, leaving just enough space to take his shoes off. The bed itself looked disconcertingly short. If he didn't bend his knees while sleeping, the soles of his feet would be pressing against a wall.

But he was too tired to think about such problems. He flung off his jacket, kicked off his trainers, then crawled gratefully beneath the freshly laundered duvet. He lay for a moment, thinking about how weird this trip had already become.

'An hour,' he heard Mum say from the next room. 'I'm setting a phone alarm. And then we'll start looking for Magnus, OK?'

'OK.' He thought for a moment. 'You told me you'd got some kind of a deal on this place. But that seemed quite pricey.'

'Did it?' There was a short silence. 'We'd better get some sleep,' said Mum.

'Mum, are you sure we can afford this?'

Silence.

He grunted, closed his eyes, and fell straight into a deep sleep.

# CHAPTER 7
## WAKE UP CALL

Mum's phone alarm shrilled from the next room.

Viggo opened his eyes and lay on his side, trying to get a handle on where he was. Things came back to him, slowly at first. He was in a bed, he knew that much, but not his own familiar one. The mattress was softer, more enveloping, and the cotton covers smelt of a different sort of fabric conditioner. His mouth was bone dry and he longed for a glass of water. He raised himself on one elbow and found himself staring blearily through a small window, which yielded a view of some mist-shrouded hills. He groaned and let his head sink back on to the pillow.

Now he remembered where he was. *Shetland*. A place called *Midgard*. Yes, they'd come here on the ferry and he'd been sick . . . he'd been horribly sick over the side of the ferry and in the middle of it all, he thought he'd seen . . .

It came at him then, in a rush of colliding images and sounds. In the midst of his recollections, he was only dimly aware of somebody coming into the room and settling onto the narrow duvet beside him. A hand ruffled his hair, then moved away.

'Wake up,' said a voice.

He blinked, shaking his head to dispel the last threads of sleep. 'Can I have another ten minutes, Mum?' he grunted. 'I'm not quite—'

'No. You need to wake up, Viggo. You need to wake up – and go home.'

Viggo blinked. 'Wait. Home?' he echoed. 'But we only just . . . ' He broke off as it occurred to him through his sleep-fogged senses that it was a man's voice that had spoken, the voice vaguely familiar yet weirdly muffled. A coldness blossomed like a flower in his chest. He twisted around to see that the figure sitting on the bed beside him was tall and gangly. He was turned away from Viggo, his face in his hands, which explained why the voice had sounded so strange. He was wearing a khaki anorak and his straight brown hair was streaked with grey.

'I didn't want you to come here,' said the man, into his hands. 'I prayed you wouldn't.'

And now Viggo knew exactly who it was.

'Dad?' he whispered.

The man didn't move. He just kept talking. 'I didn't want Magnus to come here either, but that boy . . . always so headstrong! Nothing I ever said could make him change his mind. But you, Viggo, I thought you were more sensible. I thought you'd know what to do.'

Viggo struggled up into a sitting position. He stared at his Dad's back, trying to form words but his throat was parched and, at first, he couldn't manage a sound. He reached out and placed a hand on Dad's shoulder. He could feel the warmth of him through the fabric of his coat.

'So . . . you're still alive,' he managed to croak at last.

There was a short silence, followed by a hollow laugh. Dad's shoulders moved up and down as he chuckled. 'You silly boy,' he said. 'Do I *look* as though I'm alive?'

He lowered his hands and turned slowly towards his son. Viggo stared at him, trying to hold back the scream that was building inside him like a fire. His dad's face had no features – no eyes, nose or mouth. It was a smooth, flesh-coloured blob, but somehow a voice still managed to issue from it, loud now, seeming to fill the little room with its power. 'Tell your mother this is a fool's errand. No good will come of it. You should have stayed in Edinburgh, Viggo. Tell Alison she has to go back, right away. Do you hear me? Tell her to stop following me!'

'Tell her . . . what?'

The door of the room slid open with a clunk, startling Viggo. He glanced up to see Mum, looking half asleep herself, gazing in at him through the doorway, a questioning look on her face. 'What's wrong?' she asked him.

'What do you mean?' he whispered.

'You called out for me, didn't you?'

'No, I . . .'

Viggo turned his head back to look at the place where Dad had been sitting. There was nobody there, but he thought he saw a faint depression in the memory foam mattress that was slowly rising back into position. He reached out a hand and placed a palm on the spot. The sheet felt warm to the touch.

'Dad was here,' he whispered.

Mum's eyes widened. 'You've been dreaming,' she told him.

'That often happens when you're in a strange bed.'

'No, Mum, it wasn't a dream. Come here! Put your hand there, where he was sitting.'

'Viggo . . .'

'I mean it. Hurry, before it fades.'

Mum stumbled into the room and did as he told her. She kept her hand there for a moment then gave her son a questioning look. 'It was just a dream,' she said again. 'They can feel real sometimes. Lord knows I've had enough of them over the past five years.'

'But it's still warm,' he told her. 'Isn't it?'

She gazed back at him, her face impassive. 'I'll make us some coffee,' she said. 'I think there's some on the worktop.' She straightened up and headed back to the doorway. 'We'll have a drink and then we'll head off to Jarlshof.' She saw Viggo's puzzled look and added. 'It's where Magnus was working, remember?'

She went out and he heard her moving around in the kitchen, filling the kettle, setting it down on the hob. Viggo shook his head. He put his own hand back on the mattress and moved it around, but now everything felt like it was the same temperature. He let out a sigh and dropped down again, burying his face in the pillow. He lay for a moment, trying to remember the last words his dad had used. *Tell her to stop following me.*

But they weren't following him. They were supposed to be looking for Magnus, weren't they?

He sat up again and pulled his mobile from his pocket. He switched it on and took a moment to register that there was still no signal. He gave a grunt of disgust and swung himself around onto the edge of the bed, aware now that everything was clicking back into focus, the last shreds of sleep blowing away. His trainers lay on the wooden floor where he'd dropped them and he leant forward and put them on.

From the kitchen, Mum said, 'There's a packet of shortbread biscuits here. Are you feeling well enough to eat something?'

'Yes,' he said. 'I'm actually really hungry.'

Then he got himself upright and went out to join her.

***

Viggo and Mum let themselves quietly out of the cabin and closed the door gently behind them. They looked anxiously at Leon's cabin, just a few steps away, but there were no signs of life. Perhaps he was asleep, Viggo thought hopefully. He and Mum exchanged furtive looks and then, placing their feet carefully on the wooden boards, they stepped down from the porch on to the hard earth and walked towards the parking spot. They reached Ruby, expecting at any moment to hear a shout from behind them. Mum unlocked the door and slid into the driving seat. Viggo did the same on the passenger side, closing the door behind him as gently as he could.

They looked at each other and both of them let out a breath.

'So far, so good,' said Mum.

She slid her key into the ignition, snatched in a breath and turned it. The engine started, sounding perfectly normal. 'Yes!' she whispered. She slipped her phone into its holder, switched on the sat nav and then stifled a curse as the screen failed to secure a signal. They sat there, staring at it in dismay.

'It's all right,' Mum assured him. 'If we just head back the way we came, I'm sure it'll kick in eventually. It was working fine on the way here.'

'It's something about this place,' Viggo told her. 'Something weird.'

'Nonsense,' she assured him. 'Some areas are like that. I remember when we were driving in the Highlands that time. Same thing.'

'But I'm having dreams. Weird dreams.'

'Well, that can happen when you're travelling.'

'That dream about Dad. He said . . .'

'Yes?'

'That we were to stop following him.'

Mum looked puzzled.

'And he . . . he had no features. His face was just— aaaahhh!'

The sentence dissolved into a gasp of terror as he realised somebody was staring in at him through the passenger window.

'Jesus,' gasped Viggo.

The door opened and Leon smiled at him. 'Sorry, old son, did I startle you?'

'Yes, you bloody well did! What's the idea of creeping around like that?'

Leon looked bemused. 'I was hardly creeping around. I heard the sound of an engine and came out to investigate.'

Viggo looked at the cabin and then back at Leon, trying

to work out how he could possibly have covered so much ground in what must have been seconds. Did he have starting blocks set up in there? Had he been waiting all this time for an opportunity to sprint after them?

'You freaked me out!' he protested.

'Sorry about that. Going somewhere interesting?'

'Just for a drive,' Viggo told him. 'Nowhere special.'

'Sounds great,' said Leon.

'No, actually, we're going to Jarlshof,' said Mum. She pulled a face. 'Viking stuff. I'm sure you're not interested in archeology.'

'No, I'm not,' said Leon.

'Ah, well then . . .'

'*Fascinated* would be the word I'd use. Mind if I tag along?'

'Right.' There was a terrible silence. Mum studied her hands on the wheel for a moment and took a deep breath. 'Leon, can I be absolutely honest with you?'

He smiled, as if he knew what she was about to say. 'Of course,' he said. 'I admire people who speak their minds.'

'Well then, we'd really like a little time together, Viggo and I. Just the two of us. I'm sure you understand. I don't want to be rude or anything but . . .'

'You'd rather I didn't come,' said Leon. 'I've been imposing on your good nature. I get it.'

Mum looked pained. 'Oh, but that sounds . . . I hope you're not offended.'

'Offended?' Leon seemed to consider for a moment. 'No. Not at all. Not in the least. Just . . . disappointed, I suppose. It's so rare that I meet people I get along with.'

Viggo saw to his horror that now, a single tear was trickling down Leon's face. 'I'm aware, of course, that I can be a little overbearing. Not everybody gets me, I realise that.'

'I'm not saying anything of the kind!' insisted Mum. 'Not at all. You're fine. I . . . it's just . . . we'd like some time together. *Family* time.'

'Of course. You've made yourself perfectly clear. Well, have a good trip. Without me.'

Leon turned theatrically away and started to walk slowly back towards the cabin, his head bowed, his shoulders slumped. Viggo looked at Mum with new respect.

'Go you,' he whispered.

'Had to be done,' said Mum. 'I finally found the nerve to say it.' She looked at Viggo anxiously. 'You don't think I've hurt his feelings, do you?'

'Hurt? Leon Bragg? He's tough as old boots.'

'Did you see . . .' She stroked a finger down her cheek.

'Yeah. What an actor.'

'You think that's what it was? An act?'

'Mum, please, let's go before you change your mind.'

She nodded. 'Yes,' she said. 'You're right. I'm overthinking it.' She reached down and slipped Ruby into gear.

And the engine died.

They sat there, open-mouthed, staring at the dashboard. Mum turned the key, producing nothing but a coughing sound. She tried again, and again, the engine sounding more feeble at every attempt. Leon was at the door of his cabin now, key in hand, but he turned at the sound of the car stalling, a knowing smile on his face.

He strolled slowly back to them, taking his time. He opened the passenger door a few centimetres.. 'Problem?' he asked them.

Viggo could see that Mum was mortified. 'We, er . . . we seem to be having that issue again,' she said. 'You know, like back at the ferry? She won't start. I don't suppose you could . . .'

'Pop the bonnet for me,' suggested Leon smoothly.

'Are you sure you don't mind?'

'Just pop the bonnet.'

Mum did as he suggested and Leon moved to the front of the car. Ruby's bonnet lifted, hiding him from view. Viggo and Mum stared at each other. Viggo was having a powerful feeling of *déjà vu.*

'He's doing this,' whispered Viggo.

'Don't be ridiculous. How can he be? He didn't even touch the car!'

'I don't know *how* he's doing it, but it's too much of a coincidence. Isn't it?'

'What else can it be? He's not a bloody magician, is he?'

'He's doing *something*!'

The bonnet swung down again with a dull thud and Leon gestured to Mum to try the key. She turned it and, sure enough, the engine started. Leon nodded, as though satisfied with his work. He stood for a moment, staring thoughtfully at them through the windscreen. Then he strolled to the back of the car and opened the door behind Viggo. He slid on to the back seat.

'Here's the thing,' he said. 'How can I let you go without me?

What if Ruby breaks down again? Eh? How would you manage?'

'We're with Green Flag,' said Mum. 'We have breakdown assistance.'

'Yes, but Alison, can you imagine how long it would take them to get somebody to attend to you all the way out here? You might have to wait half the day.'

'Well . . .'

'And can you afford to waste time when you should be looking for Magnus? I know how important that is to you. I only want to help.' He leant forward and placed a hand on Mum's shoulder. 'What if I promise to stay really quiet here in the back? Hmm? I won't say a word unless you ask me a question. How about that? And, you know, I've always wanted to visit Jarlshof. It's one of the most complete Viking settlements anywhere in the world.'

'You didn't see it last time you were here?' growled Viggo.

'Wanted to. Never got around to it.' Leon turned his gaze back to Mum. 'What do you think, Alison? I only want what's best for you and Viggo.'

Mum didn't say anything for a few moments. 'The sat nav . . .' she finally began.

'No need for it,' Leon assured her. 'Out of the gates up ahead and turn left. Follow the road for around twenty miles or so and you'll see signposts for Jarlshof.'

'But how do you know that if you haven't been there?' whispered Viggo.

Leon lifted a finger and tapped the side of his head. 'Excellent memory,' he said. 'Must have looked it up last time, but never got the chance to actually go.' He shrugged. 'And anyway, the sat nav will kick in again once we've gone a mile or so down the road. You'll see.'

Viggo and Mum looked at each other and Mum finally shook her head. Her expression spoke louder than words. There was no use in fighting it any longer.

She put Ruby into gear and drove away.

# CHAPTER 8
## JARLSHOF

Leon had been right about the sat nav. For the first ten minutes' drive, the screen remained resolutely blank, a single line announcing that it was 'trying to connect'. Then, without warning, it clicked in and Viggo was able to punch in their destination so they could follow the blue line. But it would have been hard to get lost since there was only one road, cutting like a knife through the ochre landscape ahead of them. Viggo studied the fields stretching away on every side, the rolling hills studded here and there with the fluffy white clouds that were sheep. High up, soaring on wind currents, he saw what looked like a bird of prey.

'Some kind of a hawk?' he wondered, pointing.

Leon followed his gaze. 'That's actually a merlin,' he said. 'A type of falcon. One of the interesting things about Shetland is the almost total absence of raptors.'

'Raptors?' muttered Viggo, thinking of *Jurassic Park*.

'Birds of prey,' added Leon.

'I was hoping to see eagles while we're here,' said Mum.

'I wouldn't hold your breath,' Leon advised her. 'White-tailed eagles used to be common, but the fulmars took over their territory and now eagles are extremely rare visitors.'

'Fulmars?' Viggo glanced back at him, puzzled.

'Cliff-nesting birds. Most people mistake them for gulls, but they're quite different.'

Viggo scowled. He wondered if there was any subject on the planet that Leon Bragg wasn't an expert on. 'So what's so great about this Jarlshof place?' he asked.

Leon chuckled. 'Are you kidding? It's one of the most remarkable archaeological sites ever discovered. The remains range from 2500 BC to the seventeenth century. There are Bronze Age, Iron Age *and* Viking remains all in one place. There's even a fortified manor house, which gave the site its name – taken from the novel by Sir Walter Scott.'

'You're like a human Wikipedia,' observed Mum, and Leon chuckled.

'You'll have to forgive me,' he said. 'I'm a sponge. I soak up information.'

Viggo smirked, thinking that 'sponger' might be a more accurate description of Leon, but realised that, whatever he was, they were pretty much stuck with him now.

'So, tell me about Magnus,' said Leon. 'I'd like to get a fuller picture of him. What was he doing in Jarlshof?'

'Oh, he was working on a conservation project,' said Mum. 'There was some kind of a . . . is the word *broch*?'

'Yes. An Iron Age roundhouse. You'll find them all over Shetland. Experts are still divided over what they were originally used for.'

'Right. Well, he was working as part of a team, trying to

shore up the wall of a broch which was in danger of falling down. There'd been a storm, you see.'

'Interesting,' said Leon.

'Is it?' muttered Viggo, irritably.

'Oh yes. That's how Jarlshof was discovered in the first place. It had been built over, covered with earth for centuries, but after a massive storm washed away some of the coastline, a small part of it was exposed. That would have been back in the 1920s, I believe. People started excavating it and gradually, over the years, they unearthed more and more of its secrets.'

They motored onwards in silence for a while. It occurred to Viggo that they hadn't seen another car in ages.

'I think Magnus had a secret,' said Mum, her gaze still fixed on the way ahead.

Leon leant closer. 'What makes you say that?'

'I sensed it. On the few occasions I spoke to him – on the phone – I got the impression he was bored with what he was doing. And I thought . . .'

'Yes?'

'That there was something he wasn't telling me. Something important that he wasn't quite ready to share.'

'And you've no idea what it might have been?'

'None.' Mum glanced at Viggo. 'You should tell Leon about your dream,' she suggested.

Viggo looked at her. 'Why?' he muttered. 'He's an expert on dreams as well, is he?'

'He seems to know about a lot of different things. He might have an opinion.'

'Oh, I'm sure he'll have that!'

'Go on, try me,' suggested Leon. 'I'm fascinated by dreams.'

'Viggo just had one about his dad,' announced Mum.

'Mum!' Viggo wasn't sure he wanted to tell Leon about it, and he wasn't sure why Mum was so ready to tell Leon things. It was as though the man had put some kind of spell on her. He noticed in the mirror that Leon was leaning forward, his elbows on his knees as though concentrating.

'Go on Viggo, tell him,' urged Mum. 'He might have an idea of what it means.'

So, reluctantly, Viggo did as she'd suggested while Leon listened.

'I think it makes perfect sense,' he said, when Viggo had finished. 'Your father disappeared in Shetland and now you are, quite literally, following in his wake.'

'I get that,' said Viggo. 'But we're not here looking for *him*, are we?'

Leon smiled. 'Are you sure about that?'

'Yeah. It's Magnus we're trying to find.'

'And why do you think Magnus is here? Could it be that *he's* looking for his father?'

Viggo thought about it and shook his head. 'Nah. Magnus has been all over the world looking at weird stuff,' he said. 'This is just his latest obsession.'

Leon looked at Mum. 'Would you say that Magnus missed his father when he left?'

'Oh yes,' said Mum. 'The two of them were very close. Viggo was a few years younger, of course, so it didn't hit him quite as hard. But, there could be something in what you're saying. I don't know why it's never occurred to me before.'

'Why do you think my dad had no face?' asked Viggo. 'In the dream.'

Leon gazed right back at him, his expression blank. 'No idea' he said.

Viggo was immediately convinced that for some reason, Leon was lying. Just for a second, there'd been a flash of recognition in his dark eyes but almost immediately, he'd made a visible effort to push it away and make his face expressionless.

'I think you *do* have an idea,' insisted Viggo.

'Sorry, not a clue, old son.'

'Why are you lying?' asked Viggo impetuously.

'Viggo!' cried Mum. 'That's rude!'

Viggo turned his gaze back to the passenger window. 'Excuse me,' he muttered. 'I thought Leon was supposed to be an expert on *everything*.'

'Not quite everything,' Leon assured him. 'And who can figure out dreams with any degree of authority? But I understand that it must have scared you.'

'It didn't *scare* me,' snapped Viggo. 'It just . . . freaked me out.' Something occurred to him. He took out his phone and saw that there was now a 4G signal. He quickly punched a question into Google. *What does it mean when you dream about somebody with no face?*

A series of dream-related sites came straight back to him so he opened the top hit and read aloud. 'A faceless person in a dream indicates a meeting with the inhabitants of another world or perhaps mirrors the subconscious mind of the dreamer.'

Leon grinned. 'Which tells you precisely nothing,' he said. 'Who writes these things?'

'Well, what about this one?' suggested Viggo, lining up another site. 'If you meet with a person who has no features, it might mean—'

'Oh, hello, what's this?' interrupted Mum.

She slowed Ruby to a halt. They had come to a level crossing in the road, the metal gates closed, red lights flashing a warning. Beside it there was a small wooden hut.

'I didn't realise there were trains here,' said Mum, looking left and right along the broad highway that crossed their route.

'Do you see any rails?' Leon asked her.

Mum frowned. 'No,' she said. 'I don't.'

'Well, let's see what happens,' suggested Leon.

They didn't have to wait long. In the sky, away to their right, a light-engined plane came into view, its white wings reflecting the sunlight. It was descending fast.

'It's a runway!' cried Viggo, and watched in amazement as the plane's wheels connected smoothly with tarmac. It raced along in front of them, decelerating as it went by.

'Sumburgh Airport is just a spit away from here,' explained Leon. 'This is the main landing strip for Shetland.'

'Amazing.' Mum shook her head. 'You must have seen it before,' she said.

But Leon didn't reply.

After a few minutes, the red lights changed to green. A man in a uniform came out of the little hut. He raised the barrier by hand then nodded them through.

'Not far now,' Leon told them, even though their destination was clearly visible on the sat nav – a vivid red marker at the end of the blue line.

*** 

Jarlshof appeared with very little fanfare. First there was a metal signpost by the roadside with the single word printed on it and they went past a curved bay with an idyllic-looking beach. Shortly after that, a large building loomed into view on the horizon. It turned out to be a hotel – though, as they drew nearer, they could see no signs of life within. Mum pulled into a spacious car park which currently held about fifteen other vehicles. The three of them got out of the Kia and stood for a moment, looking around.

'This way,' said Leon and, once again, Viggo felt convinced that the man must have been here before to be so sure of his directions. He led them through an opening in a stone wall and they walked along a straight path which crossed a rather nondescript field. At the top of it, Leon turned right and strolled through a small entrance. Viggo and Mum followed. To their right lay a low-roofed reception building and to their left was what looked like a complex labyrinth of gullies, paths and dry stone walls, topped with swathes of bright green turf. At intervals were information posts that told visitors more about what they were viewing. Small groups of tourists, dressed in brightly coloured padded jackets, were wandering in and out of sunken doorways, or peering out through rectangular openings that must once have been windows.

Mum gestured towards the reception. 'I suppose we should start by asking around in there,' she suggested.

Leon nodded, but he barely seemed to hear her. He was staring fixedly towards the ruins to his left.

'Excuse me,' he said tonelessly, and started walking away from them. He approached a flight of stone steps, went quickly down them and then ducked his head to go in through a low opening, out of sight.

Mum and Viggo exchanged puzzled looks.

'Aren't you supposed to pay before you go in there?' muttered Viggo.

Mum shrugged. 'Let's just enjoy the solitude while we can,' she whispered.

She led Viggo in through the entrance doors of the reception and approached a young woman sitting behind a glass screen.

'May I help you?' she asked, offering a professional smile.

Viggo could see she'd been expecting simply to print out tickets and pass them through, but Mum leant closer to the screen and spoke quietly to her for a few moments.

The woman nodded. She got up from her seat and went through a doorway into an adjoining room. A few minutes later, she reappeared and gestured to another door on the far side of the screen. 'Dr Glover will see you now,' she said and returned to her seat.

Mum and Viggo went through the door and into a small office, where a bearded man sat behind a desk. He was short and plump and wore metal-rimmed spectacles, a white shirt and a tartan tie. A laminated badge clipped to the front pocket of his shirt announced him as 'Dr Douglas Glover, Site Administrator'. He got up from his chair and gestured to Mum and Viggo to take the two vacant seats on the other side of his desk. Viggo glanced around the small room. Most of one wall was taken up by a notice board where various maps and diagrams were pinned. There was also a series of photographs there and Viggo immediately recognised a close-up of Magnus, staring straight into the camera lens and pulling a weird, cross-eyed face for whoever was taking the picture. Viggo elbowed Mum and pointed to the photo. She turned her head to look for a moment, then nodded.

'Mrs Ryan?' asked Dr Glover politely.

'That's right. I'm Magnus Ryan's mother. This is my other son, Viggo.'

'Pleased to meet you both.' Dr Glover nodded and sank back into his own chair. He seemed puzzled. 'How may I be of assistance?'

'Well, we're trying to locate Magnus.'

'Locate him?' Dr Glover frowned, as though unfamiliar with the term.

'Yes. We haven't heard from him since he finished working here.'

'I see.'

'I wondered if you might have any idea where he is.'

Dr Glover shook his head. 'Why would I know that?' he asked.

'Well, Magnus worked here for quite a while, didn't he?' She half-turned and pointed to the photograph on the noticeboard. 'You clearly know him. I thought he might have told you his plans for the future.'

'Well, yes, he *did* work here, for several months. But I'm sure you must also know that he left before he'd finished his tenure.'

Now it was Mum's turn to look puzzled. 'That's news to me. I was aware he was coming to the end of his appointed stay and I'd assumed that, after that, he'd return to Edinburgh, but . . .'

'You do know that he was *asked* to leave?'

Now Mum looked shocked. 'I had no idea. Who would do such a thing?'

Dr Glover clearly felt uncomfortable. 'Well, *I* did, actually. Your son was acting rather . . . oddly, I'm afraid.'

'What do you mean, "oddly"?'

'He'd fallen out with his fellow workers and was causing various upsets. I hate to be the one to tell you, but he actually had a fight with one of the other students.'

'A fight?' Mum was acting as though she couldn't believe her ears, but somehow Viggo wasn't really surprised at this news. He knew that Magnus could be volatile when things weren't going his way. 'What was the fight about?' asked Mum.

Dr Glover waved a hand. 'I'm really not sure of the details. Some petty quarrel or other.'

'Was there a girl involved?' asked Viggo, and Dr Glover gave him an odd look.

'I have no idea. At any rate, it was the final straw after a whole series of problems.'

'What kind of problems?'

'Oh, disagreements, a reluctance to follow orders. Magnus seemed to think that . . .'

'Go on,' Mum prompted him.

'He seemed to think that what we were doing here was a waste of time. I'm afraid he'd fallen under the spell of Loki.'

'Loki?' echoed Viggo.

Dr Glover looked vaguely embarrassed. 'I'm sorry, force of habit. That's what some of the students like to call him. You know, after the Norse god of mischief.'

'I'm well aware who Loki is,' said Mum tartly.

'Yes, well, his real name is Zack Strode. *Doctor* Zack Strode, if you want the full title, though most of us think it's the kind of doctorship you buy online rather than earn.'

'Hang on a minute,' said Viggo, who had just registered a name he knew very well. 'You don't mean *the* Zack Strode, do you?'

Now Dr Glover looked weary. 'You've heard of him then?'

'Of course I have,' said Viggo, but Mum just seemed confused. 'Zack Strode,' repeated Viggo, glaring at her. 'He's like . . . really famous?'

Again Mum shook her head. 'I'm sorry, I don't . . .'

'He's been all over the news lately. He's the tech billionaire guy everybody talks about. Owns the Quantum software company. They make video games and stuff. And he's just bought TallTalk!' He looked at Dr Glover. 'I have got the right man, yeah?'

'I'm afraid so. And TallTalk is just the tip of the iceberg. He has his hands in a lot of different pies. Social media, television, alternative technology, you name it.'

'What's TallTalk?' asked Mum.

'The app!' said Viggo, rolling his eyes.

Dr Glover shook his head, unable to mask his disapproval. 'Unfortunately, he also sees himself as an authority on all things Nordic. Claims to have Scandinavian ancestry.' The expression on his face suggested he didn't believe it was true. He sighed. 'At any rate, I rather think your son has become one of his devotees.'

Mum clearly didn't like the sound of this. 'But what was this Strode character doing here?'

'Oh, he just turned up one day, quite without warning. Drove up in one of those fancy electric cars that look like a cross between a spaceship and a photocopier. It was before the new season had properly begun and he breezed in, announcing that he wanted a private tour, money no object. I was against the idea to be honest – we had much more serious things to organise – but I was outvoted, particularly once my superiors found out how much he was willing to donate to our project.' Dr Glover sighed. 'Magnus was assigned to show him around the site. I gather that Dr Strode spoke to your son about some new project *he* was working on – and suffice to say, by the end of the tour, Strode had decided that Magnus would be the ideal candidate to handle it for him.'

'What kind of a project are we talking about?' asked Viggo.

Dr Glover spread his arms. 'That's anybody's guess. It's all very hush-hush. At any rate, Magnus said goodbye to Dr Strode and then marched into this office and announced that he wanted to leave. With immediate effect. I pointed out that he was required to work out his contract first, that he couldn't just go waltzing off without warning and, well, that led to bad feelings. Your son decided to make himself such a nuisance that I was forced to *ask* him to go.' He looked stricken. 'I'm sure you don't want to hear this, Mrs Ryan, but I'm afraid it's the truth. I believe he started a fight with one of his fellow workers in order to ensure that I had no other choice in the matter.'

Mum looked mortified. 'This doesn't sound like Magnus at all,' she observed. She thought for a moment. 'I don't suppose he left a forwarding address?'

Dr Glover shook his head. 'I'm afraid not. Our last exchange was . . . terse, to say the very least. I warned him that his behaviour would have to be reported back to the authorities and he told me to . . .' He grimaced. 'Well, I'll leave that part to your imagination,' he said. 'At the very least it would have caused considerable discomfort.'

Despite himself, Viggo felt a powerful urge to laugh but somehow managed not to.

'A phone number then?' prompted Mum. 'I've tried calling him on his mobile but it just rings and rings.'

'Yes, I've had the same experience,' said Dr Glover. 'Something came up, a bit of paperwork I needed him to sign, and I must have rung a dozen times or more but nobody ever answers. It's clear that he doesn't want to talk to me.' He spread his hands in a gesture of defeat. 'I wish I could be of more help,' he said. 'Did you try the 'find my phone' app?'

'I did, but it's clearly been switched off.' Mum shook her head. 'And you've really no idea where this project might be taking place?'

'No. I assume it's somewhere in Shetland, otherwise why else would Strode be here? But I can't even be sure of that.

I'm sorry if you've had a wasted trip.' He thought for a moment. 'You might try Chris,' he suggested.

'Who's Chris?'

'The other student, the one he had a fight with. Chris Scanlon.' He pointed to the noticeboard. 'That's him, bottom left.' Viggo saw a young guy around Magnus's age, with straight black hair and a neatly trimmed beard. 'He and Magnus were as thick as thieves before Dr Strode turned up … and I happen to know where you can find Chris. He's moved on to a seabird project on St Ninian's Isle.'

Mum seemed uncertain. 'I'm afraid I don't know it.'

'It's easy enough to get to.' He pulled a map from his desk drawer and opened it out. 'Where are you staying?' he asked.

'Just outside of Lerwick.'

'Ah, well, here's St Ninian's.' He tapped a jagged outline on the map. 'It's only a short drive from the town. Easy to find, and you won't need a ferry or anything. There's a tombolo.'

'A what?' asked Viggo.

'It's like a sandy causeway that never gets covered by the waves. You'll be able to park on the mainland and just stroll across. The island is tiny and quite beautiful. Worth a trip even if you don't have any success in finding Chris. But he should be easy enough to spot. The place is still secluded this early in the season and he'll be the one peering through binoculars and taking photographs of birds. Oh, and why not leave me a note of your phone number, just in case any new information should turn up?'

He offered Mum a pen and she wrote her details down

on a slip of paper. 'Thank you,' she said. 'I've put my email on there as well.'

'Not that you'll have much luck with that,' muttered Viggo. 'The Wi-Fi's rubbish around here.'

Dr Glover smiled ruefully. 'It can be challenging,' he agreed.

Mum stood up from her chair. 'Well, I suppose we may as well be on our way . . .'

'Why don't you have a wee look around before you go?' suggested Dr Glover. 'Seems a shame not to, since you've come all this way. And you'll have an idea of why Magnus wanted to work here before . . . things changed.' He opened a drawer in the desk and took out a laminated pass. 'Just show that if anybody asks to see a ticket. You can drop it at reception before you go.'

'Thank you.' Mum took the pass from him and turned to leave, but then stepped across to the noticeboard. 'I wonder . . . could I perhaps take a photo of that picture of Magnus? Just in case I need to show it to people.'

'Of course, please do.' Dr Glover stood up. 'And take one of Chris, too, it'll help you to identify him. I always like to keep pictures of our students up there each season. It helps me to put names to faces. It'll soon be time for the new cohort to arrive.' He watched as Mum took out her phone and snatched a couple of shots. 'You know, I was really impressed by Magnus when he first came here,' Dr Glover said. 'He has a quick mind and is very knowledgeable on his subject. I can see why Dr Strode thought he'd be useful. I do hope you find him. My advice would be to get him away from that man's influence as soon as possible.'

'You think he's dangerous?'

'I think he's rich, powerful and unscrupulous, which amounts to the same thing.'

He and Mum shook hands. 'Do you and your brother have the same interests?' he asked.

'Not really,' said Viggo. 'I'm an RPG guy, myself.'

Dr Glover looked baffled. 'Excellent,' he said. 'Well, er, good luck with your search.'

Viggo followed Mum out through the reception and into the open air. They stood for a moment in the pale afternoon sunlight, looking around at the weird jumble of stone and turf that stood beside them. 'I'm not sure I even *want* to spend more time here,' confessed Mum dispiritedly. 'I'd just assumed there'd be a forwarding address.'

'Are you sure?' Viggo asked her. 'It's supposed to be pretty good.' He slipped into his impersonation of Leon. 'A mixture of Iron Age and Viking!' he intoned. 'One of the most exciting archaeological finds in history!'

Mum somehow managed a half-smile. 'I wonder where he's got to?' she murmured.

Viggo nudged her with his elbow and gave her a mischievous grin. 'We could just head off and leave him here,' he suggested, but she shook her head.

'We can't,' she told him. 'What if Ruby breaks down in the middle of nowhere? I'm afraid we'll have to accept we're stuck with him.'

She was worried, Viggo could see that. She had clearly believed that finding Magnus would be an easier job than it was proving.

'Don't worry,' he told her. 'He'll show up. He always does.' He turned his head to look down the flight of stone steps which Leon had descended earlier. 'Well, if I can't persuade you to do a runner, I'd better go and fetch our mechanic.'

He saw that Mum had taken out her phone and was looking at the photograph of Magnus, studying it mournfully. She looked as though she was on the verge of tears. Viggo couldn't think of anything else to say, so he went down the steps and ducked his head to shuffle under the low stone lintel of a broch. He walked into the gloom beyond and then straightened up.

He looked slowly around. His first impression had been that the broch was completely empty, but now he became aware of a dark shape in the shadows on the far side of the circular enclosure – a man standing with his face pressed to the wall, his arms outstretched, his fists pummelling stone. In the weird echoey silence, Viggo heard the sounds he was making. And then Viggo realised with a twinge of shock that it was Leon Bragg – and he was crying like a child.

# CHAPTER 9
## THE BROCH

Viggo's first impulse was to turn around and get the hell out of there – indeed, he half-turned to do exactly that but, after a moment's thought, realised that he and Mum couldn't really leave without Leon. What if the car failed to start again? So, against his better judgement, he turned back and edged slowly closer until he was standing just a short distance from him. He waited in silence for a few moments, hoping that Leon would realise that he was no longer alone, but he didn't seem aware of anything other than his own misery. In the end, Viggo decided there was nothing for it but to speak.

'Hey,' he said. 'Are you all right?'

He realised what a stupid question it was, but couldn't think of anything better to say. Leon turned in dismay to look helplessly at Viggo, his face wet with tears, his eyes rimmed red.

'He was here,' Leon croaked, in a tiny, dismal voice that Viggo wouldn't have thought him capable of. 'Right here.'

Viggo stared back at him. 'Who was?' he whispered.

'Daniel,' said Leon. 'My son.'

There was a short silence while Viggo considered Leon's words. He had never mentioned a son before, Viggo was pretty sure about that. He opened his mouth to say so, but Leon spoke before he could say a word.

'You must have wondered why I ran off like that,' he said. 'When we arrived, I had every intention of going into the office with you. But then I heard the voice. It was coming from this broch, as clear as a bell. I had to come and look! I had to see for myself.' He stared around the circular interior, wild-eyed, as though hoping to catch a glimpse of something that was no longer here. 'When I first came in, it wasn't like this at all.'

Viggo was beginning to wonder if Leon was having some kind of a breakdown. 'What do you mean?' he asked. 'What was it like?'

'As it must have been originally. There was a wood fire burning right there . . .' Leon pointed to a blackened area that had once been a hearth. 'It lit the whole place up with this strange light and I could see that the broch was furnished with rough wooden benches and tables. There was a proper roof and . . . all these carcasses were hanging from wooden beams.' He seemed to remember another detail. 'I saw a big black pot of stew, hanging over the fire. I could smell the earthiness of it as it cooked. Mutton, I suppose. Oh, and some kind of music was playing, weird, discordant, like nothing I'd ever heard before.' His eyes seemed to grow bigger as he recalled what happened next. 'And then, all of a sudden, there was Daniel. Just sitting on a wooden bench, holding his hands out to the fire, warming himself. He turned and looked right at me and he . . . smiled.'

Again, Leon's voice erupted into tears and he had to make

a frantic effort to get himself under control. 'He spoke to me!' he gasped. 'Daniel said . . . he said he'd forgiven me!'

Viggo was bewildered by all this. 'Forgiven you for what?' he asked.

'For letting him die.'

Viggo's dream of earlier that morning came flooding back just then. The dream about his dad, sitting on the edge of his bed, issuing him with that weird warning.

'I don't understand,' said Viggo. 'Your son. How did you let him die?'

With an effort, Leon calmed himself. He lifted an arm to mop at his streaming eyes with the sleeve of his jacket, then walked over to a flat-topped boulder and slumped heavily down on it. He sat for a moment, staring at his sandalled feet, as though unsure of where to begin.

'You were right to disbelieve me,' he said. 'Of course I've been to Shetland before. I've been to Jarlshof too. It was thirty-odd years ago, mind you, and I avoid talking about it because of the memories it stirs up, but no, it's not my first time.' He shook his head. 'I was married to Steph, back then, a lovely girl. I met her in Ibiza originally and we fell head over heels in love. We married there, on an impulse, just picked a couple of strangers off the street to be our witnesses. And Daniel came along less than a year after that. He was seven when we visited Shetland. We had this beaten-up old camper van and we drove all over Europe in it, the three of us.' He smiled, remembering something. '*The Three Amigos*, we called ourselves. Like in the movie, you know?'

Viggo didn't know but decided not to mention it.

Leon took a deep breath, as if steeling himself for the next part. 'So, we were on Yell when it happened.'

'Yell?'

'The next island up from here. We found a beach. West Sandwick, it was called. It was a beautiful, sunny day and we chanced upon this perfect little cove with white sand and blue sea. It was glorious! No other people in sight. Just the three of us. But . . . we decided we wanted lunch on the sand, so Steph volunteered to take the van back to the nearest shops while Daniel and I stayed where we were and enjoyed the day. He was paddling and looking for shells and I . . . I . . .' The look on Leon's face was awful now: haunted. 'I was drunk,' he whispered.

Viggo stared at him in surprise. 'But . . . on the ferry, you said—'

'I know what I said!' snapped Leon. 'I also said that I'd come to learn that alcohol was not the answer. It was a hard lesson, believe me – the hardest I've ever had to face!' He saw the way Viggo flinched and held up a hand in apology. 'I'm sorry, I didn't mean to shout, I just . . .' He shook his head. 'I did drink back then. Indeed, I'd been drinking for most of the day, just . . . enjoying myself, you know? Steph was handling the driving and I thought, "Well, why not? We're on holiday!". So I drank a couple more beers while Daniel played and then I lay down on the sand to rest. I had him in plain sight. He was paddling in the shallows, perfectly safe . . . but then, I suppose the combination of the sunshine and booze took its toll.' He shook his head. 'I must have drifted off. God help me, I must have fallen asleep!'

He was crying again now, the sobs dragged up from somewhere deep within him – horrible strangled sounds, like an animal in pain. It was some time before he'd recovered enough to continue. 'It seemed I'd only closed my eyes for a moment and then I woke to the sound of Steph screaming Daniel's name, over and over. She was standing there, looking frantically up and down the beach and . . . he was gone – my beautiful boy – there was no trace of him. He was just . . . gone.' Leon shook his head, the expression of astonishment right there on his face, as though seeing it for the first time. Viggo felt moved enough to walk over to him, to reach out a tentative hand and place it gently on his shoulder.

'Oh God, that's awful,' he whispered.

'At first we thought he must have been abducted, you know? That somebody had come along and taken him. But his body was washed up the following day on a completely different stretch of the coast. He'd drowned, of course. The police said he must have gone out too far. There was an undertow, they said; you couldn't see it but it was there. And anyway, what kind of fool would allow a seven-year-old boy to play in the sea unattended? What kind of . . .?'

His voice gave out momentarily and he made several loud gasps as though struggling to breathe, but somehow he found his voice again. 'Of course, it was the end of my marriage. In many ways it was the end of everything I believed in. Steph moved out and wouldn't take my calls. I lost touch with her. I couldn't tell you where she went after that. And I became a kind of hermit. I shunned others, kept to myself, lived in filth and squalor in a grubby little flat in the back end of nowhere.

I never touched alcohol again. And I swore to myself that I'd never come back here. Never.'

Viggo frowned. 'So what changed your mind?' he asked.

Leon looked at him. 'Well, first of all, it was music. I finally picked up my guitar again and I started to play. And then I began to revisit some of the folk clubs I used to frequent in the old days and the people were nice enough to let me perform a few songs there. Gradually, my confidence returned. I remembered why I loved performing so much in the first place. The healing power of music. I started to busk regularly, even began to make a little bit of money. And then, one day, not so long ago, there was the voice.'

'The voice?' echoed Viggo.

'Yes. A tiny whisper in my head. I woke up one morning and it was there, whispering to me, over and over, telling me I needed to come back to Shetland, that I had unfinished business here. I didn't even realise then that it was Daniel's voice, but it was just so compelling. It told me, over and over again, that I had to return if I truly wanted to be healed, that I had to make myself do it, no matter what the cost. So eventually, I gave in to it. I booked myself aboard that ferry . . .' He looked at Viggo. 'And then, when I bumped into you and Alison, the same voice told me that I should stick with you, help you out in any way I could . . . as though helping you find Magnus would be a way of healing myself.' He waved a hand around the empty room. 'And then, just now, I heard the voice again. It was calling to me from this broch, pulling me in.' He thought for a moment. 'Daniel looked happy,' he said. 'He was only there for a moment but

I think he wanted me to know that he was at peace now. And he told me that he really wants me to help you and Alison.'

They stood there, the two of them, looking at each other in silence and then a tourist stepped in under the lintel and shuffled into the broch – a middle-aged man wearing a red quilted jacket and a baseball cap. He was holding an expensive-looking camera in his big hands and he stood for a moment, gazing at them, as though considering moving further inside and taking some photographs. But then he must have registered the intense expressions on their faces and felt the weight of the silence. Without another word, he turned, stooped and shuffled out again. They heard his footsteps crunching on gravel as he hurried away.

'Awkward,' said Leon, and it broke the spell. They both chuckled.

'I've been thinking about that dream *I* had,' said Viggo. He hadn't meant to say it, but somehow it just fell from his lips as though he'd suddenly lost control of his own voice.

'Oh yes?' Leon rubbed his eyes on the back of his hand. 'What about it?'

'I wondered if it was meant to be some kind of warning.'

'About what?'

'Like, maybe Dad is trying to tell us we're in danger?'

Leon nodded but didn't say anything.

'I mean, he said that we should stop following him. Why does he even think we're doing that? We're here to find Magnus, aren't we?'

Leon nodded. 'True. But like I said to you before, Viggo, perhaps Magnus has actually come here looking for his father.

He may not even know it, but it could be there, subconsciously, and if that's the case the line is heading towards Jonathan. Maybe it's your destiny to find your father, too.'

'My destiny?' Viggo grinned. 'That sounds like something from a *Thor* movie.'

Leon somehow managed a half-smile. 'I've yet to see one of those,' he admitted. 'Would you recommend them?'

'They're pretty cool.' Viggo sensed that Leon was trying to change the subject. He thought for a moment. 'What if I told you that what you saw in here was just a dream?' he asked.

Leon shook his head. 'It wasn't,' he said. 'I'm sure of that. And I think you know it was more than that, like when you thought you saw your father in your room. There's a fine line between dreams and visions and I was most definitely awake.' He seemed to make an effort to push his own recent experiences aside. 'How did you and Alison get on?' he asked. 'Over in reception?'

'Oh, that.' Viggo rolled his eyes. 'Well, it turns out that Magnus has got himself mixed up with this guy called Zack Strode.' He looked at Leon. 'Ever heard that name?'

Leon frowned, nodded. 'I'm afraid I have,' he said. 'I've heard too much about him lately. Every time I switch on the news. An American. Very rich, I believe.'

'That's the guy. From what I've seen online, he's a complete head banger.'

'I wouldn't disagree. A man who believes that dinosaurs never existed, that aliens founded most of the religions on our planet. A man who's rumoured to be building his own rocket ship so he can escape when the world comes crashing down around us. And the trouble is, he's rich beyond the dreams of avarice. People like that are dangerous, Viggo. And you say that Magnus has fallen in with him? That does not strike me as a good thing.' He sighed. 'So . . . do we know where Magnus is now?'

Viggo shook his head. 'We need to find this other guy who might have the answer to that. He's working on St . . . Ninny's Island?'

'St Ninian's.' Leon smiled. 'I know where that is,' he said. 'I've visited it before.'

'I think that will be our next stop.' Viggo glanced towards the exit. 'Mum must be wondering what's taking us so long,' he muttered. 'We'd better go and find her.'

'Just a moment.' Leon put a hand on Viggo's arm to keep him there. 'I don't think we should tell your mother about any of this,' he said. 'About what happened to me in here.'

'Why not?' asked Viggo.

'Because she's already worried about Magnus and has quite enough on her plate without having to listen to my troubles. Do you think we could keep the details about Daniel to ourselves? At least for now.'

'I guess.' Viggo shrugged.

'And all this stuff about dreams. It could be . . .'

'What?'

'. . . that in some places on the planet, the line between dreams and reality is paper thin, at best. I believe that line can be breached. The two things can mingle, become all tangled up in each other. I believe that Shetland is the kind of place where such things happen.' Leon got up from the stone he was sitting on. He brushed himself down and made a visible effort to calm himself. 'And Viggo, I know exactly how you and your mother feel about me.'

'What do you mean?'

'That my presence here is an intrusion on your privacy.'

'Oh, well, I wouldn't exactly say that!'

'Of course you wouldn't, because you're polite and terribly British. That's the only reason you haven't told me to get lost!'

'I don't know if . . .'

'You're doing it again! Do me a favour, will you? Stop being polite. When you speak to me, do me the honour of being straight with me, OK? And I'll do the same for you.'

Viggo nodded. 'Deal.'

'And if I'm ever out of line, tell me so.'

'I'll try.' Viggo thought for a moment. 'I would love to know one thing,' he said.

'What's that?'

'How do you do that business with the car?'

Leon looked baffled. 'Business?' he echoed.

'You know, the way you make it conk out whenever we try to go somewhere without you.'

Leon grinned. 'Viggo, if I had that ability, I'd have patented it and sold it on the internet. I'd be as rich as Zack Strode!' He shook his head. 'It's just a coincidence, I think.'

'But you always say there's no such thing!'

Leon spread his hands in a gesture of helplessness. 'In this case, I can't see what else it could be. I do have *some* talents, Viggo, but sadly I can't make a car engine obey my will. I wish I could. And please trust me when I tell you that whatever you and Alison think of me, I only have your best interests at heart.' He thought for a moment. 'I'll tell you something that *wasn't* a coincidence. I was meant to meet the two of you on that ferry. And I think Daniel called me back to Shetland because he wants me to help you find Magnus.'

He was staring into Viggo's eyes now, the power of his gaze unsettling.

'You realise how that sounds?' murmured Viggo.

'Yes. It sounds totally nuts,' admitted Leon. 'But I happen to think it's the truth. In fact, I've never felt so sure about anything in my life.'

Viggo sighed. 'Well, we'd better go and find Mum, see what she wants to do next. That's if you're ready to leave?'

Leon gazed sadly around the broch, as if to check that what he'd seen before really had gone. But it was just an empty circle of stone and shadow.

'I think we're done here,' he said.

Viggo turned and led Leon back to the entrance. They stooped, stepped under the stone lintel and wandered out into the sunlight.

They climbed the steps to higher ground and stood for a while, gazing around. Viggo finally spotted Mum at the top of a metal tower within the roofless ruins of a rectangular stone building. She was gazing out towards the sea, deep in thought. Viggo and Leon made their way along a labyrinth of paths until they were standing directly below her.

'Hey,' shouted Viggo and she looked down at him in surprise.

'Oh, there you are,' she observed. 'You two were gone a long time.'

Viggo shrugged. 'Er . . . yeah, we were . . . just chatting, you know?'

He saw an expression of surprise flicker across Mum's face. She was probably wondering why Viggo was suddenly on friendly terms with Leon, but he could hardly go into the details.

'What do we do now?' he asked her.

She smiled. 'I don't know about you two,' she said, 'but I'm *starving*. I think before we do anything else, we need to find somewhere to eat.'

# CHAPTER 10
## THE WELL

In the end it seemed to make sense to head back to Lerwick to look for a cafe. They left Ruby in a car park and wandered through the narrow streets of the town, following Google Maps to the place that had the best reviews, a cafe bar called The Well.

'Probably a reference to The Well of Urd,' observed Leon, who, Viggo thought, seemed completely recovered from his ordeal back at Jarlshof and had returned to his usual, confident self. Leon glanced at Mum, probably expecting her to make a connection but, when she didn't, he elaborated. 'It's one of the sacred wells that feeds Yggdrasil – the great tree of Norse mythology.'

'I'll take your word for it,' Mum told him. 'I only remember a few bits and pieces about that stuff. As long as the place can offer me decent food and drink, I'm happy. All we've had today is a bit of shortbread we found in the cabin.' She looked at Viggo. 'I'm surprised I haven't heard you complaining about it.'

Viggo shrugged. 'There's been too much other stuff going on to think about grub,' he said. 'But I *am* starving.'

'So what were you chatting about in that broch?' Mum asked him.

Viggo spotted an opportunity to change the subject. 'Oh look, what's going on there?' he asked, pointing.

A small group of tourists were taking photographs of each other posing in front of a picturesque stone cottage, the back part of which actually jutted up from the water in the harbour. A blue rowing boat was sitting on wooden joists by the back door as though waiting patiently to be launched.

Mum paused for a moment, gazing at the building. 'I'm pretty sure this place is featured in a TV series I used to watch,' she said. 'A crime thing. It was set here.'

Leon looked thoughtfully around. 'Hard to imagine there being much in the way of crime around here, though. It seems so tranquil.'

Viggo led them onwards, following the directions on his phone. They turned down a steep, narrow alley and emerged on to a slightly wider road. 'According to the guide book, this is Lerwick's main shopping street,' said Mum.

They looked up and down the length of it but couldn't spot any other signs of life.

'It's very quiet,' muttered Viggo. 'Where is everyone?' Nobody seemed to have an answer to that, so he consulted his phone again. 'The Well should be somewhere around . . . ah, there it is!' He pointed to a sign jutting out over a doorway and they crossed the street towards it. Mum pushed the door open and led them inside. It was immediately apparent where all the people were. Right here. The interior was packed with diners who all seemed to be happily chatting as they ate.

Rock music provided a lively accompaniment.

'Looks like we've discovered Lerwick's hotspot,' said Leon.

'Not sure we'll even get a seat,' said Mum, looking doubtfully around. A young waitress dressed in black came out from behind the bar to greet them and Viggo did a double take when he realised that it was Freya.

'Hey,' she said.

'Oh, hello,' said Mum.

'What are you doing here?' asked Viggo, before realising that sounded a bit unfriendly. 'Er ... sorry, I mean ... I thought you worked for your mum?'

Freya gave him a disparaging smile. 'I help her out sometimes,' she said. 'But this is my regular holiday gig. I'm trying to earn a little money to fund my escape plan.' She leant closer. 'Nobody in Shetland has just one job,' she assured him. 'We have to be adaptable. Table for three?' She paused and looked around. 'Give me a minute, I think somebody's just asked for their bill.'

She turned and hurried back into the chaos.

'Small world,' said Leon. He glanced slyly at Viggo. 'She seems nice,' he added.

Viggo shrugged, as though to suggest that he hadn't really noticed. 'Yeah, I suppose she's OK,' he allowed.

Leon smiled. 'I must say, I'm ready to eat. By the way, this meal is my treat.'

Viggo and Mum looked at him in surprise. 'What about your bank card?' asked Mum.

'I sorted the problem,' he said, and offered no further explanation.

A few minutes later, a group of four people moved past them, putting their coats on as they headed for the door. Then Freya reappeared and led them past rows of customers to a quieter area at the top of the main room. She indicated a freshly cleaned table, where menus waited for them. 'I'll be back in a bit to get your drinks order,' she told them, and moved off again.

'She seems friendlier today,' observed Mum, settling herself on to a chair. Leon took the seat beside her and Viggo chose a place opposite them. He grabbed a menu and started looking eagerly at the contents. For some reason, he'd expected the food here to be traditional fare, but it was anything but. The Well seemed to specialise in sharing plates featuring the likes of halloumi, kimchi and tabbouleh.

'This is a bit fancy pants,' he observed. 'I didn't even know buffalo *had* wings,' he joked, and Leon grinned.

'The old ones are the best,' he said.

Mum gave a bemused smile, looking from one to the other. 'So, you still haven't told me what you were chatting about back at Jarlshof?'

Leon didn't miss a beat. 'I was telling Viggo how much I was enjoying this trip,' he said. 'And how glad I was that I hooked up with you two. Listen, I'm sorry I headed off the way I did, without any explanation. It must have seemed rude. There was just something I wanted to check out.' He glanced at Viggo as if warning him not to comment. 'Viggo filled me in on what happened with your enquiries, though. He explained about Magnus and the Zack Strode connection.'

Mum frowned, no doubt puzzled by the fact that Viggo

was now friendlier with Leon. 'I must have been living under a rock or something,' she said. 'Because that name means absolutely nothing to me.'

'Easily fixed,' said Viggo. He'd noticed a WiFi password on the menu and within moments had called up an image from Google; a photograph of a middle-aged man in a bright orange beanie hat. He had a broad face that was dominated by a wide grin.

'That's *him*?' asked Mum. 'He looks harmless enough.'

Viggo glanced at the accompanying text. 'According to this he's worth two hundred and fifty billion dollars,' he announced.

Mum stared at him. 'Seriously?' She shook her head. 'No one person should be that rich,' she said. 'And I can't imagine Magnus being influenced by somebody like that. He's never really been interested in money.'

'No, but Strode is into Nordic stuff,' said Viggo. He studied a potted biography of Strode and found what he was looking for. 'Yeah, listen to this,' he said, and read aloud. '*Tech billionaire Zack Strode claims Scandinavian ancestry. Strode, 48, announced today that he has traced his beginnings back to ancient Norway and claims he has proof that he is a descendent of famous Viking king Ragnar Lothbrok . . .*'

Leon snorted. 'Typical,' he said. 'Why can't he just be a billionaire from Nowhere, Arizona? It's beyond me. These people get rich and suddenly feel the need to buy themselves a more interesting history.'

'You don't think it's true?' asked Mum.

'I seriously doubt it. And how would anyone be able to prove such a thing? The Vikings were a nomadic race. I read somewhere that six percent of the UK's population have Norse blood pulsing through their veins. That's approximately four million people. And how could you ever trace your lineage back to one individual?'

'Yeah, but a guy that rich would be able to pay for the best tests available.'

'And there'd be plenty of people out there just queuing up to sell him the answers he's looking for,' said Leon flatly. He adopted an American accent. 'Yes, Mr Strode, I can confirm you're Napoleon's uncle. That'll be ten million dollars!'

Just then, Freya came back to the table, carrying a notepad. 'Can I get you guys something to drink?' she asked.

Mum thought for a moment. 'I believe I'd like a small glass of white wine,' she said. She glanced at Leon expectantly.

'I'll join you,' he murmured, and, before Viggo could say anything, added. 'But I'll have the non-alcoholic variety, if that's possible?'

'Sure thing,' said Freya. 'We have pretty much everything here.' She scribbled on the pad. 'Viggo?' she asked.

'You remembered my name!' said Viggo delightedly, and then felt his face reddening. 'Er, just a Diet Coke, please.'

'Ice and lemon?'

'Er . . . yeah, sure.'

Freya grinned. 'I'll pop over for your food orders once you've had a chance to think about it,' she said, and headed back towards the bar.

Viggo was aware that both Mum and Leon were smiling at him knowingly and he went back to studying the menu intently. 'What's gochujang sauce?' he asked.

'It's Korean,' said Leon. 'Made from fermented rice, soybean and chilli, if memory serves me correctly. It's nicer than it sounds, sweet and spicy. I think you'll like it.' He turned his attention back to Mum. 'So, Viggo told me that you need to find some chap on St Ninian's Isle.'

'Yes. A former friend of Magnus, but the two of them have had some kind of a falling out. Chris Scanlon. It's not far to the island, so I expect we can go this afternoon.'

'Might not be a good idea to head there in heavy rain,' Leon advised her. 'Tomorrow morning would be better.'

Mum looked puzzled. 'Rain?' she muttered. 'What rain? The weather's lovely, isn't it?'

Leon shrugged. 'We'll see,' he said. He picked up a menu. 'Now, we'd better make our minds up about food before Freya comes back.'

\*\*\*

The food, once ordered, arrived promptly. It proved to be delicious, and the portions were on the generous side. Viggo was almost surprised to realise how hungry he was. He devoured everything on his plate and then managed to find room for a bowl of sticky toffee pudding and ice cream. As he ate, he chatted happily with Leon and had to keep reminding himself that this was the same man he had previously distrusted, whom he had spent most of the time wishing would just clear off and leave Mum alone. But after what he'd been told back at the broch, he felt he understood why Leon was the way he was – why he was so desperate to be liked. He noticed how Mum was opening up to Leon too, telling him more and more about herself and her two sons –

and also about Dad – about how strangely he'd been acting shortly before he left for that fateful trip to Shetland.

'I don't know what it was,' said Mum, 'but Jonathan seemed really anxious to get to the new excavation. He was always fired up when he took part in something like that, but this time he seemed particularly driven.'

'Where was it?' asked Leon. 'The excavation?'

'It was on Unst,' said Mum. 'The northernmost island.'

'That's where Freya's best friend lives,' said Viggo, trying to contribute to the chat.

'Is that right?' said Mum.

'That's what she told me. Hey, maybe we could offer to take her there?'

'I'm not sure about that,' said Mum. 'It's quite a journey.' She seemed to be thinking back to her previous visit. 'There are a lot of Viking remains there, more than anywhere else in Shetland, but many of them have barely been investigated. You drive across the landscape and you see them, piled up in fields, heaps of crumbling stone everywhere you look. Like they're waiting to be explored in more detail.'

'There are more Viking longhouses on Unst than there are in the whole of Scandinavia,' said Leon. 'Fact.'

'Is that right?' said Mum. 'Where do you get all this information from?'

Leon shrugged. 'I read a lot,' he said.

'Well, of course, I went up to the site where Jonathan had been based when I was last there. I talked to the administrator of the dig. He told me that Jonathan had been acting oddly in the days leading up to his disappearance . . .

that he'd stopped showing up for work on time, that he'd seemed distracted about something, which really wasn't like him. And then, one day, he just didn't turn up, and when they tried contacting him . . . nothing.' Mum frowned and stared into the wine left at the bottom of her glass. 'So when Dr Glover told me pretty much the same thing about Magnus, of course it rang alarm bells.'

'You mustn't go jumping to conclusions,' Leon advised her. 'I don't suppose there was any evidence of this Strode character being around at the time Jonathan was here?'

'No,' agreed Mum. 'At least, the name never came up.'

'But you haven't even heard of him till now,' Viggo reminded her. 'And he's all over the news like a rash lately. He's buying big companies for ridiculous amounts of money.'

'I stopped watching the news,' said Mum gloomily. 'It's too depressing.'

'I'm with you there,' said Leon.

'When I say *news*,' said Viggo, 'I mean the internet, obviously.'

Leon looked at Mum. 'But, the people your husband worked with? They must have had theories about what might have happened to him?'

Mum shrugged. 'It was five years ago, Leon. I don't really remember that much about it. I think I was in shock at the time. I had this sudden realisation that I was on my own now – that I'd have to bring up my two boys alone. And then, of course, the insurance refused to help out because no trace of Jonathan had been found. I don't mind telling you, it's been a real struggle.' She glanced at Viggo. 'I hope I made a good job of it,' she said.

'I think you did OK,' said Leon. 'What do you say, Viggo?'

'You did all right with *me*,' said Viggo grudgingly. 'Magnus . . . maybe you could have tried harder with him.'

'What do you mean?' cried Mum, in mock outrage. 'What's so bad about Magnus?'

'Where do I start?' Viggo thought for a moment. 'Well, when we were little, he always got his own way about stuff, no matter how dumb it was.'

'Maybe he just shouted louder than you did?' suggested Mum.

'Or maybe he was just your favourite?'

'Oh, now, that isn't true at all!'

Freya came back to the table. 'Can I get you guys anything else?' she asked.

Mum glanced at her wine glass and shook her head. 'I need to drive,' she said. 'So I'll leave it there. But it was lovely. We'll have the bill when you're ready.'

Freya nodded and then glanced at Viggo. 'I was thinking . . .' she said.

He looked up at her. 'Yeah?'

'That invitation to play a board game. How are you fixed tonight?'

'Should be OK,' said Viggo, trying not to sound too eager.

'Cool. Come over to the reception . . . say, around eight o'clock?'

Viggo nodded and Freya moved off to get the bill. Viggo looked at Mum. 'Is that all right with you?' he asked.

'Oh, don't worry about me,' said Mum. 'I'm sure I'll manage.'

'Well, well,' said Leon, raising an eyebrow. 'Looks like somebody's luck might be changing for the better.'

Viggo pretended to be absorbed in something on his phone, but couldn't help smiling.

A few minutes later, Freya returned carrying a saucer with a printed bill on it and a portable card machine. Leon took the bill from her and then reached into his pocket. Viggo had expected him to produce the infamous debit card but instead, he was clutching a thick wad of what looked like twenty-pound notes. Mum and Viggo exchanged surprised glances, then quickly looked away. Leon placed three notes on to the saucer. 'Keep the change,' he told Freya. 'You can put it towards your escape fund.'

'Thanks,' said Freya, with a smile. She picked up the saucer and headed back to the bar.

'That was very kind of you,' said Mum. 'There was really no need.'

'Least I could do,' said Leon.

But Viggo knew exactly what was going through Mum's mind. When did Leon have the opportunity to get his hands on some actual money? He'd claimed to have none on the ferry and they'd been pretty much in his company ever since. He seemed to have read their minds.

'Agnes cashed a cheque for me,' he explained.

'Ah.' Mum nodded and smiled. 'Well,' she said. 'Thank you. And now, we'd better get going. We need to drive to St Ninian's Isle.'

Leon didn't say anything, just followed them dutifully back through the still crowded room, towards the exit. As they neared the front doors, Viggo could see that the weather had undergone a dramatic change. The previously sun-splashed main street was now receiving a more literal soaking. Heavy rain was lashing down, bouncing off grey stone and turning the pavement into one gigantic puddle. Mum looked at Leon in amazement.

'You said it would rain,' she muttered.

He nodded. 'Can't be helped,' he observed. 'And it would be an ordeal trying to get to St Ninian's Isle in this. Tomorrow makes more sense. We can leave straight after breakfast.'

'But what if it's like this tomorrow?' asked Viggo.

'It won't be,' said Leon, and he grinned. 'Don't worry, I'll arrange it.'

# CHAPTER 11
## DATE NIGHT

Viggo stared critically at his reflection in the tiny bathroom mirror. He had showered, brushed his hair and had even indulged in a squirt of the aftershave that Mum had tucked into his washbag when they were packing for the trip. He was wearing his best *Dragondarke* T-Shirt and a pair of clean jeans. His watch told him that it was a few minutes before eight, but still he hesitated. He was thinking about what Jamie had said, about how he really needed to smarten himself up, but he hadn't brought those kinds of clothes on this trip.

Mum was sitting in the little lounge, reading her paperback. 'You're cutting it fine,' she told him, through the open bathroom door.

'Yeah, I'm just . . .' He smiled at himself in the mirror, showing his teeth, and noticed that he had a bit of food caught between two of them, so he grabbed his electric toothbrush and gave them a quick once over.

'For goodness' sake,' said Mum. 'It's not like you to be so fussy!'

'What do you mean? Are you saying I'm a slob?'

'No, stop being paranoid.'

Viggo checked his teeth again and set down the toothbrush. He attempted a welcoming smile in the mirror but decided that it just made him look slightly deranged. 'Mum, do you think I look OK?' asked Viggo.

'You look very handsome,' Mum told him.

'I don't mean that!'

'Then what *do* you mean?'

'Am I . . . like, normal looking?'

'Define normal.'

'Well, if you were Freya and you saw me, what would you think?'

'I really don't know how to answer that,' said Mum.

'What I mean is . . .'

'I'll tell you what *wouldn't* please me, Viggo. If I'd arranged to meet somebody at a certain time and they were late. Especially when the journey is only a few steps away. Now go.'

'OK.' He walked into the lounge, grabbed the box that held his travel games and went over to the door. Hesitating, he looked back at Mum. 'Will you be all right?' he asked.

'I expect so. Don't be too late. I want to make an early start in the morning.'

'Sure.' But Viggo still wasn't quite ready to depart. 'I've been thinking,' he said.

'I'd be careful if I were you. You don't want to strain yourself.'

'Very funny. But, seriously, how do you think Leon knew it was going to rain earlier?'

Mum shrugged. 'I expect he looked at the weather forecast,' she said.

'But how? When? I mean, he doesn't even have a phone, does he?'

Mum actually raised her eyes from the page she was reading. 'He must have,' she said. 'Everybody has a *phone*.'

'I've never seen him use one.'

Mum thought for a moment. 'Well, neither have I, come to think of it . . . but that doesn't mean he hasn't got one. And anyway, that kind of information isn't exclusively on a mobile, is it? Perhaps he saw it on television or in a newspaper.'

'But we've been with him the whole time. And he didn't say it *might* rain, did he?'

'Did he not?'

'No! He said it *would* rain, just like that. As though it was his decision. And then . . . did you notice how it rained just long enough to stop us from going to St Ninny's?'

'Ninian's,' Mum corrected him.

'Yeah. And then it stopped as soon as it was too late to go.'

Mum studied him wearily. 'What are you saying, Viggo? That Leon made it rain?'

'Well . . .'

'That he can actually control the weather? The same way he makes Ruby conk out?'

Viggo considered her words. 'You're right,' he said. 'When you put it like that, it does sound stupid. But it's funny, don't you think?'

She had gone back to her book. Viggo opened the door and peered out into the gathering twilight. The sky was clear now, not a cloud in sight, and the first stars were just beginning to show. 'And another thing. He said it wouldn't rain tomorrow because he'd *arrange* it.'

Mum glared at him. 'It was a *joke*,' she assured him.

'Was it though? Because it seemed to me . . .'

'Viggo, you're now officially three minutes late for your first date with Freya.'

He stared at her. 'It's not a *date*,' he assured her. 'I wish you'd stop calling it that. We're just meeting up to play *Dungeon Mayhem*.'

Mum tried not to roll her eyes. 'It all sounds very romantic,' she said.

'It's not *meant* to be romantic! We're not . . . I mean, I don't think I . . . And anyway, Freya's really into that stuff,' insisted Viggo. 'Or do you think I should have gone for *Arkham Horror*? I've brought both.'

'Viggo!'

'Yeah, yeah, I'm going!' He stepped out on to the veranda, then shut the door behind him. He paused for a moment to look at Leon's cabin, but all the lights were out and there was no sign of life in there. *Perhaps he's decided to get an early night*, Viggo thought. He stepped down onto solid ground and walked the short distance to the reception. It looked dark in there too and, for a moment, he thought maybe Freya had forgotten their plans. But when he pushed the door open he saw her sitting behind the counter, looking at a sheath of papers spread out in front of her, lit by an angle poise lamp. She looked up and smiled at him.

'Hey,' she said.

'Hi there. Are you busy?'

'Nah.' She pushed the papers away. 'Just reading through

a school assignment.' She mimed an exaggerated yawn and then gestured to an empty stool beside her. 'Come and have a seat,' she suggested. She waved a hand at the glass-fronted refrigerator behind her. 'Drink?' she asked him.

'Er, sure.' He set the board game down on the counter and settled on to the stool. 'I'll have a Coke,' he said.

'Diet Coke, right?' she said.

'Are you calling me fat?' he quipped and then, when she gave him a blank look, wished he hadn't said anything. 'You remembered from the restaurant, I guess?'

She nodded. 'One thing about working at that place, you always remember what people order.' She reached back and with well-practised ease pulled out a can and set it down in front of him. 'What did you think of The Well?' she asked him.

'Yeah, it was OK. Good food. Been working there long?'

'About a year. I do Friday and Saturday nights during term time and quite a lot more in the holidays. The money's all right and the tips add up.'

Viggo popped the ring pull on the can of Coke. 'You said something about an escape plan,' he remembered.

'Yeah. I'm hoping to go to university next year. Edinburgh, if they'll have me.'

'Cool. To do what?'

'English literature, if I can get the grades.' She studied him. 'What about you?' she asked. 'You got any plans for the future?'

He shrugged. 'I'd like to write,' he said.

'Oh yeah? Journalism?'

'Nah. I was thinking of fiction.' It sounded very easy when you put it so simply.

'Wow. Good luck with that. What kind of fiction?'

'Fantasy, maybe? Not full-on fantasy, though. Not dragons and wizards, but, like, stuff with a realistic background only with fantasy mixed in? I don't know if it would work. I mean, I've written a few short story things. My mum thinks I'm good, but I realise it's a long shot. Most of the advice seems to be that I should have a plan B – you know, a proper job – and then maybe try writing in my spare time, see if I can scare up any interest.'

'And your mum's a writer, is she?'

Viggo chuckled. 'No! What makes you say that?'

'Oh, it's just that you said she thinks you can write, so . . .'

Viggo shook his head. 'Ah, no. It's just that she's my mum and she thinks everything I do is amazing.' He thought for a moment. 'Well, most things, anyway. She wasn't keen when I said I fancied getting a drum kit.' Viggo turned his gaze towards the box of games thinking that maybe it was the right time to get started, but Freya seemed to have other ideas.

'Do you mind if I ask you something?' she said.

'No, go ahead.'

'What's the deal with Leon?'

Viggo frowned. 'The deal?' he murmured. 'I'm not sure I follow.'

'Well, no offence, but there's something seriously off about that guy.'

Viggo looked at her and nodded. 'I'm not offended,' he said. 'And, yeah, you're right.'

'I mean, I get that he's good looking and everything . . .'

'Really? Leon Bragg?' Viggo was astonished to hear this. The last thing he'd ever have said about Leon was that he was *handsome*. 'I think he looks kind of scrawny.'

'No, he's a looker, in an older man sort of way. You know, silver fox and all that . . .'

Viggo had no idea what she was talking about.

'. . . but I remember your mum said that he wasn't really *with* you. That you guys met him on the ferry.'

'Well, yes, that's pretty much what happened.'

'So how come he follows the two of you around?'

Viggo was surprised by this. He hadn't realised it was so obvious to others.

'How do you know he does that?'

'I'm kind of nosey. I was watching this morning, when you tried to leave? I'm sorry, but that was so funny! Was something wrong with your car?'

'Er, yeah, it conked out. I kind of started thinking that Leon was causing it.'

She gave him a puzzled look. 'How would he do that?'

'I don't know. But there's something really strange about him. Freya, did you see him come out of the chalet?'

'How do you mean?'

'I mean, did you actually see him come through the door? Only it seemed to me like one minute he wasn't there and the next . . .' He realised that Freya was staring at him, so he changed direction. 'But yeah, you're right, he does follow us. It was starting to get on my nerves, to tell you the truth, but then he told me about something that happened to him and I realised—'

'See, I understand that characters like that can fool certain people and, I don't know, maybe your mum is the gullible type?'

'Oh, I wouldn't say she is, not normally!'

'No? Well, here's another odd thing. Leon managed to charm *my* mum like nobody I've ever seen before.'

'Charm her?'

'Yeah. Honestly, Agnes is a real tough cookie. I mean, she hides it well, but underneath that innocent smile, there's a real ass-kicker. Sometimes we get the occasional chancers who turn up here and she doesn't normally put up with being messed around by anyone. I remember last summer, these students turned up and they were, like, really drunk and acting up. Mum handled them like that.' Freya snapped her fingers. 'Had them packed up and cleared out before their feet touched the ground. But ten minutes of chatting to *Leon* and she hands over the keys to one of her precious cabins as if it means nothing! That really isn't like her.'

Viggo took a swig of his Coke, remembering as he did so how Leon had swaggered out of reception holding the keys like some kind of trophy. 'He does seem to have a way of getting people to go along with him,' he agreed. 'And then, all that money he borrowed . . .'

Freya stared at him. 'Money?' she echoed.

'Er, yeah, you know, the cheque your mum cashed for him?'

'A cheque?'

'Yeah, it's like a piece of paper and you write on it to promise to pay.'

'I know what a cheque is! Don't see many of them these

days, but . . . you're saying that Mum cashed one? No way!'

'Way. That's how he paid for all the food at The Well.'

Now Freya seemed positively alarmed. 'My mum cashed a cheque?' she asked again, as if the words were in a foreign language she didn't speak very well. 'For how much?'

Viggo could only spread his hands in a gesture of helplessness. 'I've no idea,' he admitted. 'But see, he's been having trouble with his bank card and . . .'

Freya got suddenly up from her seat and paced over to the glass door of the reception. She stood there, staring moodily at the lights in the window of the farmhouse a short distance away.

'My dad will not be best pleased if he finds out about that,' she murmured. 'He will not be pleased at all. He really doesn't like . . .' Her voice trailed away. 'He's *in* there,' she gasped.

'Your dad?' asked Viggo.

'No. Leon!'

'What?' Viggo got up off his stool and went over to join her. He could see the illuminated rectangle of light that was the lounge window. There was Leon, sure enough, holding a glass of amber liquid in one hand. He was laughing about something and, as Viggo watched, Agnes strolled into view, talking to Leon, and then the two of them laughed together and sipped their drinks.

'That's my dad's best malt whisky,' hissed Freya. 'He doesn't let anyone have a taste of that stuff, not even his close friends!'

'It can't be whisky,' Viggo assured her. 'Leon doesn't drink alcohol.'

'He seems to be doing a pretty good impression of it,' said Freya. 'I'm going over there!'

'No, wait,' said Viggo. 'You can't just—'

He broke off as someone else moved into view, the tall gangling figure of a man, with a prominent nose and close-cropped hair. He too was holding a glass, and as Viggo watched, the three of them clinked glasses and shared a jovial toast. Freya let out a long breath. 'Jesus,' she said.

'Who's that?' asked Viggo, but he already knew the answer.

'It's only my bloody dad,' whispered Freya.

There was a long, uncomfortable silence in which Viggo became aware of the sound of a clock ticking. As he watched, the three drinkers drained their glasses.

'So . . .' he murmured at last. 'What about that game of *Dungeon Mayhem*?'

# CHAPTER 12
## TO THE ISLAND

When Viggo and Mum stepped out of their cabin the following morning, Leon was already waiting for them by Ruby. He lifted a hand to wave.

Viggo was not in the best of moods. He'd drunk coffee and eaten a breakfast of scrambled eggs on toast in almost total silence. Needless to say, the previous evening had not gone well. Freya had no longer been interested in playing a board game and she and Viggo had struggled through an awkward conversation instead. Every so often, Freya got up from her stool to prowl over to the window where she kept reporting back that Leon was still chatting and drinking with her parents, like they were his best friends in the world. Viggo had the impression that Freya somehow blamed him for the situation, which was a little unfair when it was completely out of his hands.

In the end, he'd made his excuses and headed back to his cabin, the box of games tucked under his arm. After that, he'd spent a restless night trying to get to sleep. At some point in the early hours, he'd got up to use the toilet and had taken a moment to look out towards the farmhouse, only to see that the lights in the lounge were still blazing and that Leon and his new pals were happily chatting and drinking through the small hours. Thankfully, there was no sign of Freya in there. Viggo guessed she must have gone straight to her room and left her parents to it.

This morning was bright and sunny – just as Leon had predicted – but the happy grin he was directing at his two companions made Viggo want to punch him.

'Hello, hello, fellow travellers!' cried Leon. 'I trust we're all ship-shape and ready for the trip to St Ninian's Isle?'

'Well, *I* am,' said Mum. 'But I'm afraid Viggo seems to have climbed out of the wrong side of bed this morning.'

'Oh dear.' Leon gave him an enquiring look. 'Something got your goat, old son?'

Viggo directed a withering glare in Leon's direction. 'I'm surprised to see you looking so lively,' he said.

Leon gave him a puzzled look. 'Come again?' he murmured.

'I thought you'd be suffering from a hangover this morning, what with all the late night *drinking* you were doing.'

'Drinking?'

'Over in the farmhouse,' said Viggo. 'I saw you. I thought you didn't touch alcohol?'

Mum gave him a horrified look. 'Viggo! That's very rude,' she said.

Leon waved a hand in dismissal. 'Oh, that's all right, Alison. Viggo's as entitled to get the wrong end of the stick as anyone else.' He shook his head. 'For your information, old son, I was over there with Agnes and Leif, discussing our plans for the summer.'

'Your . . . plans?' growled Viggo.

'Yes. They're thinking of laying on a bit of live entertainment for their guests this season and yours truly has been invited to organise a little concert.' He thought for a moment. 'Oh yes, and if drinking ginger ale can be described as boozing, then I'm guilty as charged.' He smiled sweetly. 'But enough about me, how was *your* evening?'

Viggo ignored the question and opened the door of the car. He slid into the passenger seat and slammed the door shut behind him.

'I'm so sorry,' Viggo heard Mum say. 'I don't know what's got into him.'

'Oh, don't worry about it. We were all teenagers once. I used to have moods that lasted for several days.'

The driver's door opened and Mum got in behind the wheel. She gave Viggo a disappointed look, then started up the engine. Leon took his regular place in the back seat, still sporting that irritating smile. Mum reversed out of the parking spot. As she turned the Kia around, Viggo saw Agnes pegging out some washing on a circular clothesline at the side of the farmhouse. She lifted a hand to wave and Mum slowed Ruby as they went by her. Leon lowered his window.

'Good morning,' he said. 'Thanks for such a lovely time last night.'

'You're welcome! Oh, I've ordered that part for the cooker, by the way. They say it could be a week before they can get it to me.'

'Oh dear. Japanese ovens,' said Leon, as though it explained everything. 'Well, let me know when you have it and we'll get everything sorted in double quick time!'

'Off somewhere nice?'

'St Ninian's Isle,' said Leon.

'Oh, you have the perfect day for it. Enjoy!'

Leon waved a hand, raised the window again and Mum drove away.

'You know the drill,' Leon told Mum. 'Turn left out of the gate and head on down the road, until the old sat nav kicks in.'

\*\*\*

It was a short and pleasant drive to their destination. The last few clouds had burnt off and the sky was a clear blue sweep from horizon to horizon. The sat nav directed them to a small car park just above the tombolo, a long stretch of vivid white sand that reached like an extended arm across turquoise water to the distant outline of the island. White waves fringed either side of the path, lapping gently at the sand. Mum pulled Ruby to a halt beside a battered-looking green Land Rover and switched off the engine.

'Look, Viggo, how beautiful!' she exclaimed.

Even Viggo, grumpy though he was, had to agree the place did look astonishing. But Leon seemed more interested in the vehicle parked beside them. He pointed to an emblem painted on to the Land Rover's side, an image of a bird with its wings spread. 'If I'm not mistaken, that probably belongs to the chap we're looking for,' he said. 'He's working for a bird society, isn't he?'

'That's right,' said Mum. 'Well spotted.'

'I spotted the bird-spotter!' quipped Leon, and Mum laughed like it was the best joke she'd ever heard, but Viggo didn't crack a smile.

They all got out of the car and Leon led the way over a small ridge and down to the fine sand of the tombolo. Viggo took out his phone and shot a couple of images, pointing out a section to Mum that looked uncannily like a man's figure, lying on his side and half submerged in the water. He glanced at Leon. 'Aren't you going to take any pictures?' he asked slyly.

Leon shook his head. 'I prefer to capture things here,' he said, tapping an index finger against the side of his head.

'Maybe you haven't got a phone?' suggested Viggo.

'Maybe,' agreed Leon.

'Well, have you or haven't you?'

Mum glared at Viggo. 'What's the matter with you this morning?' she cried. She looked at Leon. 'I'm sorry, my son seems to have forgotten his manners.'

Leon chuckled. 'That's all right,' he said. He looked at Viggo. 'In answer to your question . . .' He put a hand into the pocket of his jacket and then took it out again, holding it up for Viggo to see, the palm turned away from him. The hand was clearly empty and Viggo opened his mouth to remark upon the fact – but then, eerily, the shiny black oblong of a phone seemed to glide upwards into view from behind Leon's fingers. 'Abracadabra,' said Leon gleefully. 'Now you see it . . .' He made a theatrical flourish and the hand was suddenly empty again. 'Now you don't.'

Mum clapped her hands together. 'That was amazing!' she said.

'Oh, just a little trick I picked up,' said Leon.

Mum was clearly intrigued. 'Where would anybody pick up a skill like that?' she wondered.

'I worked alongside a magician on a Caribbean cruise,' he said. 'Back in the eighties.' He saw the baffled anger on Viggo's face and added, 'I'll teach you how to do it if you like.'

'Don't bother!'

Viggo turned away and began to walk towards the island, his head down, his shoulders hunched. 'Hey, wait for us!' Mum called after him, but he ignored her. He kept right on going, dimly aware that Mum and Leon were chatting amiably as they strolled along behind him. He felt angry and frustrated and he wasn't exactly sure why. He only knew that the trust he'd had for Leon, after hearing the story about his son, had been very short-lived. Now he wasn't sure whether he believed the stuff about the accidental drowning or even Leon's insistence that there had been ginger ale in his glass last night. Freya had said that there was something 'off' about the man and Viggo agreed with her one hundred per cent.

But what was he to do? Mum clearly trusted him now, and so did Agnes and her husband. Why couldn't they see that something wasn't right here?

It took them maybe half an hour to cross the tombolo and then the ground rose dramatically and they had to toil up a steep slope, with the fine sand slipping away beneath their feet, before they finally crested a rise and found themselves walking on a curved headland that stretched away in every direction until it culminated in precipitous cliffs. As they approached the nearest of them, the stones appeared to boil and shimmer with flocks of restless white birds, who were constantly fighting for their positions in the crevices.

'Fulmars,' Viggo heard Leon shout, because the nearer they

went to the cliffs, the more they were assailed by powerful winds, gusting in off the sea. Jagged black rocks reared upwards from the restless water, each view more astonishing than the last, but, for the time being at least, Viggo, Mum and Leon appeared to be the only visitors here.

'Let's try the other side,' yelled Leon above the tumult, and they followed him across the curve of the hill. 'You know, in the 1950s, a horde of Pictish treasure was found on this island. It dated from the eighth or ninth century and was priceless. What's more, it was discovered by a schoolboy.' He looked at Viggo. 'Somebody just a few years younger than you. Imagine how exciting that must have felt.'

Viggo shrugged. 'Whatever,' he said.

'Just think, at this very moment, a wonderful piece of treasure could be just a few centimetres beneath your feet.'

'What's your point?' asked Viggo.

'There's no point. It's just interesting, don't you think?'

They continued walking down to the cliffs and still couldn't see anybody else. They were on the point of admitting defeat when Mum spotted a lone figure, crouched on the edge of a sheer drop – a man with a camera, who was using a long telephoto lens to home in on some other birds. Not the fulmars they'd seen earlier, but little black and white creatures with brilliant orange feet and beaks.

'He's found puffins!' cried Leon, leading them closer.

After a few moments, they were standing just a couple of metres behind the man, watching him as he worked. The birds were extraordinary, with vividly coloured faces that made them look somehow clownish. Many of them had rows of tiny fish dangling from their beaks. The man was intent upon his subject and seemed completely unaware of the people standing behind him. Viggo thought about calling out to him, but the man's feet were mere centimetres from a sheer drop. It wouldn't be a good idea to startle him. They waited until he turned around, preparing to move to a new spot. He saw them and smiled absently. Viggo recognised him instantly from the photograph in Dr Glover's office.

It was Chris Scanlon. 'Thought I was all alone out here,' he shouted over the wind.

He was about to walk away but Mum stepped forward. 'Mr Scanlon?' she asked him.

He looked surprised, then worried. 'That's me,' he said. 'Can I help you?'

'I hope so,' said Mum. 'I'm Alison Ryan – Magnus's mother.'

Chris took a little time to process this information and then the worried look returned. 'Is he all right?' he asked. 'Has something happened to him?'

'I really don't know,' Mum told him. 'I'm actually trying to find him. This is my other son, Viggo. And this is . . . my friend, Leon. We've come from Edinburgh to try and locate him. I was hoping you might be able to help.'

Chris seemed to contemplate this for a few moments and he threw a wistful look towards the puffins, who were squabbling loudly over something one of them had found, but he seemed to accept that the birds would still be there later. He returned his gaze to Mum. 'Let's move inland a bit so we can hear each other talk,' he suggested. He led them away from the cliff and over the hump of a hill, then down into a small hollow, edged with rock, which provided some cover. It was only when they were out of the wind that they appreciated how loud it had been. Viggo saw an open metal case on the ground, holding a selection of other lenses. Chris unslung the camera from around his neck and set it down carefully with the other equipment, before slumping on to the ground. His three visitors found places to sit amongst the rocks.

'How much do you know already?' Chris asked them.

Mum frowned. 'We know that you and Magnus were friends and that the two of you fell out,' she said. 'Dr Glover told us that much.'

'And we also know that Magnus is working for Zack Strode,' added Viggo.

At the mention of Zack's name, Chris's face registered a scowl. It was evident that he didn't like the man one bit. 'I blame him,' he said. 'You know that Magnus attacked me?'

'Yes.' Mum looked uncomfortable. 'I can only apologise on his behalf. It's really not like him to be violent. Can you . . . can you tell me why he would do such a thing?'

Chris lifted a hand to his face and Viggo thought he could see the faint remains of a bruise on his right cheek. 'He threw a punch at me because I criticised Strode,' he said. 'Can you believe that? Magnus had just told me how the man was offering him a ridiculous amount of money to leave the project we were already working on and head off on some wild goose chase on Unst.'

'Where on Unst?' asked Leon, speaking for the first time.

Chris shrugged. 'Well, now you're asking,' he said. 'Magnus seemed to be treating it like some great secret. Whatever it is,

Magnus claimed that it was "something that would set the world of archeology on fire!"' He thought for a moment. 'What else did he say? Oh yes, that it would be "the single most important discovery in history; an artefact that would change the world, for ever!"' He smirked. 'I told him it sounded like something from a Hollywood movie and he got really angry. He told me that when I finally heard about it, I'd have to eat humble pie. Then I said . . .' His voice trailed off.

'Go on,' urged Mum.

'I said that no amount of personal wealth could disguise the fact that Zack Strode didn't have the first idea what he was talking about and, well, that's when Magnus punched me.' Again, he lifted his fingers to touch his face. 'Of course, he knew exactly what he was doing. He wanted to leave the site and he knew that Dr Glover couldn't allow him to stay after something like that.' Chris looked sad. 'But I was shocked. I had thought our friendship meant something to him. I thought we'd go on to be great pals, long after the project at Jarlshof was over, you know?'

Mum sighed. 'Dr Glover said he thought that Strode had Magnus under some sort of spell.'

'Yes, that's about right. Him and that woman he hangs around with.'

Viggo sat up and took notice. 'There's a woman?' he murmured, and he gave Mum a meaningful look as if to say, 'told you so'.

'Oh yes. Val. That's what Strode calls her. She rides around with a bunch of other women on motorbikes. They style themselves on The Valkyries, if you can believe such a thing!' He scoffed. 'But Magnus thinks she's the bee's knees. Seriously, she asks him to do something and he virtually runs to carry out her every wish!' He snorted. 'Anyway, at the moment, Strode is throwing money at the project and Magnus is his right-hand man.'

'It couldn't be, perhaps, that you're a little envious?' suggested Leon, and Chris gave him a cold stare.

'No way,' he said. 'Zack Strode is just a man with too much money who's under the illusion that it can bring him greatness. He'll soon get bored and move on to his next big thing. Building a rocket ship to go to Mars! I happen to know *that's* on his bucket list because Magnus let it slip in conversation.' He looked down towards his camera case. 'Now, if that's everything, I really do need to get some more shots while the weather's clear.'

'There must be something else,' Mum urged him. 'Unst is just too vague. Think for a moment, please. Did Magnus mention anything else when he was talking about this mysterious project?'

Chris seemed to be thinking hard. 'I don't recall any more details.'

'Please,' Mum implored him. 'It could be any little thing.'

'Well . . . shortly before we fell out, he'd been over to Unst for the day, to have a look at where he'd be working. He came back absolutely full of himself. And he mentioned the longship at Haroldswick. Do you know it at all? It's for the tourists, really; just a reconstruction of a Viking ship, sitting at the side of the road. There's a longhouse there too. Not that Strode's excavation is *there*, you understand,

I get the impression it's somewhere much more remote. But Magnus did say how he'd loved sitting behind the oars of that longship, pretending to be Kirk Douglas . . .'

'Kirk Douglas?' muttered Viggo, baffled.

'An old movie star,' Leon explained. 'Magnus was probably referring to a film called *The Vikings*.' He turned his gaze back to Chris. 'Do go on.'

'Well, he also said how amazed people would be if they knew that something so incredible was hidden away, just a short drive from that boat. So, it can't be too far from there.'

'That's useful,' said Leon.

'Oh, and . . .' He shook his head.

Mum looked at Chris imploringly, eager for any little morsel of information.

'Well, it was just a little aside really. It might not mean anything at all, but Magnus did say how lucky it was that he was within a few miles of a decent cake fridge.'

'A what?' asked Viggo.

'It's a Shetland tradition,' said Leon. 'They have these fridges set up in the most remote locations, any place where an electric cable can be run to. Somebody stocks them up with fresh cake every day and people just drop by and take a piece. There's an honesty box so they can leave money.'

'That's right,' said Chris. 'Magnus told me he'd chanced on one out in the middle of nowhere, and that he couldn't seem to drive past it without grabbing a slice of . . .'

'Chocolate cake,' said Mum, smiling fondly. 'So, you're saying, if we can find this cake fridge, Magnus won't be too far away from it?'

Chris smiled. 'That's right.' He shrugged. 'That's all I can think of. It was shortly after that when everything went wrong between us and . . . well, you know what happened next. I hope you find him. If you do, please tell him to get away from that American idiot!' Chris crouched down and picked up his camera. 'Now, if you'll excuse me,' he said, 'I've promised to get these images to my team by lunch time.' He straightened up. 'Good luck with your search,' he called as he strode back towards the cliffs.

They got to their feet and watched him approaching the edge.

'He seems like a nice fellow,' observed Mum. She looked at Leon. 'Do you think we have enough to go on?' she asked him.

'We have all we need to get us close,' he assured her. 'After that, we'll need a little slice of luck. Of course, we'll have to book the ferries before we can head off.'

'Ferries?' Viggo looked apprehensive.

'Oh, you can relax, old son, they're not big crossings. Ten minutes or so to sail over to Yell and then about the same for Unst. Honestly, you'll be fine.'

'It sounds complicated,' said Mum.

'Believe me, it's not. They're well practised at getting cars back and forth; the trip goes like clockwork. It only takes a couple of hours.'

'And the cake fridge?' muttered Viggo.

'We'll just keep our eyes open,' Leon told him. 'Come on, we'd best get back to the car.'

Viggo and Mum followed him up out of the hollow and across the curve of the headland. Viggo thought about Chris Scanlon, about how hurt he seemed by Magnus's betrayal.

He turned to look back towards the cliff and felt a shock go through him when he registered that the edge of the cliff was now devoid of life. For a moment, he imagined Chris's frail figure hurtling to his death on to the jagged rocks far below.

But then it occurred to him that Chris had probably just clambered over the cliff's edge in order to get closer to the puffins he was trying to photograph. For a moment, Viggo considered going back, just to check that he was okay, but Mum and Leon were striding onwards, heading back towards the tombolo and, after a few moments' hesitation, Viggo followed them.

# PART TWO
## UNST

# CHAPTER 13
## SEARCHING

Sitting in the passenger seat as Ruby sped along, Viggo decided that Unst looked pretty much like Yell – and that Yell had looked very like the Mainland, from where they'd started this journey a couple of hours earlier. Except, of course, that there was even less traffic here.

It hadn't started well. There'd been an irritating delay when they tried to book the ferries on Mum's phone, because she kept losing the connection halfway through. In the end, they'd been obliged to head back to the tourist office in Lerwick, where a friendly and very helpful woman called Hazel had made the booking for them by telephone (she clearly knew whoever she was talking to by name) and had worked out the crossings for them. She assured them they'd still have plenty of time to get to Unst, enjoy a good look around and be back in time to catch the last ferry of the evening. She'd also taken the opportunity to hand them a whole bunch of timetables, brochures and maps, plus something she claimed was absolutely invaluable: a typed list indicating where they might find public toilets whenever they needed them.

'I know what it's like when you're travelling and you

suddenly need to pay a visit,' she chuckled. 'So I always make sure everybody I talk to gets one of these.' Viggo had dutifully crammed the wad of paperwork into the pocket of his jacket and forgotten all about it.

They'd grabbed sandwiches from a little cafe for their lunch and then driven straight to the ferry terminal, where they'd joined a short line of cars and vans waiting on the quay. Right on cue, the ferry had come gliding into view. It was much, much smaller than the vessel that had brought them over from Aberdeen, with a section at the front that could be raised like a drawbridge to let the vehicles drive on. Viggo was delighted to discover that, once on board, there was no need to even get out of the car. They parked on the deck with their windows open and the ferry headed out across placid waters. A little more than ten minutes later, they were driving straight off again. The weather stayed warm, with barely a cloud in the sky.

Viggo couldn't help feeling a bit sorry for Yell, which seemed to be a place you drove across simply in order to get to Unst, but Leon kept pointing out idyllic-looking beaches along the way, and Viggo found himself wondering if one of them was the beach where Daniel had been lost – but then had to remind himself that he was no longer really sure if he even believed that story.

Mum had assigned Viggo the thankless task of searching for the cake fridge on his phone. The only ones he could find any reference to were back on the Mainland. He tried every search term he could think of – *Cake Fridge Unst, Cake Fridges Shetland, Unst Cakes* – to no avail, aware as he did so that he was eating into his meagre data allowance. His mood wasn't improved when an Instagram alert popped up and, when he opened the app, he saw a photograph of Jamie and the others from his regular D&D group standing outside Cineworld Fountainbridge, under a massive poster for the new *Thor* movie. Viggo couldn't fail to notice that Jamie had an arm casually draped around Emma's shoulders and that he was grinning at the camera as if he'd just won the lottery.

'Oh, that's perfect!' snapped Viggo, and switched the phone off.

Mum gave him a cautious glance. 'Found something?' she asked him.

'No,' he growled. 'Nothing you'd be interested in, anyway. Turns out my friends are having a great time without me.'

'Oh, that's nice,' said Mum, completely missing his point. 'Well, maybe we'll chance on something at Haroldswick. It's not far now.'

Soon enough, they spotted a signpost and, a few minutes later, a dark shape appeared on the horizon. As they drew closer they saw it was the Viking longship that Chris had mentioned. It was standing on trestles at the side of the road and looked exactly like the one that Viggo had thought he'd seen when he'd been ill on that awful ferry crossing. It was amazing to think that was only a few days ago. So much had occurred since then, most of it beyond his understanding, and it already felt as though he'd been away from home for weeks.

A little further on from the ship was a replica longhouse, a low building with dry stone walls and a turfed roof. Mum pulled Ruby into a little parking space opposite. After a few moments, they all got out, grateful for the chance to stretch their legs. They walked across to the main door of the longhouse, which was secured by nothing more than a simple wooden peg. Viggo turned it and swung the door open.

He stepped inside and looked along the length of the interior, noting the stout wooden uprights and the heavy roof beams, the crudely made benches and tables and, in one corner, a primitive loom. He paced the length of the building, looking for clues, his boots crunching on the shingle floor, then he went into the various little side rooms that held nothing of great interest to him. In one of them, an open window offered a tranquil view of the sea.

'This was where they kept their animals,' said a voice behind him, and he turned to see Leon studying him thoughtfully.

'Animals?' muttered Viggo. 'In the same building as *them*?'

'Of course. Milk cows, sheep, pigs . . . these would be the most valuable possessions the Vikings had. They'd want to keep them close.'

'But it must have stunk in here!'

Leon smiled. 'It was a comforting smell,' he assured Viggo. 'It let them know where their next meal was coming from.'

Viggo frowned. 'You talk as though you were actually there,' he said.

'Do I?' Leon grinned. 'I don't mean to.'

'You're like that about most things, aren't you? You talk as if you've been around for a very long time.' He studied Leon for a moment. 'How old *are* you?' he asked.

'Older than you might think,' Leon told him. 'And didn't anybody ever tell you it's rude to ask a person's age?'

Mum came into the room and looked blankly around. 'This isn't helping,' she said. 'I mean, it's nice enough, but how are we to know if Magnus was ever here?'

'We can't know,' admitted Leon. 'Not unless he left something behind.'

'I've checked every inch,' Mum assured him. 'There's nothing.'

'Let's try the longship,' suggested Leon.

They trooped back outside and walked around the building and along the road, the short distance to the ship.

Alongside it was a single information board on a stand. Viggo read the printed words aloud. *'This replica longship is called the Skidbladner. It's a detailed copy of a 9th century ship discovered in Vestfold, Norway and was constructed by a team from Sweden who planned to sail it to North America, in an attempt to emulate the deeds of famous Viking explorer, Leif Erickson.'* Viggo frowned. 'It doesn't say if they ever managed to do that or not,' he complained. 'I guess they didn't, otherwise why is it still here?'

Mum shrugged. 'This is only a replica of the original,' Mum reminded him. 'And anyway, maybe they *did* do it. And then sailed it all the way back again, just because they could.'

Viggo shook his head. 'If this was in Edinburgh,' he said, 'there'd be all kinds of stuff going on. Guided tours, books you could buy, plastic swords and shields . . .'

'I'm sure there will be more of that later in the season,' said Leon. 'But I rather like these things just . . . being here. They make the past and the present mingle together.'

'Like dreams and reality?' asked Viggo, and Mum shot him a curious look.

'What do you mean?' she asked him.

'Oh, it's just something me and Leon were talking about, back at Jarlshof. About the way the two things seem to get mixed together here – so it's kind of hard to tell them apart.'

'But we know the difference, don't we?'

Leon smiled. 'Of course we do,' he agreed. 'And it's like you said, travelling makes you dream more. It only makes sense that coming to Shetland would put Jonathan into Viggo's head. Sometimes I think we look too hard for meaning in the things that just happen to us. Maybe we need to learn to accept things without questioning what they are trying to tell us.'

He led them around the side of the boat to where a flight of wooden steps gave access up to the deck. They climbed and, one by one, stepped aboard, their feet clunking on the boards. Viggo had been initially unimpressed by the size of the vessel but, once on deck, he appreciated that it really was enormous, around sixty-five feet from nose to tail. Remembering what Chris had said, he settled himself into a seat beside an oar. He took hold of it and started churning it around in the air, as though trying to make headway on rough seas.

'How much further to Norway?' he asked in a pitiful voice. 'Are we nearly there yet?'

'Row harder!' snarled Leon and Viggo glanced up at him – then gave a gasp of surprise. He let go of the oar and was instantly aware that it was now splashing down into actual water. The bare wooden deck was lurching and swaying beneath him and Leon wasn't Leon any more. He wore a metal helmet with an elaborate nose guard and his hair hung in plaits to his bare chest. His beard was longer and there was what looked like an old scar running down one side of his face. He was staring down at Viggo, his teeth clenched. His dark eyes seemed to blaze with ferocity. 'I said, row, you dog!' he roared.

Viggo swore under his breath and scrambled back to his feet, but in the fraction of time it took him to get himself upright, everything had shifted again. The boat was back on dry land and Leon was just Leon, smiling that inscrutable smile, as though he knew exactly what had just happened in Viggo's head.

Mum was giving her son another worried look, as though aware of his current mindset. 'Are you all right?' she asked him. 'You seem . . . confused.'

'Uh . . . yeah, I'm . . . I just . . .' Viggo looked helplessly around at the miles of remote country that surrounded them. He could feel a strange sense of panic rising within him. 'What are we doing here?' he cried.

'You *know* what we're doing,' said Mum. 'We're looking for Magnus.'

'Mum, we're standing on a replica Viking ship in the middle of nowhere! Where do you think he's hiding? Do you think he might be below deck or something? We're just wasting our time.'

'Hey, hey,' said Leon soothingly. 'We can't give up that easily. We know that Magnus was here because Chris *said* he was . . .'

'Chris? We barely know him . . . and he was only guessing! We've come all this way on a wild goose chase. Why can't you admit it?'

'There's still the cake fridge,' Mum reminded him.

'Oh my God.' Viggo buried his face in his hands, then lifted his head to look at her. 'Right about now, my mates are settling down in the cinema to watch *Thor* and I'm *here* . . .' He gestured around. 'I'm stuck on this remote island in the middle of nowhere and I'm looking for a bloody FRIDGE!' His voice was loud enough to startle several birds from the cover of a nearby ditch. He watched bleakly as they fluttered into the sky, like a handful of discarded rags. He wished that he had as easy a way out of this place as they had.

'In case you've forgotten,' said Mum, 'we're looking for your brother who has disappeared. In my opinion, that's a lot more important than some stupid superhero movie.'

'What do you know about superhero movies?' snarled Viggo. 'When did you ever take the time to watch one? You were always too busy making sure that Magnus had everything he needed.'

'Look,' said Leon. 'You're getting this all out of proportion, old son . . .'

'I'm not your old son!' snarled Viggo. 'I wish you'd stop calling me that. You lost your old son, remember? You let him drown!'

Leon's eyes widened in shock for a moment and Viggo instantly regretted his words.

'Sorry, I didn't mean that . . . I just . . . I . . .'

He saw tears brimming in Leon's eyes and Mum's appalled expression, and he turned and walked quickly away. He went to the stairs and descended them at speed, his head down, his hands bunched into fists, aware that Mum and Leon were staring after him, stunned by his outburst. He went back and stood beside Ruby, his arms wrapped around himself, waiting for the others to leave the boat, to come back and start asking him questions, but there was no sign of them. He assumed they would be talking about him, Mum no doubt asking Leon what Viggo had meant when he'd said something about drowning.

He scowled and kicked a small stone which went skittering into the road. He thrust his hands into his pockets and the fingers of one of them encountered paper. For a moment he was bewildered, but then he remembered. The leaflets the woman in the tourist centre had given him. He looked around for a bin, but typically there wasn't one.

Bored now, and fed up with waiting for his companions, he pulled the papers out and went listlessly through them. Here was a flyer about the longship and the stone house which stood right in front of him, part of the *Viking Unst* project. Here was another one about a stone circle that required a long trek through the hills in order to reach it. There was the list of public toilets that Hazel had sung the praises of. And last of all there was . . .

Viggo's eyes widened in disbelief as he studied the final flyer, a crudely designed scrap of cheap paper with a simple title printed on it.

Viggo stared at it for a moment and then began to laugh, gently at first and then almost hysterically. And that was when Mum and Leon came walking slowly back from the longship, their expressions dour. They stood there, staring at him in silence, as though worried for his sanity.

'Viggo?' ventured Mum. 'Are you all right?'

'It was in my pocket the whole time!' Viggo told her. 'I didn't even look at it till now.'

'What are you talking about?'

He held the flyer up so she could read what was printed on it in big red letters.

**VISIT THE UK'S NORTHERNMOST CAKE FRIDGE!**

Leon took the flyer from him and turned it over to find the directions.

'It's up beside the Burra Firth,' he told them. 'On the way to Hermaness Hill. Another hour or so further north.' He looked at Viggo and grinned. 'Well, there's a turn-up for the books.'

'Coincidence?' asked Viggo, and started laughing all over again.

# CHAPTER 14

## FOUND

The three of them were motoring again, heading even further north as the sun began to descend towards the western horizon and the long summer twilight began.

Viggo sat staring out of the car window in silence, as the yellow grass verges blurred by him. He thought about everything that had happened to him over the past few days, the strange dreamlike quality of it all – and, not for the first time, he asked himself if that was what this adventure actually was: a series of crazy dreams conjured by his sleeping mind. Whatever they were, they had unsettled him, made him feel anxious about what else might be waiting for him on this journey.

Perhaps soon, he'd wake up in his own bed and he'd go downstairs for his breakfast and find Mum pottering in the kitchen, Radio Two burbling reassuringly from the speakers and, as he ate, she'd ask him about his plans for the day and everything that ensued – every little detail – would be completely and utterly explicable.

'Can't be far now,' he heard Mum murmur, but although she was only in the driver's seat, it seemed to Viggo that she was speaking to him across a great distance.

Leon's voice drifted in. 'If we head much further north, we'll be in the sea.'

And then Viggo heard Mum mention him by name, asking him if he was OK, but he couldn't reply because . . . he wasn't really sure if he *was* OK. He was just . . . lost, he thought, and in sore need of seeing the people he knew and cared about. Jamie and the rest of the D&D crew. And Freya, from Midgard. He really hoped he'd see her again before very much longer.

And then he was jerked rudely from his thoughts as Ruby's brakes were suddenly applied and she came to a shuddering stop, Viggo's safety belt yanking him back against his seat.

He blinked, shook his head, allowed his eyes to come back into focus.

And there it was – the cake fridge. A rectangular glass cubicle, lit from within and standing all alone at the side of the road in the middle of nowhere.

A hand-painted sign was affixed to the front of it.

ROWAN'S HOME-BAKED TREASURES

Within those glass walls, Viggo could see shelves of plastic containers, each one filled with chunks of cake and pastry. He twisted round in his seat to look up and down the seemingly endless stretch of road, but there was no sign of habitation for miles in either direction.

'How does it even have power?' he asked his companions. 'There's no building in sight.'

Leon shrugged. 'A very, *very* long underground cable,' he suggested. 'It's the only way I can account for it. Though where the other end of it is plugged in would be anybody's guess.'

'It doesn't look much,' observed Mum. 'Would anybody travel a long way to find this?'

'*We* just did,' Viggo reminded her, with a scowl.

'Yes, but are we sure this is the right one?'

Viggo reached into his pocket and pulled out the flyer. 'It's definitely the one on here,' he said. He pointed. 'See? Rowan's. And I can't imagine there are many others around here.'

'Hmm.' Leon looked thoughtful. 'Interesting choice of name.'

Viggo glared at him. 'Is it really?'

'Yes. It was a rowan tree that saved your friend, Thor.'

Viggo looked at him. 'He's hardly my friend.'

'You talk about little else,' muttered Mum, crossly. 'All I've heard on this trip is you complaining that you're missing that movie!'

Viggo ignored the dig. 'How did a rowan save Thor?' he asked Leon.

'It was when he was on his way to slay the giant Geirrod,' explained Leon, as though he was talking about the recent exploits of a good friend. 'Geirrod's daughter, Gjalp, tried to drown Thor by urinating a deluge straight at him.'

Viggo raised his eyebrows. 'She . . . wait, she peed at him?'

'Exactly. He was swept away by the force of it, but he managed to grab the branches of a rowan tree and pull himself to safety.'

'Funny how they haven't put that in any of the movies,' muttered Viggo.

'They always leave out the interesting bits,' said Leon. 'That's Hollywood for you.'

There was a short silence after that, while they all sat there, thinking about Thor trying not to drown in a river of urine.

Mum was the first to break the silence. 'What do we do now?' she asked.

'Well, I know what I'm going to do,' said Leon. He opened the rear door, climbed out of the car and then leant his head and shoulders back in. 'It's been a very long while since lunch. I'm going to treat us to some cake.' He closed the door again and strolled over to the fridge. Viggo watched him pull open the door and peer inside.

'Typical,' he muttered. 'He didn't even ask us what we *wanted*. And he'd better put some cash in that honesty box.'

'I'm sure he will,' said Mum. 'He's been a lot better since . . .'

'. . . he conned that money out of Agnes,' finished Viggo.

'We don't know that he conned her. The cheque he gave her could be genuine.'

'Yeah, and he might be planning to pay her some interest, but I doubt it.'

Mum was studying her watch. 'We don't have an awful lot of time to waste if we're going to make it back to Ulsta for the last ferry.'

'I don't even understand what we're doing here,' Viggo told her. 'Are we supposed to just sit in the car and hope that Magnus gets peckish?'

'We don't have anything else to go on,' Mum reminded him.

Viggo gave a grunt of exasperation. 'Have you tried calling him again?'

'Of course I have! I phone him every few hours. He never picks up. Probably doesn't even realise it's me calling him.'

Viggo gave her a scornful look. 'You don't believe that.

Of course he knows it's you! It tells you who's calling, doesn't it? Like, on the display?'

'Well, perhaps he's too busy to check.'

Viggo took a deep breath. 'Has it occurred to you that the reason he doesn't answer is that he doesn't *want* to talk to you.'

Mum looked hurt. 'But why wouldn't he speak to his own mother? Just to set my mind at rest.' She studied Viggo for a moment. 'Perhaps if *you* tried him again?'

'I must have rung him twenty times since you first asked me. Face it, Mum, he doesn't want to have anything to do with either of us!'

'But why? Why would he be so cruel?'

'Because that's Magnus, in case you haven't noticed.'

Mum made a sound of exasperation. 'How can you even say a thing like that?'

Viggo sighed. 'Mum, there's things about Magnus you don't know.'

She looked interested. 'Yes? Like what?'

'Oh, forget it.'

'No, come on, spit it out. I can see you want to.'

Viggo sighed. 'OK.' He thought for a moment. 'When I was little – I mean like *really* little – he used to play horrible tricks on me.'

Mum smiled affectionately. 'Oh, he could be a bit mischievous, yes, but he really didn't mean any harm.'

'You think? Mum, when I was seven or maybe eight . . .' He hesitated.

'Yes?'

'I had this little space rocket. You remember? Plastic thing.

Yellow. I used to play with it all the time. It was like my favourite toy ever.'

'Oh yes, I *do* remember!' Mum smiled wistfully. 'Whatever happened to that?'

'I'll tell you what happened. Magnus used it in one of his experiments. He opened it up, put a firework inside it, stuck it back together and then blew it into tiny pieces, right in front of me. And then he laughed his head off while I sat there crying, trying to put it back together again. So don't talk to me about cruelty.'

Mum stared at him. 'Oh, but you can't hold that against him!'

'You wanna bet?'

'He would only have been around ten or eleven years old himself. He probably didn't realise how much it meant to you.'

'Of course he realised!' snarled Viggo. 'That's why he was laughing so hard! And do you know why I never mentioned this before?'

'Well, er . . .'

'Because Magnus told me if I breathed a word to you or Dad, he would lock me in the wardrobe and throw away the key!'

There was a long, shocked silence while Mum thought about this. 'He probably . . .'

'Yes?'

'He probably thought you'd see the funny side.'

Viggo shook his head. 'Here's the thing, Mum. I never did. I never will.' He could feel himself getting unreasonably angry and was somehow unable to stop himself. 'And see, here's the problem. You never saw anything wrong because you didn't want to think that Magnus could be anything but perfect. He was always your favourite.'

'Oh, Viggo, that's ridiculous!'

'Is it? Is it really? Cos that's how it always seemed to me, Mum. Magnus got his way over everything. Whatever he wanted, no matter how dumb or how expensive, you and Dad would sort him out. But me . . . oh, that was a different story. I never get what I want.'

'Viggo, if this is about that drum kit . . .'

'It's not just that! It's lots of things, but you never want to admit the truth.'

'Viggo, please, you're being—'

Mum broke off as the rear door opened again. Leon climbed back into his customary seat, clutching three plastic boxes. 'Here we are,' he said brightly, seemingly oblivious to the uncomfortable atmosphere in the car. 'I went for the ginger cake.' He set one box down on the seat beside him. 'Always loved a bit of ginger. For Alison, lemon.' He handed the second box to her.

'My favourite,' she said.

'That's why I picked it.'

'Yes, but . . . how did you know?'

Leon shrugged. 'Call it intuition,' he said. 'I thought to myself what would a lovely, sunny lady like Alison like best in this world, and the answer came straight back to me: lemon! Cake that actually tastes of sunshine.' He glanced at Viggo. 'As for you, old son, well . . . that was a difficult one. But in the end, I decided that out of the varied selection on offer in that fridge, only one flavour would do. But did I pick the right one?'

He was holding his hand over the top of the third box. 'Let's try it this way. Viggo, what is your favourite cake in the world?'

Viggo was running out of patience. 'Oh, just give it to me, for God's sake!'

'No, no, humour me. Go on.'

'I really don't—'

'Come on. What are you afraid of?'

'Why do you keep asking me that? I'm not *afraid* of anything.'

'Then tell me your favourite cake.'

Viggo glared at Leon for a moment, trying to think of the unlikeliest flavour in existence; rhubarb and cheese perhaps, or bacon and strawberry. But then, from out of nowhere, a memory came to him, something he'd eaten only once, years ago, on holiday in Greece. 'My favourite is Greek honey and orange cake,' he said.

Leon looked dismayed. 'Oh,' he said. He frowned. 'Are you sure there isn't something else you really like?'

Viggo shook his head. 'No, sorry, Leon. You did ask what my favourite was.'

Leon sighed. 'Ah, well,' he murmured. 'You can't blame me for trying.' He handed Viggo the box. 'You don't have to eat it if you don't want to.'

Viggo smiled triumphantly and looked at the box. But his smile vanished in an instant when he saw the glistening golden wedge nestled within it. And the printed label on the lid.

**GREEK HONEY & ORANGE CAKE**

'No!' he gasped. 'No way.'

Mum leant over to look and gave a little gasp herself.

Leon giggled. 'Sorry,' he said. 'Couldn't resist the leg-pull.'

'But you couldn't have known that,' said Viggo. 'How could you?'

Leon shrugged. 'Maybe you mentioned it to me before?' he said.

'Of course I didn't! When would that have come up in conversation? "Lovely day. Yes, it reminds me of my favourite cake, Greek honey and orange." Not very likely, is it?'

Leon shrugged. 'Who knows?' he said. 'Anyway, enjoy.'

For the moment, Viggo was too hungry to care about it. He broke the seal of the plastic box, lifted the lid and took out the sticky chunk of cake. He took a big bite and the flavour seemed to explode like a bomb on his tongue, bringing back memories of that distant holiday. He'd been little and he and Magnus had raced across the silver sand on the beach, laughing and squealing, jumping in and out of the restless waves at the water's edge. And Mum had been there too, of course, younger, her hair longer. She had a turquoise bikini on and was urging them to be careful but still giggling at their antics. And Dad, of course, slim and athletic, running to the water to sweep Viggo up in his arms, the two of them laughing like maniacs, Dad tilting back his head and grinning to show that distinctive gap between his front teeth.

And straight afterwards they'd driven to this little white-painted taverna up in the hills, and the woman who ran the place had proudly brought out a slice of the cake she'd just made and had watched, smiling, as Viggo devoured every last crumb. What a holiday that had been! Viggo couldn't remember a time when he was happier – and somehow the taste of the cake had brought it all flooding back.

He looked at Mum, not usually a cake lover. She was cramming her own portion into her mouth with abandon and it seemed to Viggo that she was remembering something too, something that the sharp citrus flavour was kindling deep within her. Leon was watching them, smiling, his own box as yet unopened. He seemed very pleased with himself.

Viggo swallowed the last few morsels and snapped suddenly back to now, the three of them sitting in Ruby, staring at the upright rectangle of the fridge.

Mum had finished her own cake and was patting her mouth delicately with a napkin.

'What now?' she murmured.

'First things first,' said Leon. 'I think you should reverse a good distance down the road and park up. We don't want to make it obvious that we're staking the place out, right? If Magnus stops by and recognises your car, we could scare him off.'

Mum thought about it for a moment. 'Why would my own son be scared of me?' she asked.

'Just humour me,' said Leon.

'OK,' agreed Mum. ' We reverse and park up. And then?'

'Then we wait,' said Leon. 'And see what happens.'

'But it's already getting late,' argued Mum. 'Wouldn't we do better to drive around and try and spot the place he's working? We know it's somewhere near here.'

Leon shook his head. 'But we don't have the first idea what we're looking for. It could be a building, a cave, a well . . . or just a heap of stones in the middle of nowhere. No, I think we need to be like fishermen.'

'Fishermen?' snorted Viggo. 'What does that mean?'

'Fishermen put out some tasty bait and then they settle down to wait patiently for their catch to arrive.' He smiled. 'I really think we should park up and see what happens. Trust me,' he added. 'I have a good feeling about this.'

# CHAPTER 15
## CAKE

Viggo opened his eyes. He was cramped and uncomfortable in the passenger seat and, for a few moments, he sat there, trying to identify what it was that had woken him. And then he recognised it. Hunger. He was really, *really* hungry. More specifically, he was craving something sweet, longing for another taste of that tantalising honey and orange.

He glanced to his right to see that Mum was fast asleep at the wheel, her head tilted back against her seat. And when Viggo glanced over his shoulder, he saw that Leon was also dead to the world, stretched awkwardly across the rear seat, his head thrown back, his eyes closed. Viggo managed to get himself more upright in his seat and he reached out a hand to the windscreen, which was misted over. There was a vague halo of light up ahead of him that could only be the illuminated rectangle of the cake fridge. He wiped at the glass with his fingers and, sure enough, there it stood, looking faintly spectral in the darkness, the shelves packed with trays of goodies. Viggo glanced at the illuminated dial of his watch and realised that it was a little after ten o'clock and now far too late to think about catching the last ferry back.

But he couldn't think about that right now, because . . .

The hunger was raging within him, actually making him salivate. And almost before he knew what he was doing, he was getting out of the car and closing the door quietly behind him. He glanced up and down the moonlit stretch of road and saw no sign of another vehicle, no lights other than the shocking white orb of a full moon hanging above him like an oversized paper lantern.

He walked quickly the short distance down the road and approached the fridge. He stood looking at it in silent anticipation and then reached out to touch the metal handle. His fingers reacted to the icy chill of it, but he took a firm hold and swung the glass door open. Now he was peering into those crowded shelves – the ranks of neatly ordered plastic containers – and it seemed to him that the shelves were deeper than they ought to be, that the most tantalising cakes, the ones at the very back, were almost out of reach. He pushed himself closer so he could stretch an arm deep into the selection, ignoring the more accessible containers, because he had caught a glimpse of something right at the back, a box bigger than all the others – and his hunger was now so intense, he knew that this was the offering he wanted, even if he would have to leave extra money for it.

His stomach gurgled as he delved in and it seemed as though his arm had ventured almost its full length into those frozen depths, but finally, finally, the tips of his fingers closed on the edge of the box he wanted and he began to claw it closer, aware as he did so that he was displacing other, smaller containers – they were tumbling down in front of him and bursting open at his feet, scattering their delectable contents over his trainers – but somehow, he couldn't make himself stop. He kept tugging, pulling the big container closer and closer, until finally, it was near enough for him to get a proper grip on it and pull it free.

Now he had the box in his hands and was gazing down at the transparent lid, but the label was in a language he couldn't understand and the cake within was not the honey and orange that he'd longed for but one of those special creations you sometimes saw on YouTube, perfectly crafted to look like something completely different – a can of cola, a handbag, a trainer – but when you cut effortlessly into it with a knife you revealed the delicious, sticky layers hidden within.

And this cake, he saw, was shaped like a man's hand; big, muscular and bunched into a fist. A warrior's hand, he decided, though he couldn't exactly say why he'd thought of it as that. It had been perfectly sliced off at the wrist, where there was a tantalising glimpse of the sticky raspberry layers within. Viggo removed the lid and dropped it at his feet with the other shattered boxes. He reached into the container and took the hand by its wrist, lifting it out to study it closely and marvelling at the craftsmanship – the way the baker had so perfectly captured the various lines and wrinkles in flesh coloured icing. He saw how the fingernails glinted in the moonlight, how faint blue veins lay just beneath the surface of the skin. There was even a golden signet ring on the third finger of the hand, one that was shaped into the head of a hawk or some other bird of prey, and for some reason, this rang a bell with him. He'd seen it somewhere before . . .

and for the briefest of moments, he noticed that the cake was heavier than he had expected it to be.

But now the sense of emptiness in his gut swelled until it blotted out everything else. He was starving. He was *ravenous*. He lifted the hand to his mouth, yearning for the sweet taste of those hidden layers. His teeth closed around a knuckle and there was a moment of surprise as he registered that this cake wasn't as soft as he had anticipated, that he had to bite down really hard through that rubbery icing before his teeth encountered the cold hard touch of bone beneath.

And then his mouth filled with the warm, coppery taste of blood.

*** 

Viggo woke with a jolt and sat where he was, still aware of that weird, metallic taste in his mouth. Then he registered pain and realised that he had somehow bitten into his bottom lip and that blood was trickling down his chin. He wiped his mouth on the sleeve of his jacket and pulled down the visor to check his reflection in the mirror. He turned to look at Mum and saw that she was asleep in exactly the position she'd been in a moment earlier, only . . .

*That had been a dream, right?*

A glance over his shoulder assured him that Leon too was fast asleep.

But turning back, he noticed that the distant glow of the fridge, visible through the fogged windscreen, appeared to be getting brighter. Puzzled, he reached out to rub the glass with his fingers and saw that the fridge was now fixed in the headlights of an approaching vehicle. As he watched, the other car slowed to a halt a short distance away and Viggo thought he recognised the sleek shape of a Range Rover. He held his breath and waited, hardly daring to breathe.

The driver's door swung open and a man emerged; tall and thin, his body wrapped in a heavy waterproof jacket. He stood for a moment looking around and then moved decisively towards the fridge. He reached out to open the glass door and his face was lit by the resulting glow. Viggo instantly recognised those lean, sallow features. Now a container had been chosen and was being pulled free from its companions. As Viggo watched, the lid was torn open and the cake within pulled out.

Viggo came back to his senses, realising that he was in danger of allowing the visitor to turn away and walk back to his vehicle, so he flung open the door of the Kia and leapt out into the darkness, waving an arm.

'Magnus!' he yelled and ran towards his brother.

\*\*\*

In the glow of the fridge, Magnus's face was a portrait of astonishment. He'd been in the act of taking a first bite of the chocolate cake he'd chosen and he stood there, seemingly frozen to the spot, his mouth open, the cake suspended inches from his even white teeth. He did not look very pleased to see his younger brother.

'Viggo!' he cried 'What the hell are you doing here?'

As Viggo drew closer, he slowed to a walk, shocked by his brother's hostility. 'What do you *think* I'm doing here?' he asked. 'Duh! I'm looking for you, aren't I? And I'm already beginning to wonder why I bothered.'

Magnus gave him a worried look. 'You've got blood on your chin,' he said.

'Huh? Oh, yeah, I bit my lip.' Viggo lifted an arm to wipe at his mouth.

'Is Mum with you?' hissed Magnus, which struck Viggo as an even more stupid question than the first. Did he actually think Mum would have allowed him to come all the way out here *alone*?

In answer, Viggo turned his head to look back at Ruby and, right on cue, there was Mum, stumbling blearily out from the driver's seat, woken by Viggo's shout. She was staring at the two figures standing by the fridge. Then she recognised Magnus and ran towards him, her arms outstretched. Viggo turned his gaze back to Magnus and thought that his brother looked like a rabbit transfixed in the glare of oncoming headlights.

'Oh, here she comes now,' he said gleefully.

'Magnus!' cried Mum. 'Thank goodness!'

She crashed headlong into him, wrapping her arms around him and almost knocking him off his feet. In the process, she managed to crush the piece of chocolate cake against his chest. 'Thank heavens!' she cried. 'I was so worried about you!'

Magnus struggled to extricate himself from her embrace. 'For God's sake, Mum, what's the matter with you?' he spluttered. 'What are you doing here?'

Mum recoiled, an expression of disbelief on her face. 'I came to find you,' she persisted. 'I . . . I've been phoning you and phoning you and you never answered my calls, not once. After what happened to your dad, I was worried sick.'

'I've been busy,' Magnus told her, as though it explained everything. 'I've been working around the clock; I haven't had a chance to talk. I meant to get back to you, but . . .'

'You should have called me, Magnus, just to let me know you were all right.'

'Mum, I'm not a child!' Now he was attempting to scrape the crushed remains of the cake off the front of his jacket. 'Look at the mess you've made. Honestly!' He fixed her with a cold stare. 'You shouldn't be here,' he told her flatly. 'You need to go home.'

'*Home*?' Mum actually took a step back as if he'd slapped her. 'I don't understand. I've come all this way to find you. Aren't you glad to see me?'

'Well, yes, of course I am, but you have to understand, Mum, the work I'm doing here, it's . . . secret, you see, *really* secret. Members of the public aren't allowed.'

Viggo sniggered. 'But we're not members of the public, are we?' he reminded Magnus. 'We're, like, your family?'

'I get that,' said Magnus. 'Of course I do. But you've no idea what I'm involved in out here. It's complicated. You have to understand that I . . .' He broke off as he noticed another figure approaching from the direction of Ruby. 'Who the hell is *that*?' he cried.

'That's Leon,' said Mum. 'We met him on the ferry and he . . . he very kindly offered to help us look for you.'

'I'm amazed you didn't organise a bloody coach trip!' snapped Magnus. 'Christ!'

As Leon drew closer, he held out a hand to shake but Magnus just looked at it as though Leon might be carrying a contagious disease. He turned back to Mum. 'Let me get this straight,' he muttered. 'You met this man on the ferry and he's still with you?'

'They took pity on a lonely traveller,' said Leon brightly. 'They were kind enough to let me accompany them.' He lowered his hand. 'So you're Magnus. I've heard a lot about you.'

'Is that right?' Magnus was looking at Leon with open distrust. 'Well, I don't know you from Adam, Mr . . .'

'Bragg.'

'Whatever your name is, I'm afraid I'm going to have to ask you to leave.'

'Leave?' Leon looked slowly around and then smiled. 'Leave what? This particular stretch of road? This island? Shetland as a whole? Or how about Scotland?'

'Just this area,' said Magnus, unsmiling.

Leon shook his head and his expression hardened. 'As far as I'm aware, this road is open to anyone who cares to travel it so I don't think I'm inclined to follow your instructions. And furthermore, your mother and your brother have travelled a very long way to find you. The least you could do is be civil to them.'

Magnus stood for a moment, glaring at Leon. For an instant, Viggo thought that his brother might actually be considering punching him, just as he'd punched Chris Scanlon. But then he turned away and walked off a short distance. He began to pace back and forth on the road as though trying to figure out what to do for the best. Viggo gave Mum an enquiring look and she could only shrug her shoulders helplessly.

'This is a mess,' Magnus said, more to himself than anyone

else. 'A complete mess.' He came back again. 'Where are you staying?' he asked Mum.

'Near Lerwick,' she said. 'We were supposed to head back there on the last ferry tonight but we fell asleep. So, obviously we can't go anywhere until morning.' Her eyes filled abruptly with tears and she began to sob. 'I don't understand, Magnus. Why do you want me to leave? I was just worried about you. What did I do wrong?'

For the first time, Magnus seemed contrite. He reached out a hand and put it on her shoulder. 'You didn't do anything wrong, Mum. And, of course, I should have spoken to you before you felt the need to do something drastic like this, but try and understand, I'm under a lot of pressure here. The man I work for—'

'Zack Strode,' Viggo cut in, and Magnus spun around and glared at him.

'Who told you that?' he snarled.

'Sorry, didn't realise it was an official secret. We spoke to—'

'Dr Glover,' interrupted Magnus, managing to freight the two words with absolute loathing. 'Am I right? Or 'The Jarlshof Jobsworth' as I prefer to call him.'

'Er, yeah, him. He said . . .'

'I can imagine what he said! Pathetic little man, so concerned with his precious reputation. And of course he wanted to lay the blame on Zack. Glover saw my leaving that post as some kind of personal insult.'

'To be fair,' said Mum, dabbing at her eyes with a tissue, 'he seemed like a perfectly nice man. And he said some very complimentary things about you.'

'Oh, did he really?'

'Yes, he did! About how gifted you were, and how knowledgeable. But he reckoned that this Strode character put you under some kind of spell.'

'Hah!' Magnus seemed to find this amusing. 'He just resents the fact that Zack came to *me* with an offer and not him.'

'We also had a wee chat with your former friend, Chris Scanlon,' said Leon. 'He was of a similar opinion. He told us to tell you . . . how did he put it? Oh yes, he said that you were to get away from "that American idiot".'

'Yes, well, he would say that, wouldn't he? Chris is jealous too. Surely you could see that?'

'But Dr Glover said you hit him!' said Mum.

'I did, and I'd do it again! He was bad-mouthing Zack, trying to convince me that he doesn't know what he's talking about.' Magnus looked defiantly around at them. 'But here's the thing, he absolutely *does.* Zack is a visionary and, what's more, he has the money to back up his ideas. And he came to *me.* I'm the one he entrusted with this project and I can't let anything get in the way of that. This is my big chance, Mum, and you being here . . .' He shook his head. 'I'm sorry, but I can't let you ruin it, you must understand that.'

Mum shook her head. 'I *don't* understand,' she told him. 'How could me being here ruin anything? I can't believe that seeing your own family could jeopardise it. What is this wonderful project anyway?'

'Obviously, I can't tell you that,' said Magnus. 'I'm sworn to secrecy.'

'Well, I'll tell you something that isn't a secret,' said Mum.

'Mum, I . . .'

'Are you listening to me?'

Magnus sighed and nodded.

'It's past ten o'clock at night, we've missed our last ferry back, I'm starving and I'm bursting to use a toilet. Now, you must at least have a toilet I can use, surely?'

Magnus stared at her. 'Can't you . . . go behind a bush or something?' he asked her. 'I mean, there's nobody for miles and—'

'No, I cannot! I'm a forty-three-year-old woman and my days of going behind bushes are well and truly over. And anyway, I really don't think the use of a proper toilet is too much to ask.'

There was a long silence while Magnus pondered this. 'Wait here,' he said.

He turned away from them, pulling a phone from his pocket as he went. He walked up the road until he was out of their hearing and then punched a number into the phone. He lifted it to his ear and started talking in a hushed voice. Viggo strained to hear what he was saying but couldn't make any of it out. He looked accusingly at Mum.

'Well, this is wonderful,' he said. 'We came all this way, I missed the *Thor* movie—'

'Could you please stop mentioning that bloody film?' snapped Mum.

'I told you it was obvious Magnus didn't want to see us, but oh no, you had to book the tickets and bring us all the way out here, didn't you? And we finally find him in the middle of nowhere, acting *really* suspiciously, and what happens?

He tells us to go and take a running jump. Well, that's just great, isn't it? That's just *perfect*!'

'Try and calm down,' Leon advised him. 'Your mother only acted with the best intentions.'

'But she needs to wake up and smell the coffee!' yelled Viggo. 'This is nothing new. Magnus has always acted like this and he's not about to change.' Viggo reached out and took one of Mum's hands. 'I'm sorry, Mum, but that's just the way he is. He only cares about one person and that person is Magnus bloody Ryan. I wish we'd never left Edinburgh.'

Mum's eyes filled with fresh tears. 'I thought I was doing the right thing,' she said. 'I just kept thinking about what happened to your dad and I had to come here. You get that, don't you?'

Viggo opened his mouth to reply but at that moment, Magnus slipped the phone back into his pocket and came striding decisively back to them.

'All right,' he said. 'I've been in touch with my team . . .'

'Ooh, he has a team now!' exclaimed Viggo. 'Fancy!'

Magnus ignored him. 'I've told them to prepare some guest rooms for tonight. I'll talk to Zack and see what he wants me to do with you.'

'*Do* with us?' echoed Mum, indignantly. 'What's that supposed to mean? We're not bags of rubbish. I'm your mother. This is your brother.' She looked at Leon. 'And this is . . .' She trailed off, seemingly unsure of what their companion was. 'This is Leon.'

Magnus gazed back at her. 'It's very simple, Mum. Zack is paying for everything and he calls the shots. OK? If he says you have to leave, that's what'll happen. And don't worry, if that's what he decides, I'll have you personally escorted back to the ferry . . . in a chauffeur-driven Rolls, if you like. But Zack isn't here at the moment, so tonight, you're covered.'

'Oh, that's so good of you,' said Viggo. He looked at his companions. 'We really appreciate that, don't we guys? Hooray for Magnus and his *team*!'

Magnus frowned. 'There's no need to be sarcastic,' he snapped.

'How do you expect me to be?' retorted Viggo. 'Eh? Once again, here we are at The Magnus Ryan Show and, as usual, it's all about you.' He slipped into a simpering impersonation of his brother. 'Ooh, you're all going to have to leave, because Zack is rich and famous and of course, I have to do everything he says from now on, because for some reason I can't explain he now runs *my entire life*!'

There was a short silence. 'Have you finished?' asked Magnus quietly.

Viggo thought about it for a moment. 'I guess so,' he said. 'For now.'

'Good. You can ride with me in the Range Rover and fill me in on some of the details. Mum, you and your . . . *friend* can follow us in your car. It's only a couple of miles from here.'

'And there'll be a toilet?' Mum prompted him.

'Yes, of course. A proper one, with a door and everything.' He was about to walk towards his vehicle but seemed to remember something. He turned back to the fridge and took out another helping of chocolate cake. He looked at the others. 'Anybody else want something while I'm here?'

'Greek honey and orange,' said Viggo, and Magnus gave him a puzzled look.

'I don't think they have that flavour,' he said.

'They do. I had a piece earlier.'

Magnus examined the shelves and shook his head. 'Nope, trust me, I come here a lot. They *never* have that flavour. Chocolate?'

'Yeah, whatever.' Magnus took out another container and handed it to Viggo. He looked at Mum and Leon. 'What about you guys?'

They both shook their heads. 'I honestly couldn't eat anything right now,' said Mum, in a tiny voice. 'I've lost my appetite.' She turned away and started trudging back towards the car, her arms crossed. 'Don't forget to put something in the honesty box,' she added, without looking back. Leon studied Magnus for a moment, as if sizing him up, then went after Mum.

Magnus dug around in his pockets and finally found a crumpled ten pound note. He pushed it through the slot on top of the wooden box.

'Why does she always treat me like I'm ten years old?' he asked Viggo.

'Perhaps she wouldn't if you stopped acting like it,' suggested Viggo unhelpfully, and walked towards the Range Rover. 'Don't forget to close the fridge door.'

Magnus scowled but did as he was told, before following Viggo to the car.

# CHAPTER 16
## ASGARD

They drove through the darkness in silence while the two of them ate their cakes. The Range Rover's headlights lit up the deserted stretch of road as it unspooled like an endless length of grey ribbon in front of them. Every so often, Viggo caught sight of something racing frantically across the tarmac: a selection of plump rabbits, what looked like a large rat and, just once, the sleek silent shape of an owl, swooping low in front of them, avoiding a collision by what seemed like millimeters.

Viggo swallowed down the last chunk of chocolate cake, thinking that it was OK but not a patch on the piece he'd enjoyed earlier. It didn't help that his bottom lip was sore where he'd bitten it. He thought again about what Magnus had told him – that Greek honey and orange was *never* stored in that fridge – and he chalked up yet another question to add to the long list he already had for Leon Bragg. He crumpled the plastic carton in his hands and dropped it carelessly on to the floor of the vehicle.

'Hey, stop littering my Range Rover,' said Magnus.

'*Your* Range Rover?' muttered Viggo. 'Since when can you afford a car like this?'

'Well, yeah, technically it *is* Zack's car,' admitted Magnus. 'But he bought it for me to use whenever I need it, so . . .'

'Just like that, eh?' Viggo shook his head. 'Must be nice to have a pet billionaire to buy you things. Me, I'm still saving up for a new bike. I've got forty quid so far, which will just about get me a mudguard.'

'Yes, but when this is over, I don't get to keep the Range Rover.'

'Aww. Tough break.' Viggo mimed playing an imaginary violin. 'So who pays for the petrol?'

'Well, I do get a stipend.'

'A what?'

'A weekly allowance to pay for stuff like that. You know, petrol, food, other expenses.'

Viggo snorted. 'Boy, you've landed on your feet, haven't you? I remember when you were so poor you had to ask *me* for a loan. Look at you now!'

'It's the chance of a lifetime,' said Magnus dreamily. 'I just happened to be in the right place at the right time. Opportunities like this only come along once and you have to grab them with both hands and hang on tight, otherwise they're gone and they'll never come back again.'

'Is that why you punched Chris Scanlon? So you wouldn't miss your chance? Only, he seemed pretty cut up about it. I mean, I don't know why, but I think he actually *liked* you.'

Magnus scoffed. 'Trust me, if Zack had gone to Chris with an offer, he'd have done the same thing to me without a second thought.'

'Really? He seemed nice.'

'Nice! That boy likes to act all hard done-to, but he's just a bad loser. Where did you meet up with him, anyway? He's surely finished his time at Jarlshof by now?'

'Yeah, he was working on St Ninny's Isle.'

'St Ninian's?'

'Whatever. He was taking photographs of puffins.' Viggo thought for a moment. 'He was driving around in a battered old Land Rover, not a fancy pants vehicle like this one.'

Magnus nodded. He took his gaze from the road for a moment to give his brother a searching look. 'So, what's the story with Leo?'

'It's Leon,' Viggo corrected him. 'And that's a good question. I'm really not sure.'

'Meaning?'

'Well, at first, I thought he was just this creep who'd latched on to Mum so he could cadge meals and drinks and get a free ride. We spent most of our time trying to get away from him, except we couldn't, 'cos the car kept breaking down . . .'

Magnus gave him a baffled look, but he continued.

'. . . and then, he went and told me something about his past which made me feel, like, really sorry for him.'

'Yeah? What did he say?'

Viggo frowned. 'It was a long story. He said his son drowned, years ago, when they were in Yell.'

'And you believed him?'

'Well, yeah, I did . . . at first. Then I got the feeling that he might not have been telling me the truth . . . and now I don't know *what* to think.' He considered for a moment. 'Greek honey and orange cake,' he murmured. 'Weird.'

'What?'

'Oh, never mind. It's just that he manages to do stuff that I can't really explain.'

Magnus frowned. 'Him and Mum...they're not...?' Magnus left the line unfinished but Viggo knew exactly what he meant.

'Eww, no! At least, I don't *think* so.'

'Well, that's something, I suppose. Why hasn't Mum given him the order of the boot?'

'It's more complicated than you think.'

'How is it complicated? She's too soft. She should just tell him to sling his hook.'

'She tried that. It didn't work out.'

Magnus swallowed the last piece of his own cake and drove in silence for a while, as though thinking over Viggo's words.

'So, you're staying in Lerwick,' he said, at last. 'What do you make of Shetland, so far?'

'I don't know. It's like nowhere I've ever been before.'

'Yeah, it *is* pretty unique, right?'

'Hmm. And also kind of weird ...'

'In what way?'

'Well, ever since we left Edinburgh, I've been having these dreams ...'

'Ah, right.' Magnus nodded, as though he'd expected it.

'Mum said you always get dreams when you travel, but these ones ...' He shook his head.

'Intense?'

'Yes, very. And, I know this sounds kind of creepy, but sometimes I've been getting them when I'm not really asleep.'

He'd half expected Magnus to laugh at this but he just nodded. 'Go on,' he said. 'Give me some examples.'

'Er . . . seriously? OK, well, the first one I had, we were driving up to Aberdeen. I thought I saw a guy on a horse in the middle of the motorway. Can you believe it? A guy with long hair, waving a sword about.' He waited for the inevitable laughter but it didn't come, so he kept going. 'And then, on the ferry coming over, I thought I saw . . .' He took a deep breath. 'Like, this Viking longship sailing beside us?'

Magnus nodded again. 'Ah, yeah,' he said. 'Visions.'

'Oh, that's what Leon calls them.'

Magnus scowled at the mention of the name. There was a short pause, before he added, 'Get used to them.'

Viggo glared at him. 'What's that supposed to mean?'

'It's just something that occurs here. And the closer you get to . . . our project . . . the more that's going to happen. It's kind of like a side effect. We're still trying to work out what it means.'

'So you've been dreaming too?'

Magnus nodded. 'About Dad, mostly.'

'Yes! I had one of those.'

Magnus glanced at him. 'Want to tell me about it?'

'Well, I was asleep at the campsite we're staying in . . . at least, I *think* I was asleep, I'm not even sure about that . . . and then Dad was sitting on my bed. He . . .'

'Yes?'

'He didn't have a face. No eyes, no nose, no mouth.'

'Really?' Magnus grimaced. 'He does in *my* dreams.'

'Lucky you. It wasn't pleasant.'

'I bet it wasn't. I appreciate he wouldn't have had a mouth, but did he speak to you?'

'Yeah, he did. It was like a warning. He said . . .'

'. . . to stop following him?' finished Magnus.

Viggo stared at him, open-mouthed. 'You too?' he gasped.

Magnus nodded.

'And is that why you're here? Looking for Dad?'

'No, of course not. It never crossed my mind to do that. I'm here for the Valhalla Project, nothing else.'

Viggo grinned. 'That's what you call it? The Valhalla Project?'

Magnus seemed uncomfortable. 'I shouldn't have even said that much,' he muttered. 'It just slipped out. But yes, it's our pet name for it.'

'Sounds like something out of a Hollywood movie,' observed Viggo. 'I was supposed to be seeing the latest Marvel film back in Edinburgh. Instead, I'm here.'

'Trust me,' said Magnus. 'What's happening on Unst is way bigger than any film.' He studied his brother for a moment. 'I wish I could tell you more about it,' he admitted. 'Maybe I'll be able to, later on. We'll have to see what Zack decides when he gets here.'

Viggo grunted. 'Sounds to me like you have to ask that guy for permission to use the toilet.'

Magnus shrugged. 'Well, yes, I guess it does. But you have to understand, Viggo, it's costing millions to run this operation and I don't have any money of my own.'

'Says the guy driving around in a Range Rover!'

'Yes, but I already told you . . .'

Viggo adopted a comedy voice. 'It belongs to Zack; it's not mine!'

'Yeah, OK, I get the general idea. I mean, I'll get a big

payoff off at the end, of course, but that wouldn't cover a single piece of the equipment we're using.'

Viggo thought for a moment. 'What about all the other stuff?' he asked.

'What other stuff?'

'Leon told me that Zack Strode has some very weird ideas.'

'Oh yeah? Such as?'

'Well, like, he doesn't believe there were dinosaurs and, like, he's building his own rocket ship and weird stuff like that.'

Magnus sighed. 'When you're as wealthy as Zack, you become a target for every conspiracy theorist on the planet,' he said. 'People invent things about him, Viggo, usually in the hope that they'll get a big payoff to stop them from saying anything else. But Zack never gives them the attention they're after. His lawyers step in and shut people down.'

'So he isn't building a rocket ship?'

Magnus looked evasive. 'Well, he might be,' he admitted. 'But that's *his* business. I don't get involved in his other stuff. Not yet, anyway, but I'm hoping he might ask me to do more.' He frowned. 'What else does Leon say about Zack?' he growled.

'Only that people like him are dangerous.'

'Hmm. You sure he's not an investigative journalist or something?'

Viggo was about to insist that this couldn't be true but then realised he wasn't sure who Leon was, or what his intentions were, so anything was possible. 'Leon is a mystery,' he said. 'If you can figure him out, let me know.'

The Range Rover crested a ridge and swooped down the

track into the valley beyond. There, some distance ahead, was a huge old mansion house. The clear moonlight revealed that its roof and walls were crumbling and weathered by the years, but the many windows on the ground floor blazed with electric light.

'What's this?' asked Viggo.

'It's our base,' said Magnus, unable to conceal the pride in his voice. 'Welcome to Asgard.'

Viggo sniggered at that.

'What?' asked Magnus.

'It's just that the place we're staying in at Lerwick is called Midgard. That's like, the home of the humans, right? But you've named *your* place after the home of the gods!'

Magnus looked deflated. 'Zack came up with it,' he said defensively.

'Yeah, not that he's got a high opinion of himself or anything!'

'Oh come on, when did you turn into such a stick-in-the-mud? It's a cool name, isn't it?'

'If you say so.'

As they moved steadily closer, Viggo could see just how vast the building was. He found himself wondering how many rooms there must be in it.

'Why here?' he asked.

'It was the nearest place of any size to the site of our project. We have a whole team working on it and Zack needed somewhere to create a headquarters for them. So this was the logical choice. Mind you, it wasn't easy. We had to bring in generators for the power supply and get all the rooms cleaned up enough to be habitable. And we had to find the right people to handle the excavation. There wasn't much time and they don't work for shirt buttons. But Zack waves a hand and, hey presto! Stuff happens.'

Viggo blew air out through his cheeks.

'So how much does it cost to rent a place like this?' he wondered.

'Oh, Zack didn't *rent* it,' said Magnus, matter-of-factly. 'He bought it. For cash.'

'Cash?'

'Well, it's been abandoned for years. I expect he got it for a song.'

'He doesn't tell you how much things cost?'

'That's not my business. He has a team of accountants for that.'

'Yeah? And does he also have a team to wipe his backside for him?'

Magnus ignored that.

As they drew closer, Viggo could see that the house was enclosed by high stone walls. Up ahead of them stood a set of rusting metal gates which, Viggo was shocked to see, were guarded by two men in black military-style uniforms. Both of them had what looked like assault rifles slung over their shoulders.

'OK, now I'm getting a little freaked out,' he said. 'What's with the guns?'

'We're just being careful,' said Magnus. 'Protecting our operation. Nothing to worry about.' He pulled the vehicle to a halt and lowered his window as one of the men stepped forward with a torch. Viggo noticed that he had a camouflage-patterned mask across the lower part of his face.

'Evening, sir,' he said, his voice muffled.

'Evening, Clive. This is my younger brother, Viggo.'

The torch was directed into Viggo's face and he tried not to squint. 'He's got blood on his chin,' observed the man, suspiciously.

'I bit my lip,' said Viggo. He lifted his sleeve to give his mouth another swab.

'In the car behind us is my mother and a friend,' said Magnus. 'They've all been given clearance to enter.'

The man stepped away from the window and took out a walkie-talkie. He spoke into it briefly and seemed satisfied with the response. He stepped back and signalled to somebody by the gates, which swung silently open. Magnus drove through into the courtyard beyond, tyres crunching on gravel. He pulled up beside what looked like a main entrance, a huge wooden door at the top of a short flight of steps. The headlights illuminated an ancient metal door knocker, fashioned in the shape of a demonic-looking face – eyes shut and mouth open, as if in mid bellow.

'Well, this looks charming,' muttered Viggo.

Magnus got out and Viggo followed his example, watching as Mum drove slowly up and parked alongside the Range Rover. Viggo could see the look of astonishment on her face as she stared up at the huge stone edifice towering above her. Leon's face was expressionless as he took in the same view, as if steadfastly refusing to look impressed.

After a few moments, Mum switched off the engine and

she and Leon climbed out of Ruby. 'Magnus, what *is* this place?' she gasped. 'Those men at the gate had guns!'

Magnus opened his mouth to reply but Viggo got there first.

'Relax, Mum,' he said. 'It's just the home of the gods. No big deal.'

The entrance doors opened and a man in a frock coat and elegantly tailored pinstripe trousers came out and descended the steps. Viggo noticed that he was wearing white cotton gloves, like a character from an old film. He was clean shaven and had a thin face, with a prominent nose. His blonde hair was styled in a perfect quiff. He bowed to Magnus. 'Welcome back, sir,' he said, in a refined, English accent

Viggo glanced mockingly at Magnus. 'Sir?' he whispered, but Magnus ignored him.

The man bowed his head to Viggo, Mum and Leon. 'Welcome to Asgard,' he said. 'If you'd care to follow me, I'll show you to your rooms.'

Mum looked questioningly at Magnus.

'Just follow Jeeves,' he told her. 'He'll show you where you'll be staying. I'll catch up with you guys in a bit. There are a few details I need to sort out.'

'Jeeves?' echoed Viggo, raising his eyebrows.

The butler smiled. 'It's what Mr Strode likes to call me,' he said. 'A little in-joke, I suppose.'

'From the novels of PG Wodehouse,' offered Leon, helpfully. 'You won't have read them, Viggo; they date from the 1930s. Jeeves was the butler to an upper class twit called Bertie Wooster. The idea was that Jeeves was the real brains behind the operation, but Wooster took all the credit.' He glanced at Jeeves. 'Is that how it works with you and Mr Strode?'

Jeeves looked uncomfortable. 'As I said, it's just a little joke, sir. I have also been known to answer to the name of Martin.' He turned and led the way to the steps and, after a few moments' hesitation, Mum and Leon followed him.

But Viggo lingered for a moment, looking at his brother. 'So has Zack given *you* a new name?' he asked.

Magnus shook his head. 'Of course not. He just thinks the 'Jeeves' thing is funny, that's all.'

'It's hilarious,' muttered Viggo. 'I can hardly stop laughing.'

Magnus sighed. 'You're feeling hostile right now, and I get that. But you'll feel differently once you meet Zack. He's . . .' Magnus seemed to struggle for a moment to find the right word.

'A dickhead?' suggested Viggo.

'I was going to say *charismatic*,' said Magnus. 'But you can make your own mind up when he arrives tomorrow.'

'Where's he been?'

'California. There was a tech company he needed to buy.'

'How does anyone *need* to buy a company?' asked Viggo, baffled.

'They were in software. Potential competitors. If somebody threatens to challenge your position, you buy them out, right?'

Viggo looked at his brother in surprise. Though he'd often found himself opposed to Magnus's views, he'd never heard him come out with anything like this before.

'Oh yeah,' he said, sarcastically. 'It's dog eat dog out there.'

Magnus nodded to where Mum and Leon were waiting

at the foot of the steps. 'Go with them,' he told Viggo. 'I'll catch up with you later.'

Viggo gazed at his brother for a moment and then turned away. He walked over to join Mum and Leon. Jeeves was waiting for them by the open door, still with that vacant smile on his face.

'What do you make of all this?' Mum asked Viggo, under her breath.

He frowned. 'I was about to ask you the same thing,' he said. 'I feel like I've wandered into a James Bond movie.'

They both turned their attention to Leon, who was gazing up at the building with interest. 'Scots Baronial,' he said. 'Probably dates from around 1700. I could be wrong but it might be the work of William Chambers. It's very much in his style.'

'I wasn't talking about the *building*,' hissed Mum, irritably. 'I was asking what you think is going on here?'

Leon shrugged his shoulders. 'When I have an idea of that, you'll be the first to know,' he said. 'But for now, I believe you're in need of a toilet?'

Mum nodded, so they climbed the stairs and followed Jeeves into Asgard.

# CHAPTER 17
## THE ROOM

Jeeves opened a door and ushered Viggo into a large, empty room. Mum and Leon had already been dropped off in similar rooms along the way and, as he'd followed Jeeves down gloomy deserted corridors, Viggo had taken the opportunity to look around the old place. Only a token attempt had been made to clean the interior up. The leaded windows were mildewed and grimy with decades of dirt, and, here and there, wallpaper hung in damp strips, peeling off from the ancient plaster like lengths of tobacco-brown parchment.

But new bare cables had been laid along the hallways and into various rooms. Powerful portable lighting rigs stood at regular intervals along the route to ensure that all areas in use were properly illuminated. Viggo thought it was probably what a film set looked like and was sure it must have cost a lot of money to set up.

The room in which Viggo stood now was like the rest of the place. Once grand, it had fallen into a state of disrepair, but here too there was a lighting rig and a simple cot bed. An adjoining door led into a bathroom, which had only recently been scrubbed clean and made serviceable, judging by the powerful smell of bleach in there.

'I'm afraid it's all rather rudimentary,' said Jeeves apologetically. 'If we'd had more warning, we could have done a little more preparation. But the water still runs and the toilet flushes, which is half the battle. I hope you'll be comfortable enough, sir.' Viggo felt decidedly odd being referred to as a 'sir'. He glanced quickly around.

'It looks fine,' he said.

'The chef has been instructed and is preparing an evening meal for four. May I ask, sir, do you have any special dietary requirements?'

'Er . . . not that I know of.' He thought for a moment. 'I like mayonnaise with my chips,' he offered. 'As well as ketchup.'

Jeeves smiled. 'Jolly good. I'll come and fetch you when the meal's ready. Is there anything else I can help you with, before I go?'

Viggo thought for a moment. 'I don't suppose . . .'

'Yes, sir?'

'I don't suppose there's Wi-Fi?'.

Jeeves smiled. 'Of course there is. Mr Strode is very particular about that. You'll find our network listed on your phone as *Vahalla 1*.'

Viggo took out his phone. 'Password?' he asked.

'You won't need one.'

Zack stared at him. 'Really?'

'Oh yes, Mr Strode has his own systems in place. Don't worry, just look for the network and it will recognise you.'

And with that, Jeeves went out, closing the door behind him.

Viggo found the network easily and clicked on it. Sure

enough, it connected him instantly. As an experiment, he sent a text to Jamie.

**In Shetland staying in haunted house LOL**

Within moments, Jamie's reply appeared.

Wondered how your getting on you missed a brilliant film my dude!!!!

**Yeah, saw your post on Insta. You & Emma looked happy.**

Nah dude shes gotta boyfriend!!! Not me. ☹. When you comin home?

**Dunno stay tuned. Gotta go now. Need to eat catch ya soon.**

He switched off the phone and slipped it back into his pocket, then walked over to the nearest window and peered out through the grimy glass. He gazed down at what used to be a spacious garden, now a tangle of weeds and an overgrown expanse of lawn. As he stood there, a man in a black uniform strode past. His face was masked and he had what looked like a machine gun slung over his shoulder. He was looking around as if searching for intruders.

'Why all the secrecy?' Viggo wondered.

He stepped back from the window and walked around the room, inspecting the interior in more detail. There were bookshelves against one wall, all of them bowed beneath the weight of hundreds of old tomes, most of which looked beyond saving. The title on one spine caught Viggo's eye – *The Waking Dream* – but, when he tried to pull the volume out, he quickly realised that it had fused with all the other books on the shelf into one immovable, damp lump and he found himself wondering why they'd been abandoned here.

He moved onwards.

On one wall was a framed sepia photograph of a weird-looking man and woman standing with two children, a boy and a girl, in front of the building's main entrance. They were all dressed in what Viggo thought might be Victorian-style clothes, the man and boy wearing tailcoats and top hats, the females in weird lacy gowns and bonnets. They were staring back at the camera, unsmiling, as if asking the photographer what the hell he thought he was doing on their land. On the lowest section of the frame Viggo noticed a small metal plaque where words had been inscribed in an ornate style, but Viggo couldn't exactly make out what it said – *Thomas M . . . Laird . . . and family*? He shook his head and turned away, thinking that he'd need to spend hours scrubbing the corroded metal with a wire brush before he could make proper sense of it.

There was a tapping at his door and, before he could quite stop himself, he called out, 'Enter!' in a portentous voice. The door creaked open and Mum peered cautiously into the room, before stepping inside and closing the door quietly behind her.

'You OK?' she asked him.

He shrugged. 'I suppose so,' he said. 'Apparently the chef is preparing an evening meal for us.' He looked around and lifted his arms. 'What's this all about?' he asked her. He saw the glum expression on her face. 'Something wrong?'

'I just wanted to say sorry.'

He looked at her, puzzled. 'For what?' he asked.

'For dragging you all the way out here, only to have Magnus act like we're the last people in the world he wants to see. I feel really angry about it.'

'Mum, that's just business as usual for Magnus,' he said. 'Don't sweat it.'

'You're being nice, but I know you're mad at me too.'

'I'm not mad, just . . . confused.' He waved a hand at the old photograph on the wall. 'Come and say hello to my new friends,' he suggested. Mum walked over to join him and peered at the grim-faced figures in the pictures.

'They look like a fun crowd,' she observed. 'Imagine being stuck in a lift with them.' She glanced nervously around the room. 'You don't mind if I wait here with you, do you? I was starting to get the creeps on my own. I keep thinking there must be mice here.'

'I haven't seen any,' Viggo assured her. He waved a hand at the bookcase. 'I should think there's probably a million bugs, spiders and worms hidden in that lot, though.' He thought for a moment. 'Speaking of pests, where's Leon?'

'In his room, I suppose.' Mum looked at Viggo and then smiled. 'You don't fool me, Viggo.'

'What do you mean?'

'Ever since Jarlshof you've been acting differently towards him.'

'Have I?'

'You know you have. Chatty, more forgiving. I expect he told you, didn't he?'

Viggo looked at Mum, apprehensively. 'Told me what?' he ventured.

'You know. About his old girlfriend.'

Viggo looked at her blankly. 'His *girlfriend*?' he echoed.

Mum seemed uncomfortable as though she really didn't like talking about this. 'I did sort of promise him I wouldn't say anything to you, but ...'

'Go on,' Viggo told her. 'Spit it out.'

'Well, it's *not* Leon's first time in Shetland. He was here thirty years ago.'

'Oh, yeah, I know that.'

'He told you about his girlfriend? The one he met in Ibiza.'

'You mean his wife,' Viggo corrected her. 'Steph.'

Mum looked puzzled. 'I'm pretty sure they weren't married. And the name was Mary, not Steph. The two of them were here on holiday.'

'In a beaten-up old camper van?'

'Er ... yes, that's right. Anyway, it's a really tragic story.' Mum lowered her voice to a whisper as though afraid of being overheard. 'She took her own life.'

'Who did?'

'Mary. She jumped off a cliff. In Yell.'

Viggo stared at her. 'No, wait a minute! Leon told me about something that happened to him in Yell, but it wasn't *that*. This was about his son, Daniel, who drowned.'

Mum seemed to remember something. 'Oh yes, you said something about a son before, didn't you? When we were on that Viking longship. I thought it was a weird thing to come out with. After you'd stormed off, I asked Leon if he could explain it but he said he had no idea what you were talking about.'

'But ... no, hang on a minute. Leon must have mentioned Daniel to you, right?'

Mum shook her head. 'He never said anything about a *son*. Just this girl, Mary. She was hooked on drugs or something. And she jumped off a cliff while she was under the influence of them. Leon tried to get to her but he was . . .'

'He was drunk, right?'

'Er, yes, he was. And that's why he doesn't drink any more.'

Viggo let out a long breath and shook his head. 'That does it!' he said. 'We can't trust anything that man says.'

'Well, let's not be too hasty,' cautioned Mum. 'Maybe both things happened.'

'You really think so?' snapped Viggo, scornfully. 'Come on, what are the chances? Yell's a tiny little island, not the disaster capital of the world.'

'But Leon was crying, when he told me. Breaking his heart! I felt so sorry for him.'

Viggo felt like he'd been punched in the gut. 'When exactly did he tell you this?' he asked.

'Umm . . . it was last night, actually, when you went to meet up with Freya.'

Viggo shook his head. 'What, you mean *before* he visited the farmhouse and had drinks with Agnes and Leif?'

Mum shrugged her shoulders. 'I don't know about that, love. He knocked on my door just after you left. Said he had a really bad headache and asked if I had an aspirin. And then we got talking and it all came out, so . . .'

'How long was he there?'

'Viggo, this is starting to feel like an interrogation!' She gave him a look. 'I hope you don't think anything funny happened, because . . .'

'No, of course not! As if!'

Now Mum looked vaguely insulted. 'It's not exactly beyond the realms of belief, is it?'

'No, well, I mean . . . I don't know. I . . . I really don't want to think about that!' He ran a hand through his hair. 'Just humour me, will you? How long were the two of you talking?'

Mum shrugged. 'I don't know, an hour or so, I suppose. I do remember you saying that he was having a drink with Agnes and Leif that night, so I expect he must have gone over to them *after* he'd spoken to me.'

'But that doesn't make sense, Mum! If he was crying his eyes out with you, do you really think he'd jump straight up and go and enjoy a jolly drink with two people he hardly knows? And it *was* jolly! They were laughing their heads off in there.' He thought about it for a moment. 'Freya looked out of the window of reception and saw him, but I couldn't have been there for more than fifteen minutes, tops.'

Mum smiled. 'You must be getting mixed up,' she assured him. 'Like I said, the two of us were talking for over an hour. Leon couldn't be in two places at the same time . . . could he?'

'All I know is he's been playing us, Mum. He's been telling us both exactly what we need to hear, so we'll forgive him.'

Mum didn't seem to understand. 'Forgive him for what?'

'For following us around like he does.' Viggo thought for a moment. 'Magnus asked me before if I thought Leon might be a . . . a whatsit . . . an investigative reporter.'

Mum looked astonished. 'How does he arrive at that notion?'

'He thinks maybe Leon is looking for a story about Zack Strode.'

But now Mum was laughing. 'That doesn't make any sense,'

she said. 'We met Leon on the ferry and we didn't know anything about Zack Strode then. I'd never even heard of him!'

'No, I get that, but what if Leon knew that Magnus was working with Zack and found out we were looking for him. What if he's using us as a way of getting to him?'

'Getting to Magnus?'

'No. To Strode!'

Mum blew air out through pursed lips. 'It all sounds pretty far-fetched,' she said. She looked towards the door. 'Perhaps we should go and have it out with Leon?' she suggested. 'Ask him to explain himself.'

'No.' Viggo shook his head. 'It's best if he doesn't know we're on to him.'

'I'm not entirely sure we're on to *anything*,' said Mum. 'This is all speculation. What if he was telling us *both* the truth? Maybe he really has been that unlucky.'

'Oh come on, Mum, a drowning *and* a suicide? I know he's a pain in the bum, but that's a bit of a push isn't it?'

'So what do you suggest we do?'

Viggo thought for a moment. 'Let's just keep an eye on him,' said Viggo. 'You're right, I *had* started to trust him more after what he told me . . . and so had you. I think that's what he wants. I think he's interested in Magnus's project and if he has us on his team, he's stronger somehow.' He sighed, shook his head. 'I don't know exactly what it is but there's something about him, Mum . . . something that feels . . .' He remembered what Freya had said that evening. '. . . off,' he concluded.

Mum opened her mouth to say something else but they both jumped at the sound of a polite knock on the door.

They looked at each other and then Viggo said, 'Hello?'

The door opened and there stood Leon, smiling that contented smile. 'Time for dinner,' he announced. 'You guys ready to eat?' Viggo saw that Jeeves was waiting just behind him, his white-gloved hands clasped together. Leon was studying Viggo and Mum as if trying to figure them out. 'Are you two OK?' he asked.

'We're *fine*!' gasped Mum, managing to sound quite the opposite.

'We were just saying . . .' began Viggo.

'. . . that we're absolutely starving,' finished Mum. 'Ravenous!'

'Er . . . yeah, that,' muttered Viggo.

'Me too,' said Leon. 'Well, let's go and see what delights they have for us, shall we?' He turned away and followed Jeeves along the hall.

Viggo ushered Mum towards the door and followed her out.

Leon hung back a little, allowing them to catch up with him. 'Well,' he said. 'What else were you two talking about?'

'We were just wondering,' said Mum. 'About Magnus's mysterious project. We were trying to work out what it might be.'

'Perhaps if we keep asking him, he'll tell us,' suggested Leon.

'I don't think he'll say a word unless Zack Strode says it's OK,' said Viggo. 'It's like that guy has him on a lead.'

'But Magnus has never been afraid to speak his mind,' insisted Mum.

'That's not the impression I'm getting,' said Viggo. 'It's like Strode controls him.'

Jeeves had got to the top of the corridor and, as the others caught up, he reached out to open two huge swing doors, revealing a massive room beyond. In the middle of it there was a long wooden dining table, big enough to seat twenty people or more, but it was empty apart from Magnus, who sat in a chair at the very centre of it. Viggo saw that there were three other place settings, one beside Magnus and two more directly across from him. Lighting rigs stood in each corner of the room, their halogen beams directed on to the tabletop, but there was also a massive candelabra, with some fifteen candles burning, hanging above the centre of the table.

'Hey guys,' said Magnus. 'Take a seat. Viggo, you sit here beside me.'

Viggo did as he was told, looking down at the expensive glasses and tableware. He noted that the rolled up serviette beside the silver cutlery was thick cloth rather than paper, which struck him as an unnecessary touch out here in the wilds, but he refrained from mentioning it. He watched as Mum and Leon settled themselves into the chairs opposite.

Mum fixed Magnus with a look. 'Right,' she said, 'the first thing I want to ask is—'

She broke off as Magnus lifted a hand to silence her. 'We'll eat first,' he said. 'And then we'll talk.' He reached out and lifted a small, silver bell from the table. He shook it, producing a shrill tone that seemed to fill the entire room.

A pair of doors at the top of the room swung open and the food came in.

Viggo stared until his eyes nearly popped out of his skull.

# CHAPTER 18
## DINNER AT ASGARD

Viggo had been expecting human waiters. Instead, he watched, open-mouthed in astonishment, as a gleaming white oblong the size of a large suitcase came gliding into the room, several metres off the ground. It swept silently past the table and came to a halt in front of Jeeves, hovering steadily at shoulder height. Viggo stared at it, trying to figure out how the hell it was staying afloat. It was something like a drone, he decided. He had a small one back in Edinburgh that he sometimes fooled around with on The Meadows, but this . . . this was altogether more sophisticated. There were no signs of any propellers on it, no outlet that might be emitting compressed air to move it along. It just seemed to float, solid as a rock and eerily silent.

Jeeves walked confidently over to it and pressed a button in its side. There was a short beep and a recessed hatch slid silently upwards to reveal an illuminated interior where metal tureens were stored on racks. Jeeves took them out one by one and brought them to the diners, and then, when all four tureens were set down, he lifted the lids with a flourish to reveal generous portions of mussels, each with a side of fries, a miniature baguette and a selection of dips.

'The chef thought you might like to sample the island's biggest export,' said Jeeves. 'Shellfish.'

But the guests' eyes were still fixed on the delivery vehicle.

'Your faces!' cried Magnus gleefully. 'You all look like you've seen a miracle.'

'What *is* it?' murmured Viggo, turning reluctantly back to his brother.

'Just a little side project of Zack's,' said Magnus proudly. 'We call it Hermoor.'

'The messenger of the Norse gods,' murmured Leon. 'Very apt.'

Magnus looked at him. 'How come you know so much about mythology?' he asked.

Leon shrugged. 'I read,' he said, but Magnus didn't seem convinced.

'Lots of people read, but you seem particularly well-informed.'

'Oh, Leon knows about everything,' said Viggo. 'Mum calls him *The Walking Wikipedia*.'

'I do not,' said Mum, self-consciously. 'But he does know an awful lot of stuff.'

'Just bits and pieces,' insisted Leon. 'Picked up over the years.'

'Well, anyway . . .' Magnus pointed to the white oblong. 'What you're looking at here is just a prototype, but one day soon it's going to revolutionise postal deliveries around the world. Amazon won't know what's hit it!' He returned his gaze to Leon. 'That's not for publication, by the way.'

Leon gave him a blank look. 'I don't expect it is,' he said.

And then added. 'You seem to think I'm some kind of journalist, but I can assure you, I'm not. I'm just a simple musician.' He spread his hands. 'What you see, is what you get.'

'Yeah, right,' said Viggo, and Leon glanced at him in surprise.

There was an uneasy silence as Jeeves unloaded glasses from another compartment in Hermoor, a couple of bottles of wine and a jug of iced water. He made a special point of bringing Viggo two little dishes containing mayonnaise and tomato ketchup. 'As per your request,' he said.

'Wow, thanks,' said Viggo.

But Magnus was still talking about Hermoor. 'Here's the beauty of it,' he said. 'One section keeps things hot, the other keeps them chilled. How do we do it? That would be telling!'

'I imagine it's just a question of insulation,' said Leon, and Magnus looked annoyed.

Jeeves brought the last bits and pieces over to the table. '*Bon appetit*,' he said and then waved a white-gloved hand at Hermoor, as if dismissing it. The craft immediately reversed smoothly back the way it had come and went out through the open doors, which closed behind it.

'How does that thing even *fly*?' asked Viggo.

'Again, it's a secret,' said Magnus. He leant closer. 'I could tell you, if you like, but then I'd have to kill you.' He saw Mum's outraged look and added, 'Only joking!' Then he gestured at the plates of food. 'I hope everybody's all right with seafood,' he said. 'It was way too late for Marco to rustle up something more elaborate, so . . .'

'Marco?' muttered Leon.

'Zack's head chef,' elaborated Magnus. 'The man has two Michelin stars and owned a whole string of restaurants, before Zack made him an offer he couldn't refuse. Marco is French so he always keeps the fridges well stocked with seafood. Anyway, enjoy!'

They began to eat, Viggo reminding himself that all he'd had since lunchtime was a couple of slices of cake, which had done very little to fill him up. Jeeves moved silently around the table, dispensing drinks. Mum and Magnus opted for a glass of white wine and then Jeeves came to Leon and held up two bottles for his inspection. 'Can I tempt you, sir?' he asked. 'We have red or white.'

'No, I'll just have water, please,' said Leon.

'Perhaps they have some malt whisky?' ventured Viggo, slyly. 'Or maybe some ginger ale.' Leon gave him a puzzled look, then shook his head.

'Water please,' he insisted.

'Very good, sir.' Jeeves filled Leon's glass from the jug and then did the same for Viggo. His duties fulfilled, he took a step back.

'You can go now,' Magnus told him. 'We'll help ourselves to more drinks and I can ring the bell if we need anything else.'

'Very good, sir,' said Jeeves. '*Bon appetit.*' He turned, walked quickly to the door and let himself out.

There was a short silence, broken only by the clacking of cutlery on china as they ate.

Then Magnus paused and looked at Mum. 'So, Mum, you said you had a question for me?'

She nodded and dabbed at her mouth with a napkin.

'I have several actually. But the first thing I want to know is what you think you're doing, treating me and your brother the way you are. As though we're intruders.'

Magnus shook his head. 'I'm sorry if I gave that impression, Mum. I was startled, that's all. I really hadn't expected to see you all the way out here.'

'You wouldn't have seen us at all if you'd just kept in touch,' said Viggo. 'I told Mum it was a waste of time coming here, but she insisted.'

'Well, you're here now, so let's try and make the best of it.' Magnus pushed a forkful of food into his mouth and chewed for a moment, before speaking again. 'While you were settling in, I phoned Zack. I told him about you guys turning up out of the blue. He was worried at first; he wanted me to get rid of you . . . but I explained the situation and, in the end, he decided you could stay here – at least until he's had a chance to speak to you himself.'

'Ooh, that's big of him,' said Viggo. He looked around at his companions. 'We're all dead grateful, aren't we?'

Magnus allowed himself a half smile. 'Look, mate, I know you're annoyed but try and keep an open mind about this.' He waved a hand towards the closed door. 'You have to admit you *were* blown away by Hermoor, right?'

Viggo shrugged. 'Yeah, not bad,' he admitted reluctantly.

'Well, that's just the tip of the iceberg. Zack has some projects in development – *big* projects – that make that look like a party trick.'

'The only project we're interested in is the one that's keeping you on Unst,' said Mum.

'Project Valhalla,' said Viggo and then, noticing the sharp look that Magnus directed at him, he made a pantomime gesture of dismay. 'Oh no, I was supposed to keep that secret, wasn't I? Duh!'

Mum ignored him and kept her gaze fixed on Magnus. 'I haven't forgotten about your dad,' she continued, 'even if you have. He was working on a dig only a few miles away from here, and we all know what happened to him, don't we?' She considered her own words. 'Well no, that's the problem. We *don't* know what happened to him, because he disappeared without a trace. So naturally I'm worried.'

'About what?' asked Magnus.

'That this project – the one you won't tell us anything about – could be dangerous.'

Magnus frowned. 'Mum, I appreciate your concern. And I'll be honest with you. I don't *know* if it's dangerous, not at this stage. I really don't. But I do think it's something incredible and I feel honoured to be here now, when we're close – really close – to uncovering its secrets.'

Leon lowered his cutlery for a moment. 'Am I right in assuming that this thing you're working on is archeological?' he asked.

Magnus gazed back at him. 'No comment,' he said.

'Oh for goodness' sake!' said Mum. She lifted her glass and took a large gulp of wine. 'Surely you can tell us something more about it?'

'But he can't, can he?' said Viggo. 'He can't do anything if Zack Strode doesn't give him written permission. He probably has to ask for permission to breathe!'

Magnus sneered. 'Yeah, go on, be like the rest of them!'

'Who are you talking about?' asked Viggo.

'Dr Glover, Chris Scanlon . . . they both suffer from the same basic problem. Jealousy.'

'How can I be jealous?' Viggo asked him. 'I don't even know what it is you're doing. For all I know, you've uncovered some new formula for making better peanut butter.' He paused and smiled. 'Actually, if that's what it is, I probably *am* jealous. I *love* peanut butter.'

Magnus actually grinned at that. 'Zack will be arriving tomorrow,' he said. 'It's up to him to decide how much he wants you to know about the project. So all you need to do is get through a night's sleep.' He looked suddenly serious. 'I should warn all of you though that you may experience some very strange dreams while you're here. I was explaining to Viggo earlier, there's something about our proximity to the site which makes that happen. We're still not really sure why.'

'Viggo's been having funny dreams ever since he set off from home,' said Mum.

'Yes, he told me about them.' Magnus looked at his brother. 'It could be that you're extra receptive to them. That might be useful.'

Viggo took a mouthful of water. 'How d'you make that out?' he asked.

'We could wire you up to some equipment – if you have no objections – to help us see why you're having the dreams. I mean, I get them every few nights and they're really powerful, but you said you've been having them when you're still awake, right?'

Mum looked at Viggo. 'You never mentioned that to me,' she said, and she sounded annoyed.

'I figured you had enough on your plate,' said Viggo. He mopped up the last of his mussel sauce with a chunk of bread. 'Speaking of which, what have you got for pudding?'

Magnus shook his head. 'Ah, sorry, we don't offer anything sweet here.'

Viggo stared at him. 'Why not?' he asked.

'Zack doesn't approve.'

'What do you mean,' growled Viggo. 'I'm not making *him* eat it, am I?'

Magnus sighed. 'Zack has very strong views about sugar,' he explained. 'He believes that it's a kind of poison and he won't tolerate having it anywhere near him.'

Viggo scoffed. 'Well, that's a new one. I mean, I know it's not supposed to be good for you, but *poison*? That's a bit strong, isn't it?'

'It's just something you need to accept if you want to work for him.' He leant closer, as if to whisper, and for a moment he looked like a naughty boy owning up to an indiscretion. 'Why do you think I have to visit that cake fridge every chance I get?' He thought for a moment and then realised something. 'That's how you tracked me down, right? I bet Chris mentioned it to you.'

'Bingo,' said Leon. 'That was careless of you, Magnus. What if it gets back to Zack?'

'Who's going to tell him?' asked Magnus. 'You?'

'Oh, not me, old son. I believe in keeping secrets.'

'Is that right?' said Viggo. 'It's a shame you don't also believe in sticking to the truth.'

Leon eyed him cautiously. 'Why am I getting the impression that you're not happy with me?' he asked. 'Is it something I've said?'

Mum weighed in quickly, clearly aware that Viggo and Leon were edging close to an argument. 'So, Magnus, how is Zack getting here from . . . where did you say he was?'

'He didn't,' Viggo told her. 'At least, he didn't tell *you*. But he's in California, where he's been buying a company. As you do.' He looked at Magnus. 'What about wine?' he asked.

Magnus shook his head. 'You're too young for that,' he said.

'That's not what I meant,' he said. 'Isn't there sugar in wine?'

'Oh, yeah, normally.' Magnus picked up a half-empty bottle. 'But not this. It's from Zack's own vineyard in California. They've pioneered a special technique that substitutes all the sugar for a secret ingredient.'

'Oh, right,' said Viggo . 'Something else you're not allowed to talk about.'

'I'm sensing some hostility here,' said Magnus.

'Oh, you think?' snapped Viggo. 'Way to go, Sherlock, nothing gets past you!'

'Don't be sarcastic to your brother,' said Mum.

'You can hardly blame him,' reasoned Leon. 'I'm sure, like the rest of us, he's getting a little tired of being brushed off.'

'Says the man who has no right to be here in the first place,' snapped Magnus.

'Magnus, don't be rude,' countered Mum. 'Leon is our friend. I might add that, without his help, we probably wouldn't have found you.'

'Yes, I'm fascinated,' said Magnus, staring intently at Leon.

'What's your angle?'

'My angle?' echoed Leon. He thought for a moment and then smiled. 'Forty-five degrees?' he offered. 'Or, at a push, I could do ninety.'

Magnus sneered. 'Very funny,' he said.

'Well, I don't know what else to say. I really have no ulterior motives. I met your mother and Viggo on the ferry and it seemed to me that they needed some help. So I was more than happy to offer some. It's as simple as that.'

'But Magnus does have a point,' observed Viggo. 'What *is* in this for you, Leon?'

Leon looked at Viggo in surprise, as though feeling betrayed. 'I thought the three of us were friends,' he said, and he sounded genuinely hurt. 'Surely that's explanation enough?'

Viggo shook his head. He was aware the plan was to be low key, but somehow he couldn't stop himself from speaking his mind. 'But you see Leon, I just don't know where I am with you. I really don't. You tell me stuff and I start to think maybe you're on the level, but *then* I hear something that makes me change my mind. Like, for instance, I know for a fact that you've told me and Mum completely different stories about the last time you were in Shetland.'

'Viggo,' said Mum. 'I don't think this is the right time to ...'

'No, let him talk,' said Magnus. 'This is fascinating. Don't leave it there.'

'See, on the one hand, we have your son, Daniel, who drowned. And on the other, we have your wife, Mary, who fell off a cliff. So here's my question. Which one is it?'

Leon gazed at Viggo in silence for a moment and then

pushed his plate aside. He took a last gulp of water. 'I've had enough for one night,' he said. 'I don't know about the rest of you, but I need to get some sleep.' He stood up from the table and looked around at the others. Once again, Viggo was astounded to see that the man's eyes were glossy with tears. 'I'll see you all in the morning,' he said. He turned away and went out of the doors, letting them swing shut behind him.

There was a long silence while the three of them sat looking at each other.

'Seems like Viggo touched on a nerve,' said Magnus at last. He gazed at Mum. 'I'm not at all sure I'm happy that you're travelling around with that man.'

'I don't think you're in any position to criticise,' snapped Mum. 'All you had to do was stay in touch with me, and I wouldn't have felt the need to come looking for you.'

'I keep reminding you I'm old enough to do what I like,' said Magnus.

Mum glared at him. 'And so am I!' she snapped.

'Yeah, well. I'm sorry you feel so let down but you came here without an invitation.'

There was a long, simmering silence.

'Leon's right about one thing,' said Mum. 'It is very late and we could all do with some sleep.' She finished her wine and stood up. 'I'm bailing out. Viggo, are you coming?'

He nodded. 'Sure,' he said. He too, got to his feet. 'Does Hermoor also do the washing up?' he asked Magnus. 'Or has Zack made that *your* job?'

'No, we have others to handle stuff like that,' Magnus told him.

'Minions?' suggested Viggo. 'I think that's what they're called. It's funny, I seem to remember a time when you were against that kind of thing. You used to say that you hated capitalists more than anything else.'

Magnus glanced at his watch and Viggo couldn't help noticing that it was a state-of-the-art smartwatch that must have cost a packet.

'We'll meet back here at nine o' clock for breakfast,' he announced. 'Zack will be arriving at some point tomorrow, but I don't yet have his ETA.'

'We'll try and contain our excitement,' said Mum, tonelessly. 'Goodnight, Magnus.' She turned and walked towards the doors. 'Come on, Viggo,' she said, without looking back. 'Let's leave the great man to his *really* important work.'

'Oh, Mum, for God's sake . . .'

But she was already out of the room. Magnus transferred his attention to Viggo. 'You get it, don't you?' he asked. 'You can see why I don't want to jeopardise what I've got here.'

Viggo shrugged. 'I don't really see what you've got, except a rich guy telling you what to do with your life. But I'll try and keep an open mind until I've met him.'

He turned and headed for the door.

'Goodnight,' he heard Magnus say behind him. 'Sweet dreams.'

# CHAPTER 19
## SWEET DREAMS

Viggo opened his eyes and lay on his back, gazing up at the unfamiliar ceiling. The lighting must have gone off at some point in the night, though he was pretty sure it had still been on when he'd fallen asleep in the little camp bed. There was still light here but it wasn't the steady glare of LED.

He was surprised he had dropped off to sleep so easily. He hadn't realised how tired he was until he'd left Mum at her door and walked back to his own unfamiliar room. Then, almost as soon as he stepped inside, he'd felt the crushing weight of exhaustion settle over him like a dark, enveloping shroud. He'd only just summoned enough energy to kick off his trainers before crawling, fully-clothed, beneath the white cotton duvet. Closing his eyes, he sank like a stone into a midnight pond, leaving no ripples.

Now, however, he felt strangely alert, his senses tingling as if trying to warn him that something was different and he realised in an instant why that was the case. *He was no longer alone in the room*. He knew it with dread certainty. Hardly daring to draw breath, he allowed his head to tilt gently to one side so he could look across to the area by the bookcase.

Immediately, he saw that the entire room was different from the way it had been before. The patterned wallpaper looked clean and unblemished, and the rows of books were no longer covered in mildew. Velvet curtains masked the windows and he realised that the light now came from a series of lamps – oil lamps judging by the smell of fumes.

On a patterned rug in front of the books stood a large white dolls' house, its front hinged open to reveal a series of exquisitely furnished rooms within. Sitting cross-legged in front of it was a little girl, dressed in an old-fashioned, frilly dress, her red hair elaborately plaited, her face turned away from Viggo. He saw that in one hand, she held a tiny doll and that she was in the act of placing it carefully into one of the rooms. Then she turned to one side, as if reacting to a voice and Viggo tilted his head a little more to look in that direction, until he saw, a short distance further on, a boy sitting at a table on which were arranged what looked like regiments of toy soldiers. He was moving them around, talking as he did so – but, though his lips moved, Viggo couldn't make out any words.

He felt an instant desire to see more than he could from this awkward angle, so he gathered his courage and pushed the duvet carefully aside. He swung into a sitting position, then got himself upright, aware as he did so of the roughness of the wooden floorboards beneath the soles of his feet. This struck him as an unusual detail for what was surely a dream.

And it *was* a dream, it had to be, so for now, he was just going with it. Magnus had warned him this might happen. He pushed the thought aside and walked to the table, moving stealthily around to stand behind the boy so he could look over his shoulder and watch him as he moved the various troops across the dark wooden tabletop. The military figures were cast in metal and painted in intricate detail: old-fashioned soldiers with bright red tunics, decorated with gold epaulettes and braid. Most were foot soldiers, muskets out in front of them, bayonets fixed, while others sat astride miniature horses, the riders holding tiny swords aloft as though galloping towards some unseen enemy.

The boy continued talking as he worked and Viggo assumed he was issuing commands to his soldiers, but he still couldn't hear a word the boy was saying. He turned aside and walked across to the girl, who was also engrossed in play and, like her brother, seemed totally unaware of Viggo's presence. It was only as he came to a halt beside her that Viggo realised they were the two children from the family portrait he'd seen earlier. Perhaps, he thought, he hadn't immediately made the connection because they looked happy now, quite unlike the scowling versions captured in the old photograph.

The girl set down the doll in one of the rooms and Viggo felt a pulse of surprise go through him as he focused on the little figure and saw that it looked very like Freya, right down to a tiny pair of glasses. She was dressed in the same black outfit she'd been wearing at The Well. But before he had a chance to think more about it, the little girl half-turned and reached a hand out towards Viggo.

As he watched, transfixed, the hand grew larger and larger as it approached, until it was big enough to blot out the light. Before he could react, he felt the pinch of two gigantic fingers on either side of his waist and he was being whirled upwards into the air. He struggled helplessly in the girl's grasp – and then, in a dizzying swoop, he was thrust down again and set on to firm ground. The huge hand receded and he was left where he had been placed. It took a few moments for him to realise that he was now in one of the rooms of the dolls' house and, as he looked around, he could see the other dolls, who were all the same size as him, staring at him with sullen expressions, as though resenting his presence here. He noticed that the doll that looked like Freya was holding a tiny notepad and, as he stared at her, her painted face registered a smile and she said, 'What can I get you to drink?'

He opened his mouth to ask for a Diet Coke, but couldn't seem to form any words and then saw that Freya wasn't looking at him any more but at something *behind* him, her mouth hanging open in dull surprise.

He turned to look over his shoulder and almost screamed out loud when he saw a huge face staring down at him – the girl's face, her bright blue eyes resembling two huge orbs, her thin lips curved into a cruel smile. Now, as he stared up at her, she was pointing a finger at something behind Viggo, as though urging him to look. He wanted to tell her that there had been some mistake, that he wasn't one of her dolls, but when he tried to form words he found to his dismay that he was still unable to utter a sound. He waved his hands at her, ineffectually trying to signal that he wasn't meant to be here, but she was still intent on whatever was behind him.

A huge figure loomed alongside the girl – her brother. Now he was sinking on to his knees beside her in order to have a closer look at the dolls' house. Viggo saw to his dismay that the boy was mirroring his sister's actions, pointing in the same direction as her and that his lips were moving repeatedly, as though reciting the same word over and over again, something with three syllables, he decided. And then it dawned on Viggo what the boy and his sister were saying.

*Valhalla.*

A sense of dread flooded through him. He turned to look in the direction the children were indicating and saw to his horror that something was happening to Freya and to the other dolls in the room. Their limbs were twisting, bending, elongating as though made of soft clay, until they were parodies of the creatures they had once been. They fell one by one on to the spotless floor of the dolls' house, writhing and melting in on themselves, until they were no more than heaps of discarded clothing with viscous liquid seeping out of them.

And now Viggo looked beyond them, into the corner of the room, and he saw that where one perfectly white wall met with one smoothly sanded set of floorboards, a dark hole was opening: tiny at first, but spreading like a sickness, opening out to reveal a weird pulsing maw that seemed to beckon him to approach. Panicked, he turned back to look at the two children and saw that their faces too were beginning to lose definition as though, like the dolls, they were also melting. Their eyes collapsed in upon themselves like dying stars, their noses flattened, spread outwards, their mouths fused together. And Viggo remembered how his father had looked that time when he'd appeared in the cabin in Midgard. The same malady was afflicting the children now.

They were featureless.

Viggo turned back to the opening in the corner of the room and was shocked to see how big it was, covering most of a wall and floor. As he watched, what was left of Freya skittered into the darkness, followed by a tiny wooden chair which was all twisted out of shape. A table cartwheeled into blackness, and then a plant pot with melting flowers in it. A miniature piano was next. A four poster bed. Everything and anything that wasn't fixed down was slithering across the floorboards into the darkness.

And now, Viggo could feel it pulling at him, twisting his limbs out of shape, remoulding him, disassembling him. He reached his melting hands to his face and realised that he couldn't feel his nose or his lips. His face was a smooth, soft oval.

He was powerless to resist. He wanted to cry out but could find no sounds within him as he tumbled headlong to destruction . . .

\*\*\*

'Easy now!'

The voice spoke from right beside Viggo and he blinked himself awake with a gasp to find that Leon was standing beside his bed looking intently down at him, an expression of concern on his face. Viggo instinctively pulled the duvet up under his chin and glanced nervously around the room, which he was relieved to see had returned to its former semi-derelict state. The main door of the room was open and, once again, the LED lights were on.

'What are you doing in here?' he muttered. 'What do you want?'

Leon took a step back from the bed and held up his hands.

'Take it easy, old son,' he said. 'I heard you shouting, that's all. I came to see if you were OK.'

'But . . . your room's nowhere near mine. How did you hear me?'

'I was walking along the corridor. You were making quite a racket.'

Viggo frowned. He realised that his face was soaked with sweat and he reached up an arm to mop at his brow, noting that once again he had gone to bed wearing his clothes. It was beginning to be a habit. 'Why . . . why were you creeping about at night?' he asked.

'No particular reason. I couldn't sleep so I was just . . . having a look around.'

'That's the sort of thing an investigative reporter would do,' said Viggo, with a scowl.

Leon smiled. 'I can assure you that your brother's suspicions are completely unfounded,' he said. 'I'm no reporter. I can barely string two sentences together.'

'Well, that's not true for a start!' said Viggo.

Leon smiled. 'I think I preferred it when you were beginning to trust me,' he said. He looked at Viggo thoughtfully. 'What was your dream about?'

'How do you know I was dreaming?'

Leon chuckled. 'Are you kidding? You were shouting like a scalded cat. I'm surprised nobody else came to see what was going on.'

Viggo considered for a moment, then shifted himself into a sitting position. 'It was about a couple of kids,' he said. 'They were playing over there . . .' He pointed to where the dolls' house had been and then gasped a second time when he realised with a dull jolt of shock that it was still there, exactly as he had seen it in the dream, the front section open.

Leon must have noticed his expression. 'Something wrong?' he asked.

'That wasn't there before,' said Viggo quietly.

'The dolls' house?' Leon gave him a quizzical look. 'Maybe you just didn't notice it?'

'How could I have missed it?' snapped Viggo. 'I mean, look at it. It's huge.' He pushed the duvet back and got out of bed, noticing as he stood up, the rough feel of the bare floorboards against the soles of his feet and thinking that he'd had exactly the same sensation in the dream, if that was what it was. 'Maybe I'm still asleep,' he reasoned.

'I can assure you, you're not,' said Leon.

'Prove it,' said Viggo.

'If you insist.' Leon reached out a hand and gave the flesh of one of Viggo's arms a fierce pinch.

'Ow!' he said. He looked reproachfully at Leon. 'Fair enough,' he muttered. He approached the dolls' house carefully, half expecting it to ripple and vanish in front of his eyes, but when he reached out a hand to touch his fingertips against it, it was perfectly solid. He could see that it was ancient, the once pristine surfaces mottled with grey-green patches of mould. There was even a particularly dark blotch in the corner of one room, where it met the floorboards. 'This definitely wasn't here before,' he insisted. 'I know it wasn't.'

Leon chuckled. 'You're saying that your dream *brought* it here?' he murmured. 'Interesting theory.' But now Leon had noticed the old framed photograph on the wall and he walked over to it to take a closer look.

'They were in the dream,' Viggo told him, waving a hand at the picture.

'What, all four of them?'

'No, just the kids.'

Leon nodded. 'Thomas McKendrick and family,' said Leon. He pointed to each figure in turn. 'There's Thomas, looking all dour and prosperous. His wife, Iris, demure and obedient, as wives were compelled to be in those days. And the children, of course, Andrew and Thomasina.' He smiled. 'It takes a lot of self-belief for a father to name a daughter after himself, don't you think?'

Viggo stared at him and pointed at the picture. 'How did you manage to read their names?' he asked, suspiciously. 'I could barely make out three letters on that frame.'

Leon shrugged. 'Didn't need to read it,' he said. He turned away from the picture, as if dismissing it. 'Since I couldn't sleep, I decided to research this place and find out a little bit about its mysterious history.'

Viggo scowled, wondering why everything Leon said invited another question. 'Mysterious, in what way?' he muttered. 'And *how* have you been researching it? With what?' He thought for a moment and then remembered something. 'Oh wait. The famous disappearing phone, I suppose.'

Leon grinned and strolled over to a vacant wooden chair. He sat himself down on it. 'Thomas McKendrick was a businessman who made his fortune in the city of Dundee in the late seventeen hundreds. He worked in the tanning industry...'

'Tanning?' Viggo was mystified. 'You mean like . . . sunbeds? I didn't realise they'd been around so long.'

Leon chuckled. 'Not *that* kind of tanning, you nitwit! I mean the business of turning cow hides into leather – a charming process that mostly consisted of soaking them in urine. Hardly surprising that Mr McKendrick began to pine for fresh air and wide open spaces. He purchased a large plot of land out here and built this place after visiting Edinburgh to seek inspiration. I was right about the architect, by the way. William Chambers. Thomas and his family moved in around 1790, where no doubt they led a much quieter existence . . . until 1803, that is, when . . .' He frowned.

'Go on,' Viggo prompted him. 'When what?'

'When they disappeared,' said Leon flatly. 'All four of them.'

Viggo stared at him. 'Like my dad?' he whispered.

Leon paused for a moment as though thinking the comment over. 'Not sure about that,' he admitted. 'But it *was* mysterious.' He took a deep breath. 'It was a beautiful sunny day, by all accounts, and, this far north, that's always a cause for celebration. So the family had their groom drive them out to a remote spot on their estate, where they intended to enjoy an idyllic picnic. Their cook had packed them a hearty meal. The McKendricks and their groom, who was called Alistair, if memory serves me correctly, set off early one morning and were never seen again.'

Viggo sank into a chair opposite Leon. 'There must have been a search or something?'

'There were several. No stone was left unturned, but the months passed and, sadly, no trace of any of them was ever found. Not so much as a button.' Leon gestured around at the derelict room. 'There were no heirs to inherit the house so the place just fell into rack and ruin. The staff left – after helping themselves to whatever they wanted – and the place was left to rot. Much later, in the 1970s, there was some talk of a trust being set up to try and restore the house to its former grandeur and perhaps turn it into a tourist attraction, but alas, it all came to nothing. So, I rather think that Mr Strode got this place for shirt buttons – or at least what passes for them in his world.' He looked at Viggo. 'And that is as much as I know about the McKendricks. Now, tell me more about your dream. You say you saw the children. What happened?'

'Well, the girl was playing with these dolls . . . and one of them looked exactly like Freya . . .'

Leon raised his eyebrows. 'Is that right?' He thought for a moment. 'Well, I suppose that makes sense. She's been on your mind lately.'

'Who says?'

'I think that's been pretty obvious. Go on.'

'Er . . . well . . . and then *I* was a doll and . . .' Viggo grimaced. 'Yes?'

'We both got kind of like . . . twisted up? Like we were melting. And all of a sudden there was this hole in the corner of one of the rooms in the dolls' house and we were all like being . . . pulled into it.' He shook his head. 'I mean, it sounds loopy, but that's pretty much what happened.'

Leon nodded, as though it meant something to him.

'It all makes me wonder,' he said, 'if this secret project of

Strode's could be connected in some way to what happened to the McKendricks.'

There was a long silence while they both considered the possibility. Finally, Viggo said, 'Maybe you need to ask Magnus about it. But good luck with getting anything out of him.'

'I can only try,' said Leon. He glanced at his watch. 'But I suspect I'd better let him enjoy a few hours' more sleep. And besides, I'm curious to meet the infamous Mr Strode.' He got to his feet. 'Well, if you're sure you're OK, I may as well get about my business.'

'Hang on a minute.' Viggo stared at him. 'Why did you run off before, when I started asking you awkward questions?'

Leon shrugged. 'I didn't run off!' he protested. 'I made a strategic retreat. That's not quite the same thing.'

'Don't split hairs. You didn't like all those questions, did you?

'I felt I was being got at,' said Leon. 'By you *and* by Magnus. You can hardly blame me for being uncomfortable. And for your information, Viggo, both of those stories are, sadly, true. My son died tragically and so did my wife. I really *am* that unlucky.'

'Oh come on! On the same trip?'

'No, it was two different ones. Mary died first . . . and then, several years later, Daniel, by which time I was with Steph. Perhaps I should have made that clear when I spoke to your mother.'

'Oh yeah. And you should have also explained how you managed to be in two places at the same time. Sitting with Mum *and* having a drink with Agnes and Leif!'

Now Leon looked bewildered. 'But that's not possible, is it?'

'Well, no, it shouldn't be. And yet somehow, you managed it.'

'I think you must have got your times mixed up,' said Leon. 'To do something like that, I'd have to be magical, wouldn't I? And as you can see, I'm really quite ordinary.'

Viggo took a deep breath. 'You get angry when people don't trust you,' he said. 'But you have to admit, you do kind of bring it on yourself. I mean, I don't know what to make of you, Leon, I really don't. You say that you only want to help me and Mum . . .'

'Yes! And I've done exactly that, haven't I?'

'I . . .'

'You were looking for Magnus and I brought you to him.'

Viggo thought about it for a moment. 'Not exactly. I mean, you . . . *helped.*'

Leon shook his head. 'Think about it for a moment. If I'd left the two of you to it, you'd still be blundering around Lerwick asking useless questions. I was the one who got you here. Right?'

'Well . . .'

'It's true, and you know it! I said I would help you and I did. I kept my promise. So, really, my work is done and this is the point where I should say goodbye and leave you to it.' He frowned. 'Except that I get the strangest feeling that the two of you are in danger.'

'What do you mean?'

'I'm not sure. It's just a very powerful feeling. So until I'm convinced you're both safe, I'm afraid you're stuck with me.' He smiled sweetly and headed for the door. 'I'll see you in the morning,' he said. 'Meanwhile, try not to have any more nightmares. And if you do have them, keep your voice down.' And with that, he let himself out, closing the door gently behind him.

Viggo sat there, thinking about what Leon had said. He supposed it was true, without Leon to guide them, he and Mum wouldn't have found Magnus so quickly, if at all. So why was Viggo still reluctant to trust him? He sighed and glanced at his watch. A little after 2 a.m.. Once again, he wondered why Leon had been creeping along the corridors at such a ridiculous hour, and for a moment he even considered leaving the room and following him. But then he told himself that he still felt tired, so after one last look at the old dolls' house, he went back to the camp bed, crawled under the duvet and closed his eyes again.

He was asleep in minutes, and this time there were no dreams waiting for him.

# CHAPTER 20

## ARRIVAL

Viggo woke to a loud, shuddering sound that seemed to shake the ancient house to its foundations. He blinked himself awake and lay for a moment, listening as the sound intensified. Then he threw back the duvet and struggled out of bed. As he stood up, a shadow passed across the window. He hurried towards it to peer out through the grimy glass and saw that a big black helicopter was hovering just a short distance away. As Viggo watched, it dipped its nose and moved onwards for a short distance, before beginning to descend, aiming for a stretch of deserted land some thirty metres in front of the house. Magnus came hurrying into view from the direction of the front door and stopped a short distance from the chosen landing spot, watching as the helicopter came steadily down to earth.

At that moment, there was a polite tapping at the bedroom door and Viggo went to open it. Jeeves stood there, smiling genially. Mum and Leon were standing behind him.

'Mr Strode is just arriving,' said Jeeves, as though it was something to be joyful about. 'I've been sent to fetch you all.'

Viggo stared at him. 'Give me a minute,' he said. 'I need

to grab my trainers and take a pee!' He turned away and ran to the bathroom. Three minutes later, he was back and following the small group along the corridor. 'What's the big hurry?' he asked Mum.

She shrugged her shoulders. 'Apparently Mr Strode can't be kept waiting like ordinary people,' she complained. 'So of course we're yanked out of bed to go and worship at his altar.' Viggo could tell that she was in a foul mood.

He frowned. 'Did you sleep OK?' he asked her.

She shook her head. 'I had the most awful nightmares,' she told him. 'I really do not like this place one little bit.'

'What did you dream about?' asked Leon.

'About Jonathan. He was warning me to leave here. I'm inclined to follow his advice. And he said the weirdest thing.'

'He told you to stop following him,' said Viggo, and when Mum gave him a baffled look, he added. 'Welcome to the club.'

There was no time to elaborate. They went down the flight of mahogany stairs to the foyer, where a couple of armed guards were waiting for them, the lower halves of their faces covered. The two black-uniformed men took a position on either side of them. They unslung their guns and then one of them gestured for them to proceed. They walked together out through the open main doors, descended the short flight of stone steps and crossed the stretch of waste ground towards the helicopter. Viggo couldn't help glancing nervously at the semi-automatic weapons clutched in the guards' gloved hands. Once again, he found himself wondering what everyone here was so paranoid about.

They approached the helicopter. Its propeller was still

turning but was slowing gradually to a halt. Magnus saw them coming and lifted a hand to wave. He moved closer.

'Sorry for the early wake up, guys,' he shouted over the roar of the engine. 'I got a last minute call that Zack was ahead of schedule and I thought he'd like you to be here when he touched down.'

'I *was* hoping for breakfast first,' said Mum ungraciously. 'I don't usually agree to meet helicopters until after I've had my morning coffee.'

Magnus smiled at that. 'I wasn't aware you did it on a regular basis,' he said. 'We'll get you something soon,' he promised her. 'We'll all eat together.' He turned back to the helicopter and pointed. 'See that? That's a—'

'Sikorsky S92 Executive,' said Leon. 'Around twenty-six million dollars to buy.'

Magnus glared at him. 'How the hell do you know that?' he snapped. And then he added. 'Oh yes, don't tell me. You *read*, right?'

'It's amazing what you can pick up,' said Leon. 'I can tell you, for example, that the Sikorski is one of the world's fastest helicopters and has an effective range of four hundred and thirty-nine miles. Approximately,' he added, with a wry smile.

Magnus seemed to be about to say something else, but he broke off as the cabin door of the helicopter opened and a man climbed out.

Viggo got his first look at Zack Strode. He was a big guy, six foot or more, maybe in his mid-forties and heavy set, a once athletic physique now running slightly to flab.

He was dressed in an expensive all-weather jacket and blue jeans and he had round, pale features, his head covered by the bright orange beanie that was his trademark. His face was dominated by a wide grin, which displayed the kind of perfect teeth that could have been used as an advertisement for American dentistry. He made his way down the helicopter steps to the ground, his head lowered until he was clear of the rotor blades.

There was a pause while Zack took the opportunity to study his reception committee. Then his gaze settled on Magnus and that perfect grin grew even wider. He strode forward. 'Magnus,' he said, in a deep, booming voice. 'Good to see you again. Been too long, man.' Viggo had expected them to shake hands but Zack spread out his arms and enfolded Magnus in a fierce bear hug, almost lifting him clear of the ground. Zack held the hug for longer than was strictly necessary and then released his hold.

Viggo noticed that Magnus kept glancing towards the open hatch of the helicopter, as though he'd been expecting somebody else. 'Val not with you?' he asked hopefully.

Zack shook his head. 'Nope. She had some big motorcycle rally in Berlin to attend,' he said. 'Couldn't persuade her to come with me. Even offered to pay her!' He spread his hands in a 'what can you do' gesture. Magnus nodded, but Viggo could see that he was disappointed.

Zack put his hands back on Magnus's shoulders and gazed deep into his eyes. 'One question. Are we all ready to proceed?' he asked.

'Very nearly,' said Magnus, and – catching a look of doubt

on his employer's face – added, 'They're just running a few final checks to make sure it's safe.' Viggo thought that his big brother had the demeanour of a loyal dog desperate to please his master.

A momentary frown flicked across Zack's face and then he seemed to remember that there were others present, so he allowed his gaze to move onwards and the dazzling grin returned as he advanced on Mum. 'So, you're Alison,' he said. 'I've heard so much about you.' For a terrible moment, Viggo thought that Zack was going to try and do the hug on her, but something in her frosty expression must have warned him not to push his luck. Instead, he extended an arm and shook her hand politely. 'You must be so proud,' he said.

'Must I really?' asked Mum, disdainfully. 'I'm afraid I still have no idea what Magnus has done to deserve my praise.' Viggo almost wanted to cheer. Clearly, recent events had toughened her up, making her much less worried about hurting people's feelings.

Zack nodded, as if he totally understood. 'I'm so sorry about the secrecy, but I'm sure you can appreciate our need for it.'

'I might if I had the first clue what this is all about,' said Mum, refusing to be brushed off. 'What is it you've found, the secret of life?'

'I can assure you,' said Zack, 'when the time is right you will be one of the first to share in our discovery.' Now his gaze moved sideways to Viggo and his eyes seemed to light up. 'Oh my God, Magnus, you never told me your brother was like your mini-me!' he cried.

'We're really not alike,' protested Viggo, but Zack didn't seem to hear him.

'It's something to do with the mouth,' he said. 'Or maybe the eyes.'

Magnus chuckled. 'Viggo doesn't like being compared to me,' he said. 'I sometimes think he wishes he was an only child.'

'Magnus!' said Mum. 'What a thing to say!'

Zack smiled. 'I agree,' he murmured. 'I hope you don't think that way, Viggo. Speaking as an only child myself, I can tell you that it's a lonely life. When I was a kid I always wished for a brother.'

'Why not a sister?' asked Mum. 'But then, of course, you are known for your misogynistic remarks online, aren't you?'

Magnus audibly drew in a breath at this and Viggo found himself thinking that Mum must be really at the end of her tether to say something like that out loud, but Zack just chuckled. 'No offence intended,' he assured Mum. 'A sister would have been fine too. I guess I just wanted somebody to play sports with.'

'This will surprise you, Mr Strode, but there are some females who excel at sport.'

'Uh . . . yeah, I know that.' Zack seemed to sense that he wasn't going to win this one and quickly moved on.

Now all eyes turned towards Leon. 'And this, of course, is Mr Bragg,' said Zack. 'Funny thing.'

'What's funny?' asked Leon calmly.

'I always check out new people before I meet them,' said Zack. 'But you, you're an unknown quantity. So I did a little searching online. Some might call it paranoia, but

I just think of it as insurance. And you, Mr Bragg . . .'

'Do call me Leon.'

'You, *Leon*, don't seem to have a presence on social media.'

'Is that right?' Leon shrugged. 'Oh dear. I must admit, it's not a priority.'

'Clearly. Oh, as you might expect, I found a few other people with the same *name* as you, but not one of them with your face.'

'Well, that's probably a blessing,' said Leon with a smile. 'I wouldn't wish these sad old features on anyone else.' He thought for a moment. 'How did you know what I actually looked like?'

Zack made an apparent effort not to roll his eyes. 'I had surveillance images sent from the cameras in the house.'

'There are cameras?' muttered Viggo. He glared at Magnus. 'Thanks for the warning!'

'Why, what've you been doing?' asked Magnus suspiciously, but Viggo didn't reply.

Leon, meanwhile, seemed to be deep in thought. 'If you had images of me, then you must have had the same for Viggo and Alison,' he murmured.

Zack shrugged. 'Well, yes . . .'

'So why all that nonsense about what Viggo looks like? You must already have *seen* that he and Magnus look alike. Or was that just your attempt to create a good atmosphere?'

Zack seemed somewhat flustered, as though he'd been caught out in a lie. 'Well, a photograph isn't the same as meeting someone face-to-face,' he said.

'Fair enough, I suppose. Though I would have thought it would be enough to establish certain similarities.'

Leon smiled and stepped forward, extending a hand to shake. As he did so, Viggo was alarmed to note that the two guards instinctively raised their weapons, ready to fire, but Zack made a subtle gesture to dismiss them from taking any further action and they lowered the guns. Zack reached out and took Leon's hand in his.

'At any rate, Leon, I couldn't find a trace of you online.'

'Couldn't you?' Leon adopted a look of disappointment.

'No, I couldn't. And I looked really hard. You have never written an email, you've never posted a tweet. You don't keep a blog, and there isn't a single photograph in the cloud of anyone with your features. Even my facial recognition software couldn't identify you. How do you account for that?'

'I'm afraid I can't. It is a bit rum, isn't it? Mind you, I was only reading the other day that even the most sophisticated facial recognition has the very devil of a time when confronted by identical twins.'

Zack looked confused. 'You're saying . . . you're a twin?' he murmured.

'Oh no, they broke the mould when they made me. I'm a one-off.'

There was a baffled silence before Zack turned to Magnus. 'Well, I don't know about the rest of you, but I'm famished. I trust you have everything laid on?'

'Of course. I have some of that Columbian blend coffee you're so keen on,' Magnus told him. 'Ordered it in specially.'

'Great stuff. Well, what are we waiting for?'

Magnus turned and led the group back towards the house, where Viggo could see Jeeves standing on the steps waiting to greet them. He noticed also that the two guards had chosen to walk on either side of the small group, but as they neared the doors, Zack made a discreet motion and the two men stopped in their tracks and turned around to stand guard.

Zack saw Viggo observing this and grinned at him. 'Relax, kid,' he said. 'Everything is cool. I just believe in being careful, that's all.' He pointed back to the helicopter. 'That's how I get to ride around in a . . .'

'. . . Sikorsky Executive,' said Viggo calmly, and nearly laughed out loud at the bewildered look on Zack's face.

'How the hell did you . . .?'

'I *read*,' added Viggo, and, feeling very pleased with himself, he climbed the steps to the entrance.

# CHAPTER 21
## BREAKFAST IN ASGARD

Once again, Viggo was sitting at the massive dining table, where he and the others were all tucking into a fabulous breakfast.

Hermoor had made an even more spectacular appearance as the diners took their seats, because this time, he had an identical twin alongside him, the two of them moving side by side in perfect synchronicity. From the spacious interiors, Jeeves unloaded an absolute feast. There were tureens of scrambled eggs, bowls of mushrooms and tomatoes, a large metal platter containing beef sausages and smoked bacon. There was a rack of wholemeal toast and plenty of butter to spread on it. From the second white rectangle, Jeeves brought out jugs of freshly squeezed orange juice, cafetieres of aromatic coffee, miniature bottles of milk . . . but this morning, hunger had made Viggo almost immune to Hermoor's charms; he barely gave the two machines a second glance. As soon as he'd heaped his plate with food, he fell to eating with a vengeance and didn't even notice the two machines as they floated silently out through the open doorway.

Zack, who was sitting directly across from Viggo, gave him an approving grin.

'I remember when I was your age,' he said. 'I could eat twice my own weight without stopping to take a breath.' He slapped his stomach ruefully. 'One of these days, I'm going to get back into my exercise regime.'

Viggo stopped eating long enough to speak. 'Magnus tells me you don't eat sugar,' he said.

'That's correct,' admitted Zack. 'Well, *refined* sugar, anyway. It's not a weight-loss thing.'

'Did you eat it when you were a kid?'

Zack nodded. 'I did, actually.'

'So you weren't poisoned *then*?'

There was an uncomfortable silence and Viggo noticed that Magnus was looking daggers at him, but Zack didn't seem to mind one bit. 'Actually, I *was* poisoned,' he said.

'Really?'

'Oh yeah. In the same way that junkies are poisoned by the drugs they take. When I was your age, I was addicted to sugar. I drank cola and I ate candy, just like all my friends. I didn't realise then what it was doing to my *brain*.' He lifted a finger and tapped the side of his head.

'Your brain?' Viggo took a big bite of sausage and chewed noisily for a moment. 'But I eat sugar and my brain seems OK.'

Zack chuckled. 'Sure it does. But it's early days, yet. Sugar is a poison that works real slow, Viggo, drip by drip. You don't notice the damage because of the way it happens. But then one day, you finally wise up to what it's doing to you. You stop having sugar and gradually everything comes back, the same way you lost it, a bit at a time. You start to see clearly again; your mind works like it used to. I stopped taking sugar ten years ago and look at me now! I don't like to boast but I seem to have done pretty well for myself.'

Leon chuckled. 'But some people would argue that you're eating sausages and bacon and that animal fat is every bit as harmful as sugar.'

'Too much fat *is* bad for you,' admitted Zack. 'I wouldn't argue that point. But not as dangerous as refined sugar. That's public enemy number one.' He waved a hand over his plate. 'Besides, the meat you're eating here is completely free range. I own ranches that specialise in rearing organic meat and I won't eat anything less. All my stock is grass-fed and the animals have a happy existence.'

'But presumably they still end up being killed for food?' said Leon. 'So it isn't all good news.'

'We slaughter them humanely,' said Zack. 'That's important.'

'I doubt the animals appreciate the difference,' said Leon.

There was an uncomfortable silence which was broken by Mum, who was sitting to Zack's right. 'I'm going to ask again,' she said. 'Just exactly what *is* happening here?'

Zack turned his head to look at her. 'I'm sorry Alison, but I can't tell you that,' he said.

Mum gave a grunt of annoyance. 'You mean you *won't* tell me!'

'No, I mean I can't – because I don't really know myself. I have *expectations* of what we'll find at the site, but I can't be certain. Not yet. Not until we've . . . descended.'

'Descended?' muttered Viggo. 'So . . . this thing, whatever it is, is underground?'

Zack looked across at Magnus. 'You didn't tell me your brother was such a live wire.'

'Oh, he's full of surprises,' said Magnus, who seemed slightly put out that Zack seemed so interested in his little brother. 'But it's mostly just chitter-chatter. Take no notice of him.'

'I understand you also have an interest in all things Nordic,' said Leon.

'Yeah, that's what really gets me all fired up! You guys probably don't know this but I'm a descendant of—'

'Ragnar Lothbrok. Yes, we read about that.'

Zack grinned. 'You seem sceptical, Mr Bragg.'

Leon shrugged. 'It's a hard thing to prove,' he said. 'What if I told you I was a direct descendent of Odin? What would you say to that?'

Zack stared at Leon for a moment and then tilted back his head and laughed. 'I'd say you're deluded. But I'm all for thinking big.' He turned his attention back to Magnus. 'You said something before about last minute checks,' he muttered. 'So, when do we visit the site?'

Magnus seemed to consider the question for a while. 'Hopefully, this afternoon,' he said. 'The team needs to be sure there's no danger of another rock fall. But I've got them hard at work, they've promised to get back to me by midday.'

'Where *is* this team you keep talking about?' asked Mum. 'I haven't seen many others here.'

'They're up at the site,' Magnus told her. 'They have their own accommodation over there – tents – and they've been working in shifts, around the clock. But once they're happy it's safe to proceed, they will vacate the site and Zack and I will make the first visit.'

'I'm sure this is all lovely,' said Mum, 'but I still don't know anything about what you've found. I'm assuming it's archeological? You can tell me that much, surely?'

Zack sighed. He looked at Magnus for help.

'The thing we've found,' said Magnus. 'The thing we *think* we've found . . . it's . . .'

'The single most important discovery in archeological history,' said Viggo, in a mocking, sing-song voice.

Magnus glared at him, as if wondering where he had got the phrase from. Then it must have occurred to him that this was what he had told Chris Scanlon, and his cheeks reddened. 'Well, actually, yes, that's pretty much it.'

Zack was puzzled. 'How does the kid know that?' he asked.

Viggo saw that Magnus was in potential trouble here and reluctantly decided to help him out. 'Oh, it's what he's been talking about ever since we were kids,' he explained. 'His greatest ambition. To find some incredible buried treasure.'

Zack seemed satisfied with the answer. 'If things go according to plan, that's what'll be waiting for us down there,' he said.

'So, it *is* some kind of treasure?' asked Viggo.

'Oh, not gold or jewels or anything dumb like that,' Zack assured him. 'Something that's worth a lot more than diamonds.'

'Is the site far from here?' asked Mum.

'Stop fishing!' said Magnus. 'We can't tell you any more about it. Not yet.'

Mum made another sound of exasperation. 'Well then, I don't know why I'm still here! We may as well head back to

Edinburgh. We came to find you and we've done that. However, you've made it very plain that you wish we hadn't bothered so what's the point of us sitting around like spare parts?'

'Oh, don't be like that,' said Magnus. 'You surprised me, that's all.'

'That's no excuse for treating us like intruders,' snapped Mum.

There was a short, testy silence.

'If you don't mind,' said Zack, 'I'd rather you stayed a little longer.' Viggo noticed that he wasn't smiling now. 'Just until Magnus and I have made our first visit to the site and have had the chance to evaluate what we've got. Assuming we're happy, you'll be given the opportunity to take a look for yourselves.'

Mum glared at him. 'You're forbidding us to leave?' she cried.

Zack shook his head. 'Not at all,' he said. 'No, Alison, I'm asking you, politely, to stay a little longer. What we're doing here is highly confidential and I wouldn't want to risk any of you talking about what's going on to . . . anybody else you might meet.'

'How would we talk about it?' cried Mum. 'We don't *know* anything!'

'Well, you know I'm here and you know we're excavating something valuable and that's not the kind of information I want to go any further, right now. So, I'd be happier if you'd agree to stay for just another day or so.'

'But why should we?'

' I . . . could make it worth your while.'

Mum gave him a puzzled look. 'Whatever do you mean?'

'I could pay you for your time.'

'Pay me . . . to stay here?'

'Sure. I don't know what your financial situation is in Edinburgh, but most people are glad of a little extra assistance. I could make a donation to your bank account.'

'But that's ridiculous,' said Mum.

'Hang on a minute,' Viggo told her. He looked at Zack. 'How much are we talking about?'

Zack shrugged. 'That's entirely up to you. How much do you want?' He gazed back at Viggo, his expression calm. 'Your call.'

'Seriously?'

'Sure.'

'OK, let's say . . .' Viggo thought for a moment. The first figure that came into his head was a million pounds, which seemed a ridiculous sum, but nevertheless, he hesitated, reminding himself that Zack Strode was worth billions. But he couldn't make himself say it. Then a more realistic number came to him and he blurted it out. 'Ten thousand pounds!' he said.

Magnus gave him an angry look. 'Christ, Viggo, you can't just—'

'Sure he can,' said Zack. 'Ten thousand, huh? I admire your sass. Let me think about it.' There was a brief silence while Zack gazed across the table at Viggo. 'You think your time is worth that much money?'

'Er . . . well, I don't know. You said to name a price, and . . .'

'But do you think it's fair?'

'I . . . I don't suppose it's *fair*, but . . .'

'. . . you're worth it?'

'Er . . .'

'OK,' said Zack.

Viggo stared at him. 'Wait.' He pushed his half-finished plate away, the delicious food forgotten. 'You're saying *yes*?'

'I believe I am.'

'Zack,' said Magnus, 'you really don't have to . . .'

'I know that. But then again, why not?' He looked at Viggo. 'And I know exactly what you're thinking right now. You're thinking, "I should have asked for more!". But it's too late, kid. I'm getting you for ten thousand.' He glanced at Mum. 'And the same for you, right?'

'But . . . let me get this straight in my head,' said Viggo. His mind was racing. 'You'll give us ten thousand pounds . . . *each* . . . and all we have to do is stay here for one more day?'

'Possibly two days. Three maximum.'

'What's the catch?' asked Leon, smiling.

'What makes you think there's a catch?' asked Zack.

'In my limited experience, there usually is.'

Zack shook his head. 'Nah. Not really.' He considered for a moment, then turned his attention back to Mum. 'There's something you'd have to do first, of course. Just a small thing. I'd need you and Viggo to sign NDAs.' He saw Viggo's baffled expression and explained. 'Non-disclosure agreements. It means, if you *did* tell anybody else about what's happening here, you'd have to pay all the money back. And, of course, I'd be able to sue you.'

Mother glared at him. 'Who would sign something like that?' she cried.

'It's normal procedure,' Zack assured her. 'Everybody who works for me has to sign one.' He looked at Magnus. 'Isn't that right?'

Magnus nodded, rather sheepishly, Viggo thought.

Mum looked at him. 'You signed an NDA?' she cried. 'Why would you?'

Magnus shrugged. 'It was a condition of taking the post,' he said. 'I wanted the job so I signed. It's no big deal.'

'No big deal?' Mum seemed horrified. 'Don't you realise that it makes you powerless? What if there's something illegal going on here?'

Zack chuckled. 'Oh, there isn't, I can assure you of that. I do everything by the book; I'd be crazy not to. But a man in my position, Alison . . . I have to take care to protect myself, you can see that, can't you? There are people out there . . .' He waved a hand towards the nearest window. '. . . ruthless people just waiting for their chance to trip me up. That's why I have to be so careful.'

Viggo was staring straight ahead now, his eyes slightly out of focus. He was thinking, for some reason, about the bike he'd been saving up for. 'Twenty thousand quid,' he murmured. 'Wow. Mum, we'll be rich. I could get a really *good* bike. I could get a Rockhopper!'

'You can forget it,' Mum told him, and he turned to stare at her in dismay. 'There's no way we're signing anything like that.'

'What are you talking about?' he gasped. 'Of course we're signing it. Twenty thousand, Mum! Just to stay for a bit longer. We'd be crazy not to.'

'Maybe Alison isn't the sort of person who can be bought,' reasoned Leon. 'Perhaps she values her freedom too much to put it up for sale.'

'In my experience, everybody has their price,' said Zack.

'If ten thousand isn't enough, then why not twenty each? It's all the same to me.'

Viggo looked at him, open-mouthed. He had a sudden impulse to laugh out loud but somehow resisted. 'Twenty each?' he gasped. 'You'd give us . . . forty thousand pounds?'

'Chicken feed,' said Zack. 'I once left a waiter a thousand dollar tip, just because I liked the way he served my coffee. It's only money, kid.'

There was a long silence while Mum stared across the table at him.

'You should be ashamed of yourself,' she told him at last.

Zack looked surprised. 'Is that right?' he murmured.

'Yes, I'm afraid so. Forty thousand pounds might be chicken feed to you but there are people in this world who will work their entire lives and never have that much to spare. You know what gets me about people like you?'

'No, but I'm sure you're about to tell me.'

'You could take all that money you have and put it towards good causes. Couldn't you? You could stop people from starving. You could build houses for those who don't have them or organise clean water in villages that have to walk miles to a shared well. You could invest in finding a cure for cancer. But you won't do any of that, will you?'

Zack gazed at her. 'No,' he admitted. 'I'm not interested in that stuff. See, Alison, the way I see it, I earned that money, I created that wealth, and I figure I should be free to do whatever I want with it. Oh, every day, people come to me with their hard luck stories, "Ooh, I'm so poor, I can't seem to get a break!" But I tell them, "Do what I did. Use your mind

— 253 —

to gain access to those things that will generate income." But do they do it? No. Because they don't have my business brain. Of course, you could take the forty thousand I'm offering you and put *that* to good causes. Now there's an idea! Except, I think that when it comes down to it, you won't. Money is like that, Alison. We all think we'd use it responsibly, but when we get it . . . we don't.'

Leon lifted a finger. 'Excuse me for interrupting . . .'

'Yeah?'

'I seem to remember reading something about you.'

Zack's eyes narrowed suspiciously and the grin faltered. 'Oh yeah, what's that?'

'Well, correct me if I'm wrong but I understand that your great grandfather was a very successful businessman.'

'Uh . . . yeah, but . . .'

'A man who made his fortune from exporting slaves from Africa to work in the cotton plantations of the United States.'

'Ah, that's ancient history,' snapped Zack.

'Oh no, I wouldn't say 'ancient'. In world terms, it's a relatively recent occurance. In turn, all of your great-grandfather's money was handed down to his son, who – I believe – continued in the same vein. And then, I think, years later, when the slave trade had finally been abolished, your father made *his* money from slot machines, isn't that right? He had a gambling empire that was famous all over America – casinos, arcades, betting shops . . .'

'What is your point?' growled Zack.

'Only that you inherited a fortune from your father when he died. Millions, in fact. So, though you have grown your personal wealth by investing in new technology and so forth, the fact is, you were born rich. You've never experienced poverty.'

Zack seemed eager to move on. 'I can't be held responsible for what my ancestors did,' he insisted. 'That was all a long time ago. And there's nothing toxic or illegal about any of the companies I've invested in.'

'No, but I did read some criticism about you not paying your taxes, so . . .'

'Can we change the subject?' asked Zack, making it clear he wasn't in the mood to discuss it any further. He turned his attention back to Mum and took a moment to remember how to smile. 'So,' he said. 'Going back to what we were discussing earlier. Am I to assume you're turning down my generous offer?'

Mum stared at him a moment longer then slowly lowered her gaze to look at her hands. She looked, Viggo thought, thoroughly ashamed of herself. 'No,' she murmured. 'No, I can't do that. Of course I can't. Because the sum you're talking about would change my life. It would pay off all my credit card debts and set me free. I . . . I could even get a new car.'

Viggo stared at her. 'You'd sell Ruby?' he gasped.

'She's more than ten years old, Viggo; she's only held together with rust.' She looked back at Zack. 'I accept your terms,' she murmured.

Zack nodded, as though he'd known all along that she'd go his way. 'Excellent,' he said. 'If it's any consolation, Alison, I think you've made the right decision.' He looked at Magnus. 'Straight after we've finished eating, print up some NDAs and get them across to your mother and to Viggo.'

Now he turned his attention to Leon. 'What about you?' he asked. 'Same deal?'

Leon smiled and shook his head. 'I have no intention of leaving just yet,' he said. 'It's just starting to get interesting. So, I'd be perfectly happy to stay on a little longer.'

'Ah, good, so . . .'

'But I don't need to be *paid* for my presence here. It's awfully generous of you, but no, thanks all the same. I'm good.'

Viggo looked at him, astonished. 'But . . . he'll give you the money anyway. All you have to do is sign a form.'

'I understand that,' said Leon. 'And of course it's tempting. It really is.'

Zack smiled confidently. 'I know what he's doing,' he told the others. 'He's holding out for a bigger payment.' He shrugged. 'All right then. What *is* your price?'

Leon shook his head. 'You don't understand me at all,' he said. 'The freedom to talk is not something I'm prepared to sell at *any* price.' He looked at Magnus. 'So I'll save you some printer ink. Don't bother preparing a form for me.' He turned back to Zack. 'And please don't insult me by raising your offer. I'm really not interested.' He looked down at his plate and speared a sausage with his fork. 'You are right about one thing,' he told Zack.

'Oh yeah, what's that?'

'This organic beef is absolutely delicious.'

Leon pushed a chunk of sausage into his mouth and chewed enthusiastically while Zack stared across the table at him in stunned silence.

# CHAPTER 22
## THE DECISION

After they'd finished eating, everybody headed off to their respective rooms to consider what had just happened. Viggo was in a state of high excitement at the prospect of becoming suddenly wealthy, but Mum seemed tortured by the idea, as though she'd agreed to something terrible. Only Leon appeared to be really happy, even a little jubilant, after telling Zack exactly what he could do with his money. Viggo really didn't get it. It wasn't as if Leon was wealthy, he was always struggling to find the funds for whatever he needed to do. This had been his chance to make some easy money and in Viggo's opinion, he'd totally blown it.

'I don't understand,' he told Leon, as he and Mum trudged alongside him towards their rooms. 'All you had to do was—'

'Leave him alone,' snapped Mum. 'Leon can do whatever he likes. Actually, I admire his decision. I wish I'd had the guts to do it.'

'Hey, you're not thinking of changing your mind are you?' muttered Viggo, suspiciously.

Mum scowled. 'I've got a headache coming on,' she said. 'I think I'll try and get some sleep.'

'Good idea,' said Leon. 'Meanwhile, I'll explore this place a little more.' And he turned along the next corridor as if he didn't have a care in the world.

'Imagine turning down all that dosh,' said Viggo, shaking his head. 'What an idiot.' But Mum didn't reply. She looked as if she might burst into tears at any moment. 'Please tell me you're not having second thoughts about this,' Viggo implored her.

'I just need time alone to get my head straight,' said Mum, and she strode away along the corridor.

Back in his room, Viggo couldn't relax. He stood in front of the dolls' house and pondered its sudden appearance here. He knew it hadn't existed before he'd had the dream about it, and so he asked himself, had his weird visions somehow made it real and brought it here? And, if so, could he bring other things? What if he dreamt about a Rockhopper, for instance? He imagined waking up to find it standing in the room, brand new and shining. Wouldn't that be something?

He was just crouching down to take a closer look at the dolls' house when somebody rapped on his door, and, just as he stood up, Magnus strode into the room, looking self-important and carrying a sheet of paper.

'That the ND whatsit?' asked Viggo excitedly, hurrying over to him.

'The NDA.' Magnus corrected him. 'Yes, this is it.' He seemed irritable about something. 'I can't believe you pulled that stunt back there,' he complained.

'What stunt?'

'You know perfectly well! Asking Zack for money like that!

You cheeky little sod! I didn't know where to put myself.'

Viggo took the sheet from him. 'You're just mad cos you didn't think of it,' he said. A new thought occurred to him. 'How much is Zack paying *you*?'

'That's my business,' snapped Magnus. 'And besides, this may surprise you, but not everything is about money.' He watched as Viggo made a valiant attempt to read through the tiny print on the page. 'I wouldn't bother,' he said. 'It's all corporate-speak. Basically, it just says that you can't tell anybody about *anything* that happens here. And Viggo, if you do decide to sign it, you'll have to keep your word.'

'What happens if I don't?'

'You know perfectly well. Zack will sue for every penny you and Mum have got.'

'Fair enough, I suppose.' Viggo sighed, dreamily. 'Anyway, I wasn't thinking about blabbing. I'm just thinking about my new bike.'

'What new bike?'

'The one I'm going to buy when the money comes through.'

Magnus looked weary. 'And to think you called *me* a capitalist,' he complained.

'I'm not usually,' said Viggo. 'But, like . . . he's giving it away! I'd be stupid to say no. I still don't get why Leon turned him down.'

'I don't get Leon full stop,' muttered Magnus.

Viggo thought for a moment. 'So, you've signed one of these things, right?'

Magnus nodded.

'And he didn't pay you anything to do it?'

'Will you please stop going on about money?'

'But come on, think about it! Zack will give me all that dough just to keep quiet about what's going on here. Which will be easy, cos I haven't got much idea anyway.' He thought for a moment. 'Why was he so keen to employ you?' he asked.

'Why do you think?' snorted Magnus. 'I know my subject.'

'Yeah, but you said it yourself, this is a big operation; he can afford the best people on the planet. Instead, he went for you.'

'Thanks for the shout out,' muttered Magnus. He shrugged. 'Once you get to know Zack, you'll understand that he operates purely on instinct. He told me that from the first moment he spoke to me, he knew that I was the right person to head this up.'

Viggo made a heart shape with his hands. 'Aw, it was love at first sight!' he trilled.

'Yeah, very funny.' Magnus reached into a shirt pocket and took out a pen. 'Just sign the form.'

Viggo frowned, but took the pen and went across to a nearby table to add his signature on the dotted line. 'When do I get it?' he asked.

'Within thirty days,' said Magnus.

'What about Mum. Did she sign?'

Magnus nodded and waved another sheet of paper. He still had a scowl on his face. 'The way she acted you'd think I'd asked her to sign away her firstborn child. That's me, by the way. In case you were wondering.'

'First isn't always best,' Viggo reminded him. He noticed

Magnus's glum expression. 'What's up with you?' he asked. 'You should be happy about this.'

'Happy! You're a chancer, that's all. And you showed me up good and proper.'

'Yeah, but think about it. The next time you need money for one of your crackpot schemes, you can come to me.'

'Oh, that's big of you. Assuming you haven't spent it all on bicycles.'

Viggo studied him for a moment. 'There's something else, isn't there?' he murmured. 'Something you're not telling me.'

Magnus gave him an aggrieved look. 'Zack told me to ask you if ...'

'Yeah? Spit it out.'

'... if you wanted to come with us.'

Viggo was puzzled by the question. 'Come with you where?' he asked.

Magnus took a deep breath. 'Where do you think? To the site.'

'What, you mean ... like, underground and everything?'

'Yeah, I know, stupid, right? I'll tell him you're not interested.'

'Whoa, hang on a minute! Let me think about it. Why does he want me along?'

'God knows! He seems to have some weird notion that you're in tune with it all. He has this theory that kids have a strong connection to the paranormal.'

'Is that what's down there? Ghosts and stuff?'

'No. Not exactly.' Magnus made a dismissive gesture. 'Anyway, Zack told me to ask you. Now I have and you're not interested, so that's fine.'

'Wait a minute! When are you going?'

'I'm expecting a call from the people at the site any time now. As soon as it comes through, me and Zack are heading off for the first recce.' Magnus thought for a moment. 'You'd need to OK it with Mum,' he added. 'If you decide you're in.'

'Don't talk soft,' said Viggo. 'If I tell *her* about it, there's no way she'll let me go. She still thinks I'm a kid.'

Magnus sighed. 'I wonder where she could have got that notion?' he muttered.

Viggo gave Magnus a sharp look. 'Oh right. That's what you want, isn't it? You don't want me there and if Mum says no, that's your excuse. "Ooh, sorry Zack, Alison says NO!"'

Magnus scowled. 'If you want the truth, I think it's a stupid idea, you coming along. I told Zack: *Viggo's just a kid. He knows nothing!*'

'Oh, now it's you bigging *me* up!'

Magnus ignored the remark. 'Zack's weird. Like I said, he acts on instinct – and when he gets something into his head, he will not let it go. I can't imagine why, but for some reason he's impressed by you.'

'You're jealous,' said Viggo with a grin.

'Don't be ridiculous. Jealousy doesn't come into it. I just think it's ridiculous. I mean, you're fifteen; you're not old enough to make a decision like that. And it could be dangerous.'

'Dangerous, like how?'

'I honestly don't know. The truth is, we've no clue what's waiting down there.'

'But what do you *think* is there? You must have some idea.'

Magnus shook his head. 'It could be nothing at all.'

'You don't believe that. Why would you have spent so much

time working on it if you think it's just a hole in the ground?' He thought for a moment. 'Maybe I *should* go with you. Maybe Zack's got the right idea about me.'

'What's that supposed to mean?'

'Maybe I *do* have a connection.'

'Oh yeah? How do you make that out?'

'See that?' Viggo pointed across the room to the dolls' house. 'Do you ever remember seeing that before?'

Magnus stared at it for a moment, then shook his head. 'I don't think so.'

'But you've been in this room before, haven't you?'

'I suppose.'

'So, here's the thing. That dolls' house wasn't here until *I* brought it.'

'What do you mean, you *brought* it?'

'I dreamt about it last night and when I woke up . . . there it was.'

Magnus laughed. 'Get lost! You're making it up.'

'I'm not though. It's like I was telling you before. I keep having these dreams and they're not like ordinary ones. And this time, I woke up from one and the dolls' house was just standing there. And listen! You know who was playing with it in the dream?'

Magnus shrugged. 'Don't tell me. Somebody from one of your D&D games?'

'No, nothing like that.' Viggo crossed the room and indicated the framed portrait on the wall. 'These two kids. The children of Thomas and Iris McKendrick, who used to own this house.'

Magnus stared at him suspiciously. 'Where did you get those names from?'

Viggo tapped the frame. 'They're written right here,' he said. Magnus crossed the room to take a closer look. He grunted.

'I can't make head nor tail of that,' he protested.

'Neither could I, actually. But Leon already knew about them. He told me they disappeared, the whole family. They went off on a picnic one day and were never seen again. This was like back in the 1800s or something.'

Magnus scowled. 'Leon again. How come he knows so much about everything? I've been working here for months and it's the first I've heard about these people. What's his deal? I don't trust him. You saw how he turned Zack's money down like it meant nothing?'

'Yeah. That *was* weird.'

'Mum hated the thought of it too but in the end, even *she* couldn't bring herself to say no. But Leon Bragg?' He adopted a posh accent. '"Oh, the freedom to talk is not something I'm willing to sell". Like he's the Scarlet frickin' Pimpernel or something.'

'The who?'

'Never mind. You just make sure you don't tell him anything he might report back to others.' Magnus moved across to the dolls' house and crouched down to take a closer look at it. He reached out a hand and tapped experimentally at the walls with his fingers. 'It's solid enough,' he said. He shook his head. 'It must have been here all along but for some reason, you didn't notice it.'

'Are you kidding? Look at the size of it! How could I miss that?'

'Viggo, I added a writing desk to my room at home and you didn't notice it for six months!'

Viggo opened his mouth to reply but the phone in Magnus's back pocket started buzzing. He took it out and lifted it to his ear. 'Yes?' he said expectantly. There was a pause and Viggo could hear the insect-like buzz of an unfamiliar voice at the other end of the line. 'OK, thanks. We'll be with you in twenty.' Magnus signed off and clicked another number – somebody answered almost immediately. 'Zack?' said Magnus. 'Vahalla is code green. I repeat, code green. I'll meet you downstairs in five.' He signed off again and returned the phone to his pocket.

Viggo stared at him. 'Vahalla is code green?' he echoed. 'Seriously? Have you been watching old episodes of *Thunderbirds* or something?'

He'd been hoping for at least a grin, but Magnus didn't react. 'OK,' he said. 'I need to get moving. It's your choice. Are you coming or staying?'

'Can I think about it for five minutes?'

'We don't *have* five minutes. It's now or never.'

'I'm not sure I . . .'

Magnus turned and started for the door, as though dismissing him.

'Just give me a couple of minutes!' Viggo shouted after him. 'There's something I need to do.'

Magnus didn't even look back. 'If you're not there, we'll go without you,' he called back.

'I'll be there! Just . . . wait, OK?'

Viggo pulled his phone from his pocket and dialled Mum's number. He knew all too well that she always kept her phone on silent, tucked away in her bag, and rarely ever had it with her. He was gambling on her not hearing him and, sure enough, after a couple of rings it clicked to voicemail and he heard her recorded voice apologising for the fact that she couldn't come to the phone right now.. For some reason, he opened FaceTime and left her a message, talking quickly, not sure of what he needed to say, but realising that if anything bad should happen to him, she wouldn't even know where he'd gone. After what had happened to Dad, he couldn't do that to her. He just couldn't.

It all came out in a breathless rush and all the time he was terrified that she would actually answer the phone and interrupt him. Thankfully, she didn't. He gasped out the last few words and rang off, then shoved his phone back into his pocket.

'Love you Mum,' he murmured, then heard Magnus shout up to him from the staircase. He ran after him and caught up with him halfway down the big staircase. Magnus half-turned to look at him, his eyebrows raised.

'You're sure about this?' he murmured.

'Yes,' said Viggo. 'Definitely. But listen, if Mum gives me earache about it later on, you'll help me explain it to her, right?'

Magnus considered for a moment, then shook his head. 'You're on your own,' he said. 'So if you can't handle it, go back now.'

But Viggo stayed with him and they descended the staircase side by side.

# CHAPTER 23
## HEADING OFF

They emerged from the front entrance to find Zack already waiting for them on the steps. He was dressed in what looked like a black combat outfit, complete with sturdy leather boots and motorbike gloves. But he still wore the orange beanie, which, Viggo thought, looked decidedly odd. Magnus's Range Rover was parked on the gravel, just a short distance away. Zack nodded to Magnus and grinned at Viggo.

'You decided to come,' he observed. 'Good. I was hoping you would.' He glanced at Magnus. 'Did you get those NDAs?'

Magnus nodded, reached into his fleece and handed the papers to Zack.

'Great,' he said. He gave them a brief look over, then folded them and slid them into a concealed pocket in his jacket. He looked at Viggo thoughtfully. 'Remember, we have a deal,' he said. 'You don't talk about what you see to anyone. Agreed?'

'Agreed,' said Viggo.

'Excellent.' Zack turned his head to look at Magnus. 'We got an extra helmet for the kid?'

'There are spares in the boot,' said Magnus. 'One of them should fit him.' He walked to the Range Rover, opened the driver's door and slid in behind the wheel.

Zack went around to the passenger side so Viggo climbed in behind Magnus.

'Last chance to change your mind,' murmured Magnus, studying Viggo intently in the rearview mirror. Viggo thought about it for a few moments, then shook his head.

'I'm good,' he said.

Magnus started up the engine and they drove away from the house without looking back.

\*\*\*

They sped along a narrow dirt track, the hills stretching away on every side of them, with no sign of a building in any direction. It was a dry day but the skies were piled with heaps of tumbled grey clouds that seemed to threaten rain. They had come this far in total silence and Viggo was beginning to get antsy.

'So . . . how did you find out about this thing . . . whatever it is?' he ventured.

Magnus gave him a glare in the rearview mirror, as if warning him to keep his mouth shut, but Zack didn't seem to mind. 'It's OK,' he said. 'The kid's coming with us, he deserves to know a little more.' He turned to look back at Viggo. 'A contact of mine found a map,' he said. 'He's a professor at Yale and he discovered a scrap of old parchment hidden away in the back of an ancient book on Norse mythology. There were coordinates on there, which he was able to pinpoint to Unst. Of course, he really should have handed it to his employers, but he knew of my interest in such matters.' Zack grinned. 'He also knew that he was coming up to retirement and didn't have much of a nest egg put aside. So he offered it to me at a price.'

'Couldn't it be some kind of forgery?' asked Viggo suspiciously.

Zack grinned as though he liked Viggo's style. 'First thing that occurred to me. I had it checked out, of course, carbon dated and everything. It was created some time in the 1600s.' He reached into his jacket and pulled out a square of paper inside a transparent protective cover. He handed it back to Viggo. 'That's just a photocopy,' he said. 'The original is in a safe place, but I like to carry that with me. There's an interesting little poem there too . . .'

Viggo took the sheet and studied it thoughtfully. It had been drawn in ink and was faint with age, the original black faded to grey. The map had been drawn over a grid of vertical and horizontal lines. Viggo decided that the little oblong to the bottom left of it, which was marked 'MANSE', could only be the old house that Zack had rechristened Asgard. Away to the top right of the map was a single cross with the letter 'V' beneath it and, below that, what looked like random numbers, which Viggo could make neither head nor tail of.

'What are these?' he asked, tapping them with his index finger.

'Coordinates,' said Magnus. 'Lines of latitude and longitude. That's how we were able to pinpoint the location.' He glanced at Zack. 'I told you he knows nothing,' he said, apologetically.

'Yeah, funnily enough, we don't do any of this in school,' snapped Viggo.

Zack laughed at that, but Magnus just looked annoyed.

Viggo turned his attention to the poem that Zack had mentioned, which was written across the top of the page in strange loopy handwriting.

*Behold the bough that marks the place*
*And there the seeker's path you trace.*
*Descend the steps beneath the ground*
*Where famed Yggdrasil's roots are found.*
*Walk on in silent contemplation . . .*
*Valhalla is your destination.*

'Wow,' said Viggo.

Zack looked at him. 'What do you make of it?' he asked.

'Not sure.' Viggo frowned. 'This . . . Yggdrasil,' he murmured. 'I'm not even sure if I'm pronouncing it right . . .'

'You're not,' Magnus assured him.

Zack smiled encouragingly. 'Never mind that. What about it?'

'Isn't that like a famous tree or something?'

Zack looked impressed. 'You've studied Norse mythology?' he asked.

Viggo shook his head. 'No, but I'm pretty sure Leon mentioned it at one point.'

Zack and Magnus exchanged worried looks. It was clear that both of them were very nervous about Leon and hated to be reminded of his existence. 'How did it happen to come up?' asked Magnus.

Viggo thought for a moment. 'We went to this cafe in Lerwick,' he explained. 'It was called The Well. And Leon said it was probably a reference to the Well of . . . Ern?'

'Urd,' Magnus corrected him.

'Yeah, that. And then he said it might also refer to this . . .' He pointed to the word and had another go at saying it aloud. 'Eeg-draz-eel? Is that right?'

'Close enough,' said Zack. 'What do you make of the poem's ending?'

'Well, it seems to be saying that following the tree's roots will take you to Valhalla. That's like the home of the gods, right?'

Zack nodded. 'Yup,' he said. 'You got it in one.' He extended a gloved hand to take the map back and replaced it carefully into his jacket.

'But . . . what's down there?' asked Viggo.

'That's what we hope to find out,' said Zack. He grinned. 'If everything goes according to plan we could be sending out postcards from there pretty soon.'

'Postcards from Valhalla,' murmured Viggo. 'Cool.'

The Range Rover crested a rise and moved down into the valley below. Some distance off, Viggo could see a collection of big yellow vehicles waiting at either side of the dirt track – various bulldozers and tractors and pieces of equipment he couldn't even put a name to. Men and women in hard hats and high-viz jackets stood around as though waiting, some of them smoking cigarettes, others sipping mugs of tea or coffee. Magnus slowed as he approached the cluster of workers and one of them, a lanky middle-aged fellow, detached himself from the others and came forward to meet them. Magnus brought the Range Rover to a halt and clicked the button to open Zack's window. The man stooped to peer in at them. 'Right on time,' he said, in a broad Scottish accent. 'You two ...' He noted Viggo in the back and amended his query. 'You *three* all ready to go?'

'We are,' said Magnus. 'You've cleared the site?'

The man nodded. 'Completely. And we've double-reinforced that entry tunnel, just to be on the safe side.'

'Nobody else has taken a look down there?' asked Zack sharply.

'Nobody, Mr Strode. I was very insistent about that. Told them they'd be dismissed if I found out they'd been snooping. And they have sensors hidden in their overalls. If anybody tried to go further than they're allowed, they'd kick off the alarms. I know how important it is for you to be first, so I made sure every angle is covered. We'll all stay at a distance but, if you should need us, you just have to dial in a code red and we'll be there in minutes.'

Zack nodded. He took a deep breath and then nodded to Magnus, who put the car into gear and drove on, leaving the workmen behind. After travelling for another hundred metres or so, they came to a ridge and, from here, the ground sloped steeply down. A bulldozer could have negotiated it, but not a Range Rover. Magnus pulled the vehicle to a halt.

'Now we continue on foot,' he told Viggo, and climbed out of the car.

Viggo did as he was told and Magnus went around to the boot. He opened it, revealing a jumble of equipment in the back. He pulled out what looked like a climber's helmet, equipped with a light on the front, and handed it to Viggo.

'This looks about your size,' he said. 'Just tap this button here to switch on the light.'

Viggo placed the helmet on his head and it seemed to fit him fine. He tested the button but Magnus switched it straight off again. 'Save your power for when you need it,' he said. Magnus located another helmet and handed it to Zack as he came strolling around the side of the vehicle.

Zack removed the beanie hat and in the few seconds it took him to don the helmet, Viggo noticed that the man was virtually bald, just a few wisps of hair left around his ears and the back of his neck. He pushed the beanie into his pocket and then looked at his companions. 'Well,' he said, 'I guess it's time.' He took out a rucksack and slung it around his shoulders. 'I can't believe we're finally about to do this,' he said, and Viggo thought he had the wide-eyed look of a little boy about to visit an adventure playground. 'Over a year of preparation, hundreds of thousands of dollars paid out and it all comes down to this one moment.' He looked at Magnus. 'You realise it might all have been for nothing,' he added. 'It could be one of the most expensive wild goose chases in history.'

Magnus smiled. 'I've got a good feeling about it,' he said. 'You lead the way.'

Zack nodded, and then the confident grin was back on his face. 'Let's do this,' he said.

He turned and started to descend the rocky track. As he moved away, Viggo noticed something worrying. Zack was wearing a leather holster from which the handle of a gun protruded.

Viggo glared at his brother. 'He's armed!' he hissed under his breath.

Magnus shrugged. 'Not taking any chances,' he said calmly. 'We don't know what we'll find down there. Now listen, stay behind me at all times. If I tell you to head back, don't hang around. Just run. You hear me?'

Viggo nodded and watched as Magnus went after Zack, placing his feet with care on the steep path. For the first time, Viggo had a terrible sense of impending danger. Magnus seemed to sense it and turned to look up at him. 'Stay by the car if you're worried,' he murmured.

Viggo shook his head. 'No way,' he whispered. 'You're not leaving me behind.'

And he followed his companions down the slope.

# CHAPTER 24
## YGGDRASIL

After a short distance, the ground levelled out again and they were walking along the bottom of a wide gulley with walls of rock rising sheer on either side of them. Then, up ahead, Viggo saw a place where the ground had been cleared, the earth rutted with tyre tracks, big mounds of dirt and rock piled around it. A great shape reared up from the centre of the cleared space: a weird, twisted stump that appeared to be made of grey stone and yet had all the properties of a tree, pretty much the first one Viggo had seen since his arrival in Shetland. There was a stout, gnarled trunk which rose straight up for perhaps eight metres or so before diverging into what appeared to be several branches, all of which were broken and ended in jagged stumps. It put Viggo in mind of a giant hand, reaching up from the dirt.

'That's it?' he murmured incredulously. 'That's what all the fuss is about?'

Zack glanced back at him in surprise. 'You're disappointed?' he asked.

'I was expecting something . . . bigger,' said Viggo. 'Cooler. It's supposed to be the tree of the gods, isn't it? Is it even made of wood?'

'Petrified wood,' Zack told him.

'What, you mean, like, scared or something?'

'It's fossilised,' explained Magnus patiently. 'Turned to stone. We've tried carbon dating it, but it's off the scale. Can't seem to get a reliable fix on it. But it's old. Very old. As in, millions of years. We're pretty sure that this is Yggdrasil.'

'The great tree of Norse mythology actually exists,' said Zack. 'Think about that for a moment. Awesome, huh?'

Viggo had been about to say that the tree was one of the ugliest things he had ever set eyes on, but he just smiled and nodded.

As they made their way closer, Viggo could see that, deeper into the cleared ground, the tree's roots had been exposed. In one place, they had been excavated enough to form a rough arch, an opening that resembled a natural doorway. Viggo also saw that metal reinforcing struts had been installed around the entrance to shore it up.

'When we first found it,' explained Magnus, 'there'd been some kind of a rock fall.' He pointed through the opening. 'The entrance was plugged with rubble for quite some distance. It had to be carefully dug out, a little bit at a time. But only far enough to clear the obstruction. I was very insistent about that. I told them, this is Zack's project and he's earnt the right to be the first to explore the place.' And he glanced at Zack, as though seeking approval.

But Zack was already leading the way down into the declivity. He got to the entrance and stood for a moment, peering into the darkness. Then he turned and gestured to Magnus. 'Let's get some pictures of me before I go in there,' he suggested. He adopted a pose in front of the opening, his arms crossed, his legs widely spaced, that confident grin back on his face. Magnus fished his phone out of his pocket and took the role of photographer, shooting off what seemed like a whole sequence of photographs, until Zack finally waved a hand to signal that it was enough.

'OK,' he said. He reached up a gloved hand and tapped the button on his helmet, switching on the light, then turned back to peer into the opening. 'This is quite a moment,' he announced. 'I'm feeling excited.' Viggo caught a brief glimpse of shadowy red walls within, the moving light seeming to make them undulate. 'Stick close behind me, guys,' said Zack, and he stooped to step under the arch. Magnus switched on his own light but paused for a moment to look back at Viggo.

'If for any reason you get freaked out,' he murmured, 'just retrace your steps and wait for us by the car.' For the first time in ages, Magnus seemed less than sure of himself. He turned away and followed Zack through the opening. Viggo hesitated for a moment, telling himself that it wasn't too late to change his mind, but knew in that same moment that he would never forgive himself if he missed this opportunity. And besides, if he *did* chicken out, Magnus would never stop reminding him about it. He reached up a hand, tapped his own helmet switch and moved towards the entrance. He took a deep breath and stepped inside.

He stood for a moment, disorientated, and saw that the beam of light had picked out a central core of thick roots, all twisted and tangled around each other, leading straight down. Light flashed to his left and he turned his head to see that the others were moving away from him, heading down a steep incline. It took Viggo a few moments to figure out what was happening. He finally realised that around the roots, there was a kind of huge spiral staircase, which cut downwards through solid rock – a series of roughly hewn steps that had somehow been sculpted out of the stone. It reminded Viggo of an old church tower he'd visited some years back, though this was on a much bigger scale. He caught a glimpse of Magnus's face, glancing back at him from under the light on his helmet, and Viggo gave his brother a thumbs up before following, placing his feet carefully on the steps, aware of occasional bits of gravel slipping under the soles of his trainers. Looking down, his lamp picked out the fact that the steps had only recently been scraped free of dirt and rubble and he told himself that this must be the section that the workmen had already cleared, the part that had been obstructed by a rock fall. To his right, the tangle of petrified roots continued downwards. They were as thick as tree branches, intertwined with each other, as though fighting for supremacy as they burrowed deeper and deeper to whatever lay below.

Viggo found himself wondering who had made these steps. Everything about them spoke of ancient times and he suspected that no machinery had been employed to cut them out of the solid rock, just hours of hard toil with hammers and chisels.

He heard Zack's voice up ahead, announcing that he had now reached 'the flag'.

'What flag?' asked Viggo, aware that his own voice had acquired an eerie echo.

'It marks the point where the team stopped excavating,'

said Magnus, matter-of-factly. 'From here on in, it's undiscovered territory.'

They continued onwards, moving deeper and deeper beneath ground. Viggo became suddenly aware of how hot it was down here. Drops of sweat ran from under the brim of his helmet and into his eyes – and there was a powerful, sulphurous odour too, that seemed to rise in waves around him. 'You smell that?' he asked nervously and heard Magnus grunt a reply.

'Yeah. It's nothing to worry about.'

'How do you know?'

'I have a whole bunch of gadgets attached to my belt. They'll detect anything dangerous and warn me about it in advance. If that happens, we just turn around and head back. I've got breathing apparatus in the Range Rover. We'll put that on and give it another try.'

'You've thought of everything, haven't you?'

'I believe so. Now pipe down, we need to— What the . . .?'

Viggo bumped suddenly against Magnus's rucksack and realised that his companions had come to a sudden halt, the combined beams of their lamps directed at something that was tangled in the column of roots to their right. Both men were breathing hard. Viggo tried to focus on whatever it was they were looking at and then the beam of his light settled.

'Holy cow,' he heard Zack say.

Something was caught up in the roots, as though imprisoned by them. It was a skeletal figure, rotted down to bare bones, hands clawing at something out of its reach, jaws open wide and blind eye sockets staring. The figure was still partially clad in the tattered mouldering remains of what had once been a green satin dress.

'Iris McKendrick,' said Viggo quietly.

There was a short puzzled silence.

'What's he talking about?' asked Zack.

'Huh? Oh, somebody he thinks used to live in Asgard,' muttered Magnus. 'He showed me a framed photograph in his room. Viggo claims this woman disappeared some time back in the 1800s.'

'There'll probably be others,' Viggo assured Magnus. 'Her husband and the two children. Oh, and maybe even Alistair, the coachman.'

'You're telling me that others have been here before us?' asked Zack incredulously. He didn't sound happy about it.

'We don't know for sure that's the case,' said Magnus.

'Well, what's this then?' demanded Zack, pointing at the skeleton. 'Scotch mist?'

There was some shuffling up ahead and now Zack was leaning sideways to stare up the steps at Viggo. 'Where did you get the information from?' he snarled. He glared at Magnus. 'And why is this the first I've heard of it?'

'To be fair, he only mentioned it to me just before we set off,' explained Magnus. 'I didn't know anything about it, I promise you. Viggo says . . .'

'Go on!'

'He says that Leon Bragg told him.'

Zack muttered something under his breath that sounded suspiciously like a curse. 'I'm going to have a long talk with

Bragg when we get back from here,' he said. 'I need to know who the hell he's working for.'

'I'm not sure he's working for anyone,' said Viggo.

'What's that supposed to mean?'

'I don't think anyone would trust him enough to give him a job.'

There was a long silence while they stood there, staring at each other in the uncertain light. Zack looked like he was about to have a tantrum, but somehow he made an effort and managed to get hold of himself. 'Come on,' he said at last, 'let's keep going.'

They moved onwards again but it wasn't long before they found the next skeleton, another full-sized figure, a man this time, tangled in stone branches just as his wife had been. The remnants of a striped blazer hung around his shoulders.

'How did these people ever find their way down here?' asked Zack.

'They went off on a picnic,' said Viggo. 'And were never heard from again.'

'But we researched this area. It never came up, not in any of the reading I did.'

'Me neither,' Magnus assured him.

'So how does Bragg know about it?'

Another long silence.

'I'm getting a bad feeling about this,' muttered Zack.

They moved on again and once more they stopped, a few steps further down, at the sight of two smaller skeletons trapped in the roots, their bony arms wrapped protectively around each other, their faces pushed into each other's shoulders. There were still tufts of hair on the skull of the girl. In the glare of the electric light it was hard to be sure, but Viggo thought it might have the same chestnut tones as the girl he'd encountered in his dream.

'I don't like this,' he said. 'It's getting too weird.'

'Head back up and wait for us,' suggested Magnus. 'You don't have to be down here.'

But Viggo shook his head stubbornly. Having come this far, he wasn't about to give up. When Magnus followed Zack, Viggo stayed close behind him, matching him step for step.

They seemed to walk for a very long time after that, the heat steadily rising until Viggo's clothes were sticking to him like wet flannels. Just as he was beginning to wonder if they'd ever stop descending, he turned a final circle and saw they had reached the bottom of the steps and that, from here, the ground levelled off and opened out. He was able to stand beside Magnus and Zack as they gazed around what appeared to be a huge underground cavern. Above them, the great tangled plug of roots rose upwards towards the surface – but here on level ground, they angled sharply and stretched horizontally away across a hard earth floor towards a distant circular opening in a wall of solid rock. It looked too symmetrical to be a product of nature. A dull red pulsing glow was coming from the opening and, for a moment, Viggo was reminded of the dream he'd had about the weird opening in the wall of the dolls' house.

Zack gave a jubilant cry and started eagerly towards it. Viggo and Magnus followed him – but they all slowed again as their combined lights picked out something sprawled on the ground ahead of them. Viggo saw that it was a man.

'Maybe that's the coachman?' ventured Viggo, but Magnus shook his head.

'Not unless he's been dressed by The North Face,' he said.

Viggo saw that he was right. The figure was wearing colourful contemporary clothing, an outdoor jacket and leather walking boots. He wore a helmet with a lamp attached, though it was evident its light must have died a long time ago. He was lying on his side. Though the flesh of his face was shrunken and wizened, it hadn't yet rotted through to the skull like the bodies they'd found earlier. Viggo noticed that one of the man's legs was lying at an odd angle, a jagged stump of bone protruding from waterproof material. His head was twisted to one side and his face seemed frozen in an eternal grimace of pain. As Viggo came closer, the beam of his lamp illuminated the face in more detail and he could see that the man's teeth were visible and that there was a distinctive gap between the two top incisors.

'What the hell is this?' asked Zack, bewildered, his voice echoing in the silence.

But Viggo was scrambling breathlessly forward, flinging himself down on to his hands and knees beside the fallen figure. A powerful surge of excitement flared within him. He could hardly believe what he was seeing. It was five years since he'd seen this man.

'Dad!' he gasped. He looked up at Magnus who was staring down at him, bewildered and apparently speechless. 'Magnus, can't you see? It's Dad!'

# CHAPTER 25
## REUNITED

There was a silence so deep that Viggo was aware of his own words echoing around the cavern and then bouncing back to him, eerily distorted.

*It's Dad! It's Dad! It's Dad . . .*

Magnus finally snapped out of his spell. He ran forward and kneeled beside Viggo, his breath emerging in a series of ragged gasps. 'Dad,' he hissed, and his voice was little more than a sigh. 'Oh God!' He reached out a hand and placed it on the dead man's shoulder. Then he was crying, tears pouring down his face. 'Oh Dad. I never thought I'd see you again!'

'What the hell is happening here?' demanded Zack, apparently furious that his great adventure had been sidelined by something inexplicable.

Magnus somehow managed to get hold of himself. He looked up at Zack, his face shiny with tears. 'It's my dad,' he gasped. 'Don't you remember, I told you about him? He disappeared in Shetland five years ago.'

'Your *dad*?' Zack didn't seem able to understand the simple word.

"Yes,' said Magnus. He gestured around. 'Don't you see?

He must have found the same map! Maybe there was another copy?'

'I was told mine was the only one,' insisted Zack stubbornly.

'Yes, but whoever sold it to you couldn't know that for sure.' Magnus glanced around. 'Don't you get it? Dad must have come here looking for the same thing as us. Only five years ago.' He gestured at the corpse's damaged leg. 'It's broken; he clearly fell, injured himself.' He gestured back towards the staircase behind him. 'And then I guess the rock came down behind him and sealed him in . . . oh, Jesus, he would have been trapped down here alone! I don't suppose anybody else knew where he was.' He gave another ragged sob and Viggo could only imagine what a horrible, slow death it must have been. Instinctively, he reached out and put an arm around Magnus's shoulders.

Zack was still trying to piece it together. 'You . . . *knew* about this?' he asked Magnus. 'You knew he was down here? You used me to get to your old man?'

'No, no, of course not! I had no idea. But this *is* him; I'd know him anywhere.' Magnus was still looking at Zack and, as he did so, Viggo leant in closer to his father, steeling himself to take a more detailed look. He saw now that, half covered by the body, there was a tattered notebook lying on the ground, open to a page with words written in Dad's meticulous hand. Without really thinking about it, Viggo grabbed the book and surreptitiously slipped it into his own pocket. It occurred to him that Zack might want to claim the notebook for himself and that didn't seem right, not before Viggo and Magnus had a chance to read its contents.

They would be Dad's final words.

Zack was staring down at Magnus, his hands on his hips. He looked furious.

'Well, see now . . . you're just going to have to leave him here,' he said. 'We can decide what to do about him later . . .'

'*Do* about him?' Magnus was puzzled. 'What do you mean? It's my *dad*, for Christ's sake. Obviously we're going to get him back up to the surface.'

Zack shook his head. 'No, no, we need to go on,' he said, speaking slowly as if to a child. 'This is an unexpected development, but we can't let it get in our way.' He pointed towards the circular opening in the rock. 'That looks like the obvious route forward. We have to go through that opening, find where it leads.'

'But . . .' Magnus shook his head and waved a hand at the body. 'I can't just leave him here, can I? It's my *dad*! We've spent years wondering what might have happened to him, hoping and praying he'd get in touch. He never did. And now we know why.' He turned to look at Viggo. 'Give me a hand, we need to get him out of here.'

'Never mind about him!' snarled Zack. He pointed again to the opening. '*That's* why we're here. That's what all the work was for, the reason I spent millions of dollars on this project. We're going that way.'

'We can come back to it,' Magnus assured him. 'There's no hurry; it's not like it's going anywhere. Right now, we have to—'

'You're not listening to me!' Zack's voice had risen to a shout that seemed to fill the entire cavern. He pointed down at Dad's prone figure. 'You think he matters?' he sneered. 'Forget him, he's a technicality. Just leave him where he is and come with me. We could be on the verge of something really important here. Something big. Just do the job I'm paying you for!'

Magnus bowed his head for a moment. He was breathing hard. 'And I'm saying it can surely wait a little longer. You need to let me—'

'You think I want to be associated with *that*?' asked Zack, pointing again at Dad's corpse. 'If anyone up above gets a look at the body, word will get out. All kinds of people will come sniffing around.' He shook his head. 'No, no, I can't allow myself to be associated with this. I won't.' He started pacing around as though trying to reason it out. 'And besides, I was supposed to be the first one here!' Viggo thought he sounded suddenly like a little boy about to have a temper tantrum. 'I mean, none of this is what I expected. We've just found the skeletons of an entire family and then you tell me your old man was here five frickin' years ago! I spent a fortune organising this! Millions of dollars. This was supposed to be *mine*!' He shook his head again. 'So, you listen to me, kid. I know this isn't what you want to hear – I appreciate it's going to be hard for you – but we need to leave him down here. We'll find some way of concealing the body . . .'

'Concealing it?' cried Magnus. 'What the hell are you on about? We're not doing that! We'll take him back up, so he can have a decent burial and my mum can have closure.'

'The hell with your mother!' yelled Zack. 'Damned woman, coming here and poking her nose in where it isn't wanted!

I can't allow you to take him up where others will see him. I *won't* allow it.'

Magnus got slowly to his feet and walked across to face Zack. Viggo watched the encounter nervously.

'You won't allow it?' echoed Magnus. He shook his head. 'Who do you think you are?'

'I know exactly who I am. I'm one of the most powerful men on the planet and I'm the one calling the shots here. I *own* you, and I'm telling you to do the job I pay you to do.'

'You *own* me?' Magnus glared at him, and for a moment Viggo thought he might be about to throw one of his famous punches, but somehow he managed to get control of himself. 'OK,' he said. 'This is easily fixed. I quit.'

Zack glared at him. 'You *what*?'

'You heard me. I quit. Me and Viggo are going to carry my dad back up to the surface. If you want to continue on without us, then be my guest.'

'Nobody quits on me,' growled Zack. 'I bought you. You hear me? I'm ordering you to stay.'

'I already told you,' snapped Magnus. 'I don't work for you any more. You're on your own.'

'You won't be paid!'

''Who cares? Stuff your money.'

Magnus turned away and started to walk back to his brother, but stopped when he heard a sharp click behind him. Viggo saw that Zack had pulled the gun from its holster and was pointing it at Magnus.

'Do your job,' he said.

Magnus turned slowly around. There was a long silence

while the three of them stared at each other in the uncertain light.

And then Viggo turned his head at the unexpected sound of somebody whistling a cheerful tune. It seemed to be emerging from the open mouth of the red tunnel on the far side of the cavern. As Viggo studied it, in stunned disbelief, he saw that something was moving about in there – and, as he watched, a slight figure emerged from the opening and came ambling out towards them, hands in pockets, apparently without a care in the world.

As they all watched, speechless, as the figure moved steadily closer, still whistling and clearly amused by the baffled expressions on their faces. Leon had no lamp or any other form of lighting but he seemed perfectly able to pick his way across the rocky ground without stumbling, even in those ridiculous leather sandals. He came to a halt just a few metres away from them and said, 'Well, well, fancy meeting you guys!'

Zack reacted by swinging the gun away from Magnus and aiming it instead at Leon's chest. 'What are you doing down here?' he muttered.

'Waiting for you, of course,' said Leon cheerfully. 'And I have to say, that's not a very polite welcome. It's a good job I'm not easily offended.' He transferred his attention to Viggo, who was still crouching beside Dad's body. 'So,' he said. 'I see you finally found what you were looking for. I'm glad to have been of help.'

'Help?' murmured Viggo. 'But . . . I wasn't looking for my dad.'

'Of course you were,' said Leon. 'You just didn't realise it.'

'Who the hell *are* you?' growled Zack. 'Who do you work for?'

Leon seemed to consider the question for a moment. 'I'm whatever you want to call me,' he said. 'And I don't really work for anyone. But I *do* like to help people. I'm funny like that.' Again, he smiled at Viggo. 'Remember when I met you and your mother on the boat? I said I'd help you find your brother, didn't I?'

Viggo nodded silently.

'And then, when we found Magnus, I realised that my work wasn't finished. I knew that I could help a little more . . . that both of you needed to find your father. Tell me, I'm dying to know. How does it feel?'

Viggo thought for a moment. 'It feels . . . incredible' he murmured. 'I mean, sad too, but . . . now we know he didn't just leave us. I'd forgotten how much I wanted to find him, back when I was little.' He looked at Magnus. 'What do you say?'

Magnus nodded, lifting an arm to wipe his tears on his sleeve. 'It feels like a weight coming off,' he whispered. 'Knowing that he couldn't help what happened. That he was prevented from ever coming home to us. It feels like a blessing.'

Zack shook his head. It was clear he was becoming impatient. 'This is all very touching,' he said, 'but I haven't finished asking questions.' He took a step closer to Leon. 'What were you doing in my tunnel?' he demanded.

'*Your* tunnel?' Leon looked amused. 'I'm sorry, I didn't realise you owned it.'

'I made all this happen,' said Zack. 'We wouldn't be here if it wasn't for me.'

'Point taken, but I'm afraid no amount of money can buy what's on the other side of that entrance. I was just down there taking care of business. The truth is, this whole place is something that should have been shut down a long time ago. But you know how it is with those irritating little jobs. You keep putting them off, don't you? "I'll do it later", you tell yourself. But you never quite get around to it. And besides, there was a good reason to keep it going a bit longer. Now the boys have found their father, there's no reason not to shut it down.'

Zack was losing his patience. 'What in God's name are you talking about?' he roared. 'How did you even get in here before us? There was a twenty-four-hour guard on this place. You . . .'

Leon lifted a hand to his lips to silence Zack. 'Listen carefully, because there isn't much time,' he said. 'In about ten minutes, this whole place is going to come down around you. I strongly advise that you're not here when it happens.'

'Yeah, right,' sneered Zack. 'And how exactly is that going to come about?' His eyes widened as though something had just occurred to him. 'You've planted explosives?''

'Oh, nothing so crude. The mechanics are complicated and I doubt I could explain them to somebody of your limited intellect. Just trust me when I say, it *will* happen and nothing is going to stop it. I'm quite sure that if the three of you work together, you'll be able to get Jonathan's body safely up to the surface before everything collapses. But I wouldn't hang about.'

'The hell with that!' snarled Zack. 'I'm going down that tunnel. I paid for the privilege. I need to see what's down there.'

'Trust me, you really don't,' Leon assured him. 'It's not something for the eyes of a man like you. A man who prizes money above all else. A man who has lived his life spending it without a thought for the consequences. A plunderer.

A charlatan.' He pointed again to the tunnel. 'That's a place for the mighty, for the champions, for the ones who have earnt their right to be there. You? I hate to break this to you, Mr Strode, but you're nothing.'

'You say that,' snarled Zack, 'but I could have you snuffed out like a candle!' He snapped his fingers in front of Leon's face.

'Not if you die here,' Leon assured him. 'And you will die, very soon, if you don't head for the surface *now*. There are things in that tunnel that will boil your brain inside your skull. Creatures that will feast on your flesh, others that will fling you headlong into madness. And your millions won't save you from any of it. In there, material wealth is worthless; meaningless. Of course, if you insist on going in, then who am I to stop you?' He stepped aside and gestured towards the opening. 'Go ahead. Explore! Suffice to say, if that's your choice, you'll never live to tell anybody what you've seen. And I should have thought the examples you've witnessed on your way ought to tell you that humans have no place in this realm. Look what happened to the McKendricks. Lured here by the thought of the treasures they might find. And that was when it was much easier to gain access . . .' He broke off at the sound of a deep rumbling. Thin columns of dust began to spiral down from the ceiling. 'I really hate to hurry you,' he said, 'but I'm afraid the process has begun.'

'You're bluffing,' said Zack.

'Suit yourself.' Leon looked at Viggo and Magnus. 'Boys, I'd get a move on if I were you. Don't make the mistake of thinking you owe Strode anything.' He turned and began to stroll back towards the tunnel, whistling that same jolly tune.

'Stay where you are!' roared Zack. 'I'm warning you.' He was still holding the gun but now it was trained on Leon's back.

'Viggo,' snapped Magnus. 'Give me a hand here.' He moved to Dad's body and took a firm grip of his shoulders. Viggo went to get the legs. He had a moment of overwhelming repugnance, but then reminded himself that this was still his dad, that he deserved to be finally released from his prison. He and Magnus lifted the body clear of the ground and Viggo was amazed to find that Dad didn't seem to weigh half as much as he'd expected, though it was still a struggle supporting that lanky frame between them. 'Zack,' shouted Magnus. 'We could do with some help here . . .'

But Zack was still staring at Leon's retreating figure. 'Come back!' he roared. 'That's an order! If you don't stop now, I'll shoot.'

Leon didn't bother to turn his head. He just lifted one arm in a carefree wave.

'Last chance!' yelled Zack.

Leon kept the arm raised but changed the gesture, leaving just the middle finger upright.

Zack pulled the trigger. The sound of the shot seemed to fill the entire cavern like a crack of thunder and Viggo's eyes could scarcely credit what happened next. Something impossible.

Leon's body literally broke apart and reassembled itself into a flock of flapping, black shapes – crows, Viggo thought, though in the uncertain light he couldn't be absolutely sure.

As he watched, wide-eyed in astonishment, the birds flew away towards the tunnel and were absorbed into that perfect circle of red. Viggo glanced at Magnus, but he'd been facing away from the action, concentrating on the task of carrying Jonathan. By the time he turned his head to look for the source of the noise, it was all over – but he couldn't miss Viggo's astonished expression.

'What?' he gasped. 'What happened?'

Viggo could only stare back at him, open-mouthed.

'Birds happened,' he whispered.

The sound of the gunshot faded and was replaced by a deeper, more ominous, rumbling. Viggo could feel the ground starting to shudder beneath his feet. He and Magnus looked at each other in alarm, then started up the spiral steps, struggling to carry Dad's long body between them.

Viggo heard Zack shout a curse and then he too was running back towards the steps, clearly with the intention of pushing right past Viggo and Magnus, but at the last moment, Magnus threw out a hand and grabbed Zack by the arm, yanking him closer.

'We're struggling here,' he said. 'Help us.'

'Why should I?' snarled Zack. 'You've messed up this whole damned thing.'

Magnus pushed his face closer to the American's. 'I'm not asking you,' he yelled. 'Give us a hand or I swear I'll knock you flat and leave you down here.'

A thought flashed through Viggo's mind. *Go Magnus!*

There was a long terrible moment while the two men stared at each other through the rain of dust that was sifting down from above. Viggo was uncomfortably aware of solid stone shaking violently beneath him.

'We're running out of time,' he warned them.

Zack grimaced and reluctantly took hold of Jonathan's body around the waist. Together the three of them started back up the steps, aware, as they stumbled onwards, that the stones around them were beginning to break apart. Large chunks of rock started to fall, smashing into pieces as they hit the ground, flinging up fragments of grit that stung their faces. Viggo was aware of dust clogging his nostrils, making his eyes water, but he gritted his teeth and kept on going, though the sweat spilt from every pore. He realised it would make a lot more sense to let his Dad fall and run on without him, but he'd waited five years for the chance to see him again and he wasn't going to let him go a second time . . . and besides, he needed to get Dad's body back to Mum. They couldn't leave him down here in the darkness.

Now they were plunged into a maelstrom, a world that was literally breaking apart around them, threatening to fling them to the ground, to bury them beneath tons of falling earth and stone. Viggo caught a fleeting glance of the McKendricks' skeletons, which appeared to be dancing a gleeful jig within their prison of roots, their teeth set in rictus grins, their outstretched limbs falling to bits. A stone caught Viggo a glancing blow on the arm and he couldn't hold back a yell of pain. For an instant, he nearly let go of Dad, but he gritted his teeth and clung tenaciously on.

Somehow, the three of them kept on going, hurrying up around the spiral, tripping, skidding, coughing, until, after what seemed an eternity, they saw above them a haze of light where the sun still poked its fingers through billowing grey curtains.

'Come on!' roared Magnus, his eyes fixed on the light.

'We won't make it!' bellowed Zack, but they didn't slow their pace.

A wide gap appeared in the steps ahead of them but Magnus wouldn't let them slow their pace. 'JUMP!' he roared and they launched themselves across the open space. They seemed to hang in the air for a very long time before their feet slammed on to rock on the far side of the chasm.

Suddenly, improbably, they burst out of the entrance into fresh air and, gasping for breath, they carried Jonathan's corpse to a safe distance. They climbed up out of the declivity and laid Dad on the ground, then turned back to look down at the site. Viggo saw the ancient doorway tremble and collapse, the reinforcing struts bending like warm toffee, great clouds of red dirt bursting outwards into the clean air as the whole thing imploded on itself – and then Yggdrasil too was shattering, crumbling, falling into fragments. There was one last roar and then the whole edifice was gone, leaving only a great mound of red soil to mark where it had stood.

Silence gradually settled while Viggo and Magnus stood, their arms around each other's shoulders, watching the last dust clouds drift back down to earth.

'That was close,' said Magnus, wiping his eyes.

'I thought we were done for,' whispered Viggo, and Magnus nodded and gave him a hug.

'We brought Dad back,' said Magnus, and his face was wet with tears.

And then they both turned at the sound of a voice behind them.

Zack had walked away a short distance and pulled out his phone. He spoke two words into it. 'Code Purple,' he said, and rang off.

He turned to look at the brothers.

'OK,' he said. 'This is how we're going to handle it.'

# CHAPTER 26
## THE DEAL

Zack somehow made it all sound so reasonable.

'Right,' he said. 'First of all, I need to apologise to you both. I completely lost it down there and I'm sorry about that, I really am. I wasn't thinking straight. You'd just found the body of your father. I get that. It's momentous.'

'But calling in a Code Purple?' murmured Magnus. 'Really?'

'What's a Code Purple?' asked Viggo.

'It means everyone pulls out immediately,' said Magnus, still looking daggers at Zack. 'The work crew, the people back at Asgard, everyone. They all head back to where they came from and this is never spoken of again. Or did I get it wrong?'

'No, that's pretty much it,' admitted Zack. 'It's 'Game Over'.'

Magnus stared at him. 'But why? Why would you do that? We were so close.'

Zack shrugged. He waved a hand towards the pile of dust that was the site. 'Yeah, but we need to wake up and smell the coffee, Magnus. All that time and energy spent on getting down there and now what's left of the site? Dust. Even the tree of Yggdrasil is gone! No proof that it was ever there. And besides . . .'

'Besides what?' growled Magnus.

Zack looked sheepish. 'The moment I saw that first skeleton I began to have second thoughts about the whole thing,' he admitted.

'Are you kidding me?' Magnus looked baffled.

'Don't you get it? I wanted to be the first, that's all. And now it turns out I'd only be the *sixth*. That's not a position I feel comfortable with.'

'But the others all died. You'd be . . .'

'The first one to survive?' snapped Zack. 'There's no guarantee of that. Who's to say the same thing wouldn't happen to me? You heard what Bragg said. Humans aren't meant to go into that tunnel; they can't survive in there.'

'But *he* was in there, so . . .' Magnus realised the implications of what he'd just said. 'You're saying Bragg is some kind of . . .?'

'I don't know what he is,' admitted Zack. 'But you both saw what happened when I pulled the trigger on him, right?

Magnus looked puzzled, but Viggo nodded. 'That was weird,' he admitted, 'but kind of cool.'

'What *did* happen to him?' asked Magnus. 'I missed it.'

'He kind of . . . turned into birds,' said Viggo, and realised even as he said it, how ridiculous it sounded. 'I think they were crows. They all flew back into the tunnel.'

Magnus stared at him. 'What are you talking about?' he snapped. 'Birds?'

Zack grinned. 'Kid's not lying,' he said. 'I saw it too. That's something I'll never be able to explain. Not if I live to be a hundred years old. And you know what? It scared the hell out of me.'

'Why did you *shoot* him?' whispered Magnus. 'For Christ's sake, Zack!'

'I guess I wasn't thinking straight. But no court is going to convict me of killing him. Like Viggo said, he turned into *birds*! Try telling that to a police officer!' He shook his head. 'None of this has turned out the way I expected.' He looked down at the wizened body stretched on the ground between them. 'And then this,' he murmured. 'I sure didn't see this coming and, from what you told me down there, you didn't either.' He stood gazing down at the body for a moment. 'But we can make it work,' he said. 'It's just going to mean bending the truth.'

'Go on,' said Magnus. He took off his jacket and laid it gently over his dad's body.

'First rule. You don't tell anyone that you found your father down there.' Zack pointed to the great mound of earth that had previously been the entrance to the underworld. 'You understand what I'm saying? You make up a story. You say that you and Viggo went out on a hike and you chanced upon the body lying in a gully, half covered by bracken. You rehearse the story first, make sure you both say exactly the same thing, and you stick to it whatever questions are fired at you. You call the authorities and let them come out to collect the body.' He waved a hand around. 'There's plenty of remote spots in this area, just choose somewhere away from the site. It'll take a little time but they'll eventually deliver a 'death by misadventure' verdict and they'll release the body into your care. Then you'll be able to get him home and give him a proper burial.'

Magnus scowled. 'And how am I supposed to get Dad to this . . . remote spot?' he asked.

'In the Range Rover. You can have it. Think of it as a farewell gift.'

'But . . .' Magnus pointed back to the rubble behind them. 'We can't just pretend that didn't happen,' he said. 'The portal is still down there. You realise that's what it is, right? A portal. An entrance to another world.' He waved his hands at the heap of earth. 'It can be dug out again.'

Zack frowned. 'I'll think about that,' he said. 'If we do commit to the job, it will be much more than a simple digging-out process. It could take years to get back down there. And if we go again we'd need to do it armed, ready to fight whatever's down there. But the way I figure it, it's not going anywhere. We'll always know where to find it. And right now, I have other projects waiting on me, big projects.'

'Like your space rocket?' suggested Viggo, and Zack gave him an odd look.

'No comment,' he said. He turned his attention back to Magnus. 'Look, I understand how frustrating it must be for you – and I know you said you were quitting – but I'm not accepting your resignation. I'm just asking you to wait for a while. A year, maybe two . . .'

'Two years!' Magnus looked like he might be about to burst into tears.

'The time will soon pass. And, if I decide to give this another go around, I'll call you.'

'Not *if*' snapped Magnus. '*When!* You have to do it, now we know it's there.'

— 309 —

'That's for me to decide. But listen, kid, this is real important. You don't do anything about it yourself. You hear me? And you don't speak about it to *anyone*. Not so much as a whisper. Same goes for you, Viggo. If either of you blab, I'll find out about it and I'll put my lawyers on to it. And Magnus, if I give the say so, they will bury you and the rest of your family so deep you'll never claw your way out. Trust me on that.'

Magnus glared at him. 'You'd do that to us?' he gasped. 'Really?'

'It's nothing personal,' Zack assured him. 'Just sound business sense.'

'What about Mum?' asked Viggo. 'What do we tell her?'

'The cover story,' said Zack. 'She doesn't know where you've been.'

'Umm . . . actually, she does? I . . . left her a message, telling her where I was going.'

Zack glared at him. 'You did *what*? Why?'

Viggo shrugged. 'I don't know. I guess I thought I needed to. Just in case something went wrong.' He thought for a moment. 'And it kind of did, right?'

'And Mum knew that you and I were going to the site,' Magnus reminded Zack.

He pondered for a moment. 'All right,' he said. 'What's done is done. No point in crying over it. You guys are going to have to convince her to go with the cover story.'

'She'll never agree to that,' said Viggo.

'She will if you make her understand it's for the best. Don't forget I have those signed NDAs right here in my pocket. Play ball with me and they *will* be honoured. That's my promise to you both. You guys will have the money to do whatever you want.'

Magnus pointed to the remains of the site. 'But I wanted to do *that*,' he said.

Zack shrugged. 'That's the way the cookie crumbles,' he said. 'Find other things to interest you until the time is right.'

Viggo and Magnus looked at each other. Viggo could see that his brother hated the idea of walking away from this but was smart enough to know that he'd been offered something that might just work.

'All right,' he said. 'We'll try it your way. But promise me something in return.'

'I'm listening.'

'When you decide it's time to come back to this project, you'll offer *me* the chance to work on it with you. Nobody else. Me.'

'I already said I'd do that,' reasoned Zack.

'Yes. But you have to promise.'

'It's almost as though you don't trust me,' said Zack.

'I know enough about you that you'll honour a promise,' said Magnus.

Zack grinned. 'OK then,' he said. He extended a hand and he and Magnus shook on it. 'Right, let's get your dad into the back of the Range Rover,' suggested Zack. 'There are some ground sheets in there we can cover him with. Then I want you to drive me back to Asgard to meet the helicopter.'

'You're leaving already?' asked Viggo incredulously.

'Like I said, there are places I need to be. We'll keep

your dad's body hidden and you'll explain to Alison what's happening. Then the three of you will drive to the place you're going to 'find' him and take it from there. Don't forget, act astonished in front of the people who come to collect him. You can't believe the coincidence! They'll go for it.' He shook his head. 'Like you said, Magnus, we were close. And maybe one day, when I've figured out all the angles . . .' He considered for a moment, then seemed to snap out of his reverie. 'Come on,' he said. 'We need to get out of here.'

'What about Leon?' asked Viggo. 'He's still down there.'

'He can stay there as far as I'm concerned,' muttered Zack. He looked at Viggo. 'You saw what happened to him when I pulled the trigger. You think a few tons of rocks are going to bother him?'

Viggo thought about it for a few moments. 'I suppose not,' he admitted. 'So . . . what is he, exactly? Is he, like, some kind of . . . god?

There was a brief silence while they all considered this. But nobody had an answer.

They moved to Jonathan's shrouded body and lifted him clear of the ground, then carried him up the slope to the waiting vehicle. Magnus opened the back of the Range Rover, pulled things out and then he and Viggo arranged the body carefully inside, before covering it with blankets and equipment. Magnus closed and locked the rear door before they took their seats in the vehicle. He turned it around and drove back the way they had come.

As they approached the diggers and other vehicles, Viggo saw that everything was already being packed up and prepared for departure. The leader of the team lifted a hand to wave as the Range Rover went by, but Zack didn't even acknowledge him.

They drove the short distance to Asgard and, here too, Viggo saw that the operation was being dismantled. Uniformed men were loading electrical rigs into the back of hired vans and the black helicopter was parked on the grass a short distance from the house. Jeeves was waiting by the steps, the very picture of a faithful servant.

Zack opened the passenger door and got out, then leant back in to look at Magnus. 'You're still young,' he said. 'That site isn't going anywhere. Maybe one of these days we'll head back and give it another shot.'

Magnus nodded but he didn't say anything.

Zack closed the car door and walked straight across to the helicopter. He went up the steps and into it and Jeeves gave Viggo and Magnus a brief wave before following him. The door of the craft closed and the rotor blades started to turn, slowly at first, but gathering speed until they were a blur. The helicopter lifted straight upwards and hovered for a moment, as if Zack were taking a last look at his abandoned project. Then its nose dipped and it moved away at speed. Viggo and Magnus watched until it was no more than a tiny speck in the distance.

Viggo turned his gaze towards the house and saw that Mum was coming out from the courtyard, looking baffled. She had her phone in her hand and it occurred to Viggo that she had probably just seen his message. She spotted the Range Rover and started towards it.

Viggo watched her approaching, a sinking feeling in his gut. He glanced back at the jumble of equipment behind him, but for the moment, nothing was visible.

'Are you going to tell her?' he asked Magnus. 'Or shall I?'

There was a brief silence while Magnus considered the question. 'We'll tell her together,' he said. They got out of the vehicle and went to meet her.

# EPILOGUE

Viggo rode his new bike to the cemetery and took care to secure it to a railing with the fancy lock that Mum insisted he should always use.

He wandered down to Dad's grave and stood looking at it for a few moments. Mum had chosen something simple: a small black marble block with a short epitaph inscribed upon it.

*Jonathan Ryan – finally at peace.*

Viggo moved over to a wooden bench a short distance away from the grave. He'd had the afternoon to himself and had gone out for a cycle ride. Something had steered him in this direction.

The late August sunshine was warm on his face and he felt content.

Zack had made good on his promise. The money had appeared in Mum's bank account one morning without so much as a word, paid in via a transfer from a bank in California. Since it was exactly thirty days since the Ryans had left Shetland, it was evident where it had come from, though oddly, it was listed as a tax-free cash prize from a lottery Mum had never heard of.

Zack had been right about Dad. A verdict of 'death by

misadventure' had eventually been arrived at and Mum had arranged for the body to be flown to Edinburgh, while the three of them had driven back the same day – Mum and Viggo in Ruby and Magnus in the Range Rover that was now officially his. A few days later, there'd been a small funeral at a local church. A few of Dad's old university pals had shown up, together with some rarely seen relatives, all of whom had wanted to know more about what had happened to him, but who accepted the well-rehearsed answers they were given without query.

For some reason, Viggo had been sure that Leon would show up at the funeral, but there'd been no sign of him and he'd felt strangely disappointed by the non-appearance.

He reached into his jacket pocket and took out Dad's notebook. He had shared it with Mum and Magnus shortly after their return to Edinburgh and both of them agreed that Zack would never hear about it. For no apparent reason, Viggo was now its custodian and he carried it with him everywhere. Of course, he'd read and re-read the contents many times. It was a journal, beginning with an excited note about the map his father had discovered tucked away in an ancient book he'd found in a little library in Shetland, a mouldering tome about Nordic Mythology. There was no sign of the map itself, but from Dad's description it was clear that it was a copy of the same one that Zack had paid a fortune for. The rest of the journal was a breathless account of Dad's plans to sneak away from the dig he was working on, to secretly make his way to the place marked by those coordinates so he could investigate. He had caught a bus to a spot as close as he could and then trekked for miles across open country until he was finally there.

But the part that Viggo found most affecting was the final page, a barely legible note scribbled by somebody who was in such pain he could hardly write. It was a brief, poignant farewell to his family.

*Alison, Magnus, Viggo.*

*I doubt you'll ever read this. I realise now I have been a complete fool. I kept it all a secret, you see, and now nobody knows where I am. My leg is broken and a rock fall has blocked my way out. I cannot get a phone signal down here and the GPS isn't responding. All hope gone. I am sorry, not for myself, but for failing you all.*

*Alison, you were the best thing that ever happened to me. I love you. And boys, you always made me so proud to be your father. I know you will both achieve great things. Please remember me with affection. I want to tell you*

That was where the note ended. Viggo wanted to believe that his father had slipped into unconsciousness at that point, that he had slept and felt no more pain, before the last traces of his life ebbed away from him. The scribbled words on the page blurred as Viggo's eyes filled with tears and he returned the notebook to his pocket. Somebody handed him a tissue and he took it gratefully, mopping at his eyes, then looked up in surprise.

Leon was sitting beside him on the bench, gazing down

at the grave. 'I like it,' he said. 'It's just enough. I suppose Alison chose it. She has excellent taste, don't you think?'

Viggo stared at him, open-mouthed. '*Now* you show up?' he cried. 'After all this time?'

Leon turned to look at him. 'I'm sorry, old son,' he said. 'I've been rather busy. After spending so long with you and the others, a lot of work had built up. You're looking well.'

'And you're looking better than the last time I saw you. You were busy turning into a flock of birds, I seem to remember.'

'Hmm. A tad theatrical, I know, but I couldn't resist it. I like your new bike, by the way.'

'It's not the one I wanted,' complained Viggo.

'Is it not?'

'No. Mum said it would be ridiculous to spend that much, but I managed to talk her into letting me have my sixth choice. She said she wanted me to put most of the money aside for when I go to uni. She said it would be there to build my future.'

'An excellent idea. Do you know what you're going to study?'

'Not fully decided. Whatever it is, it'll include Norse Mythology.'

'Oh ho! But I thought that was Magnus's thing? Did you ever get to see that *Thor* movie, by the way? The one you kept banging on about?'

'I did.' Viggo frowned. 'It wasn't that great, to be honest. Bit of a letdown.'

'That's a shame. You'd looked forward to it for so long. Perhaps that was the problem. The things you wait the longest for often turn out to be the biggest disappointments.

— 310 —

But not, I suspect, finding your father. So, why this sudden interest in all things Nordic?'

Viggo shrugged. 'I did some reading. Started to get into it. I know who *you* are, by the way.'

'Me?' Leon looked intrigued. 'Do tell me,' he said.

'Well, for ages I thought you were Loki. The god of mischief. All those tricks you kept pulling on me, it seemed to make sense. And I also checked out Bragi, the guy with the harp, the one you talked about on the ferry . . . but he didn't quite seem to fit.'

Leon looked disappointed. 'Why not?' he asked. 'He's supposed to be a poet, isn't he? A skilled talker, a musician . . .'

'Yeah, and there's plenty of that about you. But even so, it seemed too obvious. And then I remembered one of those dreams I had.'

'A dream?'

'Yeah. We were in a boat, the two of us. You were standing behind me, working this long oar thing. So I checked that out online and there you were. Harbard. Or Greybeard, the Ferryman. He's known for taking people on journeys, for guiding them to their destinations. I read into it some more and it said that Harbard is actually one of Odin's disguises – and that some scholars link him to Loki anyway. And then I remembered something you said to Zack. "What would you say if I told you I was a direct descendant of Odin?" That's what you said, isn't it?'

Leon stroked his own beard thoughtfully. 'I think you flatter me,' he said.

'So are you going to tell me if I'm right?'

Leon thought for a moment, then shook his head. 'Nah. I prefer to leave you wondering. But I do like the fact that you're so interested in all things Norse. I'm sure you'll give Magnus a real run for his money before too long. How *is* your brother, by the way?'

Viggo rolled his eyes. 'He's spending his days in the National Library of Scotland up in the Special Collections room. Some new project he's working on. Won't tell me a thing about it. But he did let something slip.'

'Oh yes? Pray tell.'

'Whatever it is, he's working with Chris Scanlon on it.'

'Chris . . . Scanlon?' Leon pretended to have forgotten the name for a moment, but Viggo wasn't fooled for a moment. 'Oh right, the seabird guy. The one he had a difference of opinion with. Well, well, there's a turn up for the books.' Leon chuckled. 'And Alison?'

'She's taken Ruby to the garage. Says she needs a complete overhaul this time. I told her, "Mum, you talked about buying a *new* car. You could have whatever you fancy, brand new, straight out of the factory". But she's having none of it. She insists that Ruby's been with her a long time and she's sticking with her.' Viggo shook his head. 'I don't know why I'm telling you this, you know it all anyway, don't you?'

Leon smiled. 'Humour me,' he said.

Viggo thought for a few moments. 'What I still don't understand,' he said, 'is all that stuff you told me and Mum. The stuff about your son Daniel and what happened to him. And about your girlfriend or your wife or whatever she was supposed to be. Was there truth in any of that?'

— 312 —

Leon looked apologetic. 'It was *all* true,' he said. 'But not my truth.'

Viggo stared at him. 'What's that supposed to mean?' he asked.

'They were other people's stories,' he said. 'On my travels, I encounter them and sometimes I borrow them, absorb them, claim them as my own.' He shrugged. 'I know it's not fair but . . . sometimes I use them to persuade others to come along with me. At that point on our journey together, I sensed that you distrusted me and I knew that, if I was ever going to convince you to go where I wanted you to, I needed you to be on my side. Alison was in a similar place. Using those stolen stories was simply a means to an end. I hope you can forgive me for that.'

Viggo frowned. 'I'll have to think about it,' he said. 'You lied to us.'

'And would you have come along with me if I hadn't?'

Viggo frowned. 'Probably not,' he admitted.

'And if you hadn't come with me . . .'

'We wouldn't have found Dad. Yes, I get that. Doesn't make it right though.'

Leon smiled. 'No, I suppose not.' He studied Viggo for a moment. 'Was there anything else you needed to ask?'

'Just a couple of things. How were you in two places at one time? And . . . the thing with the car. The way it kept conking out. That *was* you, right?'

Leon's face remained impassive. 'I have to have *some* secrets,' he said.

'Ah, you're impossible!'

They both chuckled.

'So,' murmured Leon. 'What else is new in the life of Viggo Ryan?'

Viggo felt his cheeks reddening. 'I, er . . . got a text from Freya.'

'Did you now?'

'Yeah. She's coming to Edinburgh. Soon. She's planning to study at Napier Uni next year. She wants to meet up.'

Now Leon's smile opened out into a broad grin. 'It's all coming together,' he said. 'I'm delighted to hear it.'

'You sound like you care,' said Viggo. 'About what happens to me.'

'I do. I care about all my travelling companions.'

'So what are you, exactly? Are you, like, a god?'

Leon scowled. 'Never much cared for *that* word,' he admitted. 'I'm more of a traveller than anything else. And a meddler. Sometimes, I just can't resist getting involved.'

Viggo thought for a moment. 'I'm glad you finally came back,' he said. 'I wanted to thank you.'

'Thank me?'

'Yes. For helping us, all three of us. I don't think we realised, back when it started, how much we needed to find Dad. It was like I'd been carrying this emptiness around inside me for five years, and I'd kind of forgotten it was there. And finding Dad somehow cured me of that. It made me feel whole again.'

'You're more than welcome. But Viggo . . .'

'Yes?'

'I hope you understand. The site is closed now. I truly hope that you won't be tempted to visit it again, under any circumstances. The things that are waiting down there are not for any human to experience. They'd destroy you, just as they destroyed your father and that poor family from the old house. Promise me you'll stay away.'

'I . . . can't promise,' said Viggo. 'But I promise I'll *try*.'

Leon gave him a stern look. 'Viggo . . .'

'I know if Zack ever gets in touch with Magnus, he'll want to go. And I'll probably want to be with him when he steps into that portal.'

'Zack?' said Leon. 'I believe I heard something about him. Isn't he making a journey into space any time now?'

'Yeah, that's right. Just a short trip to start the ball rolling but everyone says he's got his eyes on Mars. What would that be like, I wonder?'

'Hopefully it will keep him occupied for a very long time. Hey, maybe something will go wrong and he'll be marooned up there!' Leon gave out a long sigh. 'You humans,' he said. 'You're impossible. And yet, despite everything, there's something about you that I can't help liking.' He seemed to remember something. 'Oh, yes, I brought you a wee present. All the way from Shetland.' He made a theatrical flourish and, as if by magic, a plastic food container appeared in his hand. 'I seem to remember you have a liking for this stuff.'

Viggo took the box eagerly and tore off the lid. The gooey orange chunk of cake looked inviting. 'You remembered,' he said. 'Wow, thanks for . . .'

He looked up and the other end of the bench was empty again. He turned his head to make a quick search of the graveyard but there was no sign of Leon anywhere. Viggo did notice a large black crow, perched on a stone wall a short distance away, which gave a short, harsh squawk and then flapped away. Viggo gazed after it for a few moments, then returned his attention to the box on his lap. He reached into it, lifted out the cake and took a big, hungry bite.

It tasted incredible.

Then, chewing happily, he leant back in his seat and thought that he felt happier now than he had in years.

# ACKNOWLEDGEMENTS

I've been a published author for many years now and I learned early on that the creation of a new novel is always a team effort - so once again, it's time to offer thanks to the many people who helped me bring *Postcards from Vahalla* to fruition.

As ever, I'm indebted to Hazel Holmes and her intrepid team at UCLan Publishing, for granting me the opportunity to bring my latest brainchild into print - as ever, I'm not exactly sure where the idea for this book came from, but once it bubbled up from somewhere deep inside, I knew I would have no rest until it out there. Thanks also to Daisy Webster for the eye popping cover artwork which I think really captures the essence of the book.

Thanks are also due to Susan Singfield, who as well being a brilliant proofreader, was also an invaluable help when it came to filming and editing the bonus content for the book. Shetland is an extraordinary place and the week Susan and I spent there, visiting the locations for the story will linger long in our memories. We were welcomed everywhere we went.

Thanks to the very talented Finn Shearer who agreed to be Viggo for a bonus scene that's only briefly alluded to in the actual book – and thanks also to gifted baker Louise Campbell who shows readers how to make their very own Greek honey and orange cake. (My only regret is that I wasn't around when the finished cake was ready to be sampled!)

Special thanks must go to Creative Scotland, whose generosity bought me the time to work on the book without interruption and I particularly want to thank Alan Bett who helped me through the tricky process of applying for a grant. Though I've published millions of words in a career that spans more than forty years, filling out forms is still something I struggle with.

Finally, I can't wind this up without once again thanking my home from home, the National Library of Scotland which once again provided me with the perfect place to write.

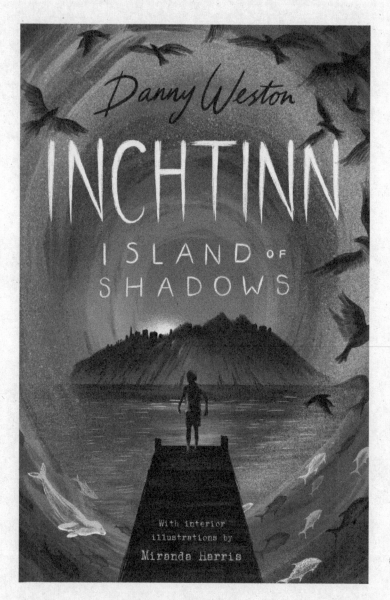

The Witching Stone
I don't believe in witches!
I don't believe in witches!
I don't believe in witches!
Danny Weston

THE FOREST BELONGS
TO THE WALKERS . . .

ENTER AT YOUR PERIL

# A HUNTER'S MOON

*Danny Weston*

The
Black
Air

Jennifer
Lane

Who can say
what's real, what's not,
and what should
stay buried?

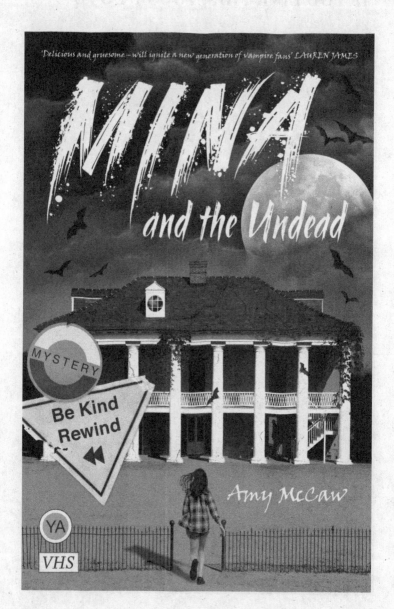

'Delicious and gruesome – will ignite a new generation of vampire fans' LAUREN JAMES

# MINA
## and the Undead

MYSTERY

Be Kind
Rewind
◄◄

*Amy McCaw*

YA

VHS

'Mina is back with bite in this action-packed romp of a sequel.' KENDARE BLAKE

# MINA
## and the Slayers

MYSTERY

BE KIND
REWIND

YA

VHS

Amy
McCaw

BRYONY
PEARCE

Black magic just met
its match . .

RAISING

HELL

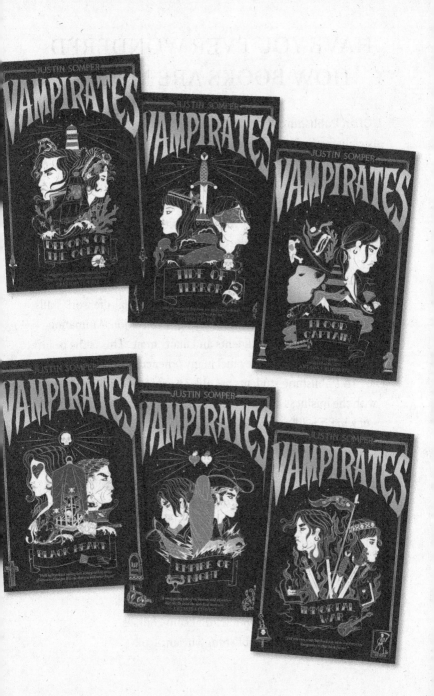

# HAVE YOU EVER WONDERED HOW BOOKS ARE MADE?

UCLan Publishing is an award-winning independent publisher specialising in Children's and Young Adult books. Based at The University of Central Lancashire, this Preston-based publisher teaches MA Publishing students how to become industry professionals, using the content and resources from its business; students are included at every stage of the publishing process and credited for the work that they contribute.

The business doesn't just help publishing students though. UCLan Publishing has supported the employability and real-life work skills for the University's Illustration, Acting, Translation, Animation, Photography, Film & TV students and many more. This is the beauty of books and stories; they fuel many other creative industries! The MA Publishing students are able to get involved from day one with the business and they acquire a behind-scenes experience of what it is like to work for a such a reputable independent.

The MA course was awarded a Times Higher Award (2018) for Innovation in the Arts, and the business, UCLan Publishing, was awarded Best Newcomer at the Independent Publishing Guild (2019) for the ethos of teaching publishing using a commercial publishing house. As the business continues to grow, so too does the student experience upon entering this dynamic Masters course.

www.uclanpublishing.com
www.uclanpublishing.com/courses/
uclanpublishing@uclan.ac.uk